Praise for Layla

A beautiful book—at once nostalgic and fresh—that will go straight to your heart and lodge there.
Alethea Black, Author of *I Knew You'd Be Lovely*

I love *Layla*. I will give this novel, a precious gift, to my friends whose psyches were shaped by the idealism, hope, and chaos of "the sixties." As a student of that period, I will also beg younger friends to read this emotional page-turner. Layla's coming to terms with her parents' dangerous activism is heart-wrenching due to Keating's delightfully drawn characters. This novel also serves as a compelling lesson in our values and how drastically they've changed. It serves as a better history than any essay or screed.
Susan Braudy, Author of *Family Circle: The Boudins and the Aristocracy of the Left*

Céline Keating's deftly plotted novel takes readers on a gripping journey along the underground railroad of post-'60s radicalism. I fully empathized with Layla and her search for a father lost in history. Every adult has to reinterpret the story of her childhood. Keating beautifully demonstrates the courage it takes for each of us to face that bittersweet truth.
Larry Dark, Director, The Story Prize

As the Great American Nostalgia Machine works to convert the idealism and anger and, yes, the naiveté of the Sixties into a cartoon of funny hair and flowery shirts, Céline Keating's novel *Layla* provides a strong antidote by sending her eponymous heroine on the road in quest of the realities of her parents' past. As Layla James drives cross-country, following the cryptic directions of her late mother, she meets a wide and sharply drawn group of veteran radicals who all play a part in the search for her mysterious father. Is he alive or dead? Was he an innocent or a criminal? Were her parents who she thought they were? Keating keeps the pace fast and the suspense high as Layla's discoveries add up, bringing real change into her own young life. You'll want to ride with her every mile of the way!

Robert Hershon, Editor, Hanging Loose Press and Author of 12 collections of poetry, most recently *Calls from the Outside World*

In *Layla*, Céline Keating has produced a fast-moving story of family secrets, political intrigue, and a young woman's coming of age. *Layla* is a rare combination of a novel that is both suspenseful and insightful, narrated by a character who is charming, intelligent, appealing, and most importantly, honest. Her search for the truth about her father and for meaning in her own life is a gripping tale and a memorable read.

Con Lehane, Author of *Death at the Old Hotel*

Céline Keating's debut novel, *Layla*, is a triumph of political literature. With mastery, Keating has fashioned a thrilling and moving tale of a young woman forced to discover the secret history of her family. Set in contemporary time, *Layla* reaches back into the tumultuous 1960s. It's the perfect novel for anyone in search of a serious, compelling read, but Keating's deep socio-political knowledge of the period, combined with her narrative skills of pacing and mystery, also makes this a perfect choice for American Studies courses; it is as informative as it is impossible to put down.

Marnie Mueller, Author of *Green Fires, The Climate of the Country*, and *My Mother's Island*

Layla's ambivalence towards her parents and their idealism is evoked in beautiful prose and telling details. The novel brings to life the complexity of family dynamics with all its conflicts, dangers and rewards. The reader travels with Layla as she searches to understand her past and present and comes out of the journey wiser.

Nahid Rachlin, Author of memoir *Persian Girls* and novels *Foreigner* and *Jumping Over Fire*

Layla's story unfolds like a finely calibrated psychological mystery. In her search for the truth of her parents' past, she enters a world of subterfuge and danger, cold-hearted judgment and unexpected kindness. With each new revelation about her past, Layla—the disaffected daughter of 60s' activists whose apolitical nature is matched only by her scorn for what she considers to be her parents' antiquated passions—begins to peel open, onion-like, finding new respect for the powerful forces that shaped her and developing passions of her own. In *Layla*, Céline Keating has created an unforgettable character who is by turns exasperating, funny, courageous and fiercely loyal. Layla's journey toward understanding of her past and present evokes both the idealism and danger of the '60s, which resonate to this day.

Susan Segal, Author of *Aria*

In Céline Keating's auspicious debut, the political and the emotional collide, as one generation's raison d'être—the radical politics of the '60s—becomes their offspring's burden. What results is a wrenching look at the human costs of activism and the resiliency of love.

Helen Schulman, author of *A Day at the Beach* and *This Beautiful Life*

To learn more about Céline Keating, please visit her website: celinekeating.com

Layla

Céline Keating

Plain View Press
P.O. 42255
Austin, TX 78704

plainviewpress.net
sb@plainviewpress.net
512-441-2452

ISBN: 978-1-935514-77-0
Library of Congress Number: 2010940934

Cover photograph by Abbas Rahbar
Cover design by Susan Bright

Acknowledgements

I am so pleased to have the opportunity to express my gratitude to so many people: to Pamela Bicket, Merren Keating, Alan Reich, Robert Rosenberg, and Jody Winer for reading and giving suggestions on the manuscript; to Andrew Beierley, Anne Gibbons, Craig Kayser, Molly Mikolowski, Abbas Rahbar, and Christine Tansey for helping the manuscript reach an audience. A huge thank you to Pam Knight and Sherry Pilisko, who picked up the reins at Plain View Press after the tragic death of publisher Susan Bright, and have given it their heart and soul. Last, much thanks to The MacDowell Colony for the precious gift of time to work on this novel.

For Mark and Merren, for who you are

For Chloe and Daria, for who you will become

Chapter 1

My name is Layla. My mother said my father insisted they call me that as soon as they knew I was a girl. He thought the song by Eric Clapton, when he was with Derek and the Dominoes, was the best R&R single of all time. I loved knowing it meant so much to him to name me. My mother, though always eager to talk about the world and its problems, shied away from anything personal, and so the main thing I knew about my father was that he was dead.

They were '60s people, my parents. And that's what's brought me to this waiting room where I sit, rubbing my hands over my goose pimpled arms, steeling myself. After this long, rough summer, I think I finally get what it means to suffer the consequences of your choices.

My mother was always trying to convince me that we are all tied up in history and politics – who we are, even what we think. The personal is political, she would say, and, all politics is personal. She was a Women's Studies teacher, an antiwar activist, a placard-wearing, union-ballad-singing Leftie. She was always pointing things out in the paper or on the news, trying to "engage" me. But I wouldn't engage. I resented the politics that took so much of her attention. And I believed – I wanted to believe – that I could escape being shaped by anyone or anything I didn't choose.

I no longer believe in escape.

The door opens, and a guard beckons. I stand so quickly I bang my knee, but the sharp pain helps clear my head. Was this what my mother was hoping for with her elaborate scheme, the promise she asked of me – that by drawing me in to her secrets,

I'd end up every bit as implicated as she was? Forced to become involved, to take a stand? Because wasn't that her point – that we're all, in some way or another, implicated?

Still, I want to believe that it was much simpler, something that doesn't have to do with politics at all: that my mother wanted to give me what I had been denied, and that she wanted my forgiveness.

O

We were close once. I cuddled up to her in her bed if I had a nightmare, or she encircled me in her arms as she read to me, the book open on my lap. On Saturdays we walked to Riverside Park and she hoisted me up on the balustrade to look at the Hudson River and count the boats. In the playground she would push me as high as I wanted on the swings or watch me scrabble to the top of the cement dinosaur. She took me to shows in the winter – the circus or the Nutcracker – and to Coney Island and City Island in the spring. In summer we watched the rollerbladers doing fancy moves in Central Park, and rowed into the middle of the lake, licking ice cream.

It was fun then. She was fun.

I didn't know when that changed, when everything she said became boring, why she annoyed me so. I had wanted her to give me space, to let up. I couldn't wait to get away.

I didn't mean I wanted her to die.

The day my mother told me she didn't have long to live, I grabbed the railing of her hospital bed and shook it so hard I set the bed rocking. My mother was a fighter, tough, strong. "You had chemo! You had your breast cut off!" I lowered my head to the railing; the metal was cool against my forehead. How could my only parent, the woman who had lectured me about breast self-examination, about health as a feminist issue, my own warrior mother, let herself be felled?

"Layla, please," my mother said, and a look I knew well, of exasperation warring with patience, crossed her face. "Try and accept it."

"No," I wailed, "no." I backed into the cloth curtain that separated her from the patient who shared the hospital room, knocking into the bedside tray, utensils clattering. My mother hadn't even told me the cancer had recurred until the end of the school year, so that I wouldn't be distracted from final exams and graduation. She'd hidden the effects of the chemotherapy from me as long as she could, and covered her bald head with a jaunty, red-print bandana. She'd always been like that – secretive, insistent on her privacy – and it infuriated me.

"Layla, come here."

I shook my head; my feet wouldn't come unglued from the floor. She had beaten the cancer once, years before. She would beat it again. I wouldn't let her leave me.

"Please," she said. She closed her eyes and her head fell against the pillow, the bandana slipping to reveal the dome of pale skin. A look of pain and exhaustion crossed her face, and I saw how sallow her skin had become, how sunken her eyes. I dropped into the chair next to the bed.

"I need to talk to you," my mother said, her eyes still closed. "It's important." Her eyes fluttered open. "We have to keep our voices down."

"She's not here," I said. Her roommate's bed was empty.

My mother shook her head, put a finger to her mouth, and gestured for me to come closer. When I leaned over she hissed into my ear, "The room is bugged."

I sat back hard in the chair. The morphine? Or worse: Had the cancer spread to her brain?

"Layla," she put her hand on my arm, "I need you to promise something. Promise you'll go ahead with the trip."

"How can that matter now?" My voice had a raspy, strangled sound, like a swimmer desperate for air. I had agreed to go cross-country with her to visit friends from her radical college days.

All winter she'd worked out the details. As soon as I graduated from college we would drive to the Adirondacks and Boston, then west to California. My mother said she wanted to share with me more of her life from when she was my age. Ever since the war began in Iraq, and the antiwar rallies, my mother couldn't stop talking about Vietnam.

But I suspected that the trip was really about us – that she wanted to get past some of our differences, to make peace before I left home. Without her, it made no sense to go.

"You don't understand," she said, her voice so faint I could hardly hear. She coughed and struggled to sit up. My throat constricted. I tried to get my arm around her back, felt her angel bones through the cotton nightgown I'd given her when she had gone back to the hospital the week before. Its sprigs of pink-flowered cheer mocked me.

"The trip will give you answers." She looked at me tellingly.

"To what?"

"Your father," she mouthed soundlessly.

"My fa – ?" I began, but she put a finger over her lips. I had nagged her all my life to know more about my father, but she'd always said there wasn't much to tell. He had died soon after I was born.

"I don't understand."

"Layla, you have to trust me. Just say yes. Please?"

I opened my mouth to protest, but I saw her eyelids droop. "O.K." I said. I could feel her relief as she sagged against me. "There's something for you," she whispered. "In the drawer there." I rummaged in the cabinet by her bed and found an envelope with my name and the words "Personal and Confidential."

"There will be a letter for each place you visit. It'll be as if I'm with you."

My eyes smarted, and I turned away. I stared out her window, at the grimy glass, the puke-beige building opposite. Why was New York City so filthy? Why didn't anybody ever clean these buildings? Along the sill was a line-up of get-well cards and wan bouquets. I wanted to sweep them to the floor.

"One more thing." I felt her light tug on my sleeve. "Try and deal with your anger. It doesn't serve you in any way."

I felt my eyes well up, my face grow hot. I turned away, shoulders hunched, like a child hugging a stuffed animal to herself from someone who threatened to take it. My mother was always at me about why I was angry. But I didn't want to let go of it. I liked the rush of energy it gave me. And down deep I wasn't sure I would know who I was, what I would find inside myself, if I weren't angry.

"You'll try?"

I nodded, but I couldn't look at her. A memory of my most recent outburst the night before she was readmitted to the hospital, before she told me she was sick again, flooded my mind.

I had been oblivious to her all semester, caught up in the photography club I'd joined my senior year at Barnard and a new group of friends. I woke up every morning thinking about shadows and framing and shutter speeds, eager to rush outside to shoot pictures. I had always been only an average student; it was exciting to finally find something I was actually good at.

But that night the boy I was dating and I broke up, and even though it was mutual, I came home feeling coated with the familiar clammy discomfort of failure.

My mother was on the couch wrapped in an old beige terrycloth robe, watching a movie. She looked worn, not so pretty any more. I turned away.

My glance fell on the TV.

"God, not *Salt of the Earth* again." I dumped my backpack on the floor, flopped into a chair, and put my feet up on the coffee table.

"Can you move your feet? You're blocking my view."

"It's so sentimental. Not to mention preachy."

"Do you mind? I'd really like to watch it."

"The heroic struggle of the poor Mexican workers in all their black-and-white glory – God!"

"What's gotten into you?" she snapped. "Can you just leave me alone to enjoy this?"

"Fine!" I jumped up, flinging my head, enjoying the sweep of hair against my cheek. My hair was finally long enough for flinging, and I'd been doing a lot of it lately. I made sure to slam the door to my room for extra theatrical effect.

Now, next to her frail body, shame made my skin hot and itchy. How could I have been so cruel? My mother sighed, a little whisper of a sound, like the air escaping from an empty plastic bag. Suddenly I wanted to throw myself against her, to allow the kind of closeness we hadn't had for years, but I didn't. It had been a long time since I'd given my mother anything, and then only begrudgingly. And so I didn't console her in death. Or myself. But at least I made her the promise she asked.

"I wish I could say more," she said, so softly I almost thought I imagined it. I felt a gentle pressure on my hand, and finally moved to hug her. But her eyes were closed; she was asleep.

Later I would say the words, I thought. When my mother woke up I would tell her I was sorry, sorry for all the times I'd been so mean, for all the aggravation I'd ever caused her. Somehow I would tell her.

I was at the candy machine when I saw her doctor hurrying toward me. The pack of Raisinetts slipped from my hand. And though I raced through the hospital corridors as fast as I have ever raced, it was too late.

"I'm sorry," the doctor said. My mother lay very still. I stroked her forehead and whispered that I loved her. I pretended that she was alive, and could hear.

O

It was late when I left the hospital. The doctor, who kept asking if there was someone she could call, finally settled for putting me in a cab. I wanted desperately to talk to my best friend, Jenny, but it was 3:30 a.m. My mother's sister and parents would have to be told, too. I didn't think my mother had even let them know the cancer had returned. It seemed both pointless and cruel to contact them in the middle of the night.

I crawled into bed, burying myself under the covers, craving forgetfulness. I was jolted awake from nightmares. It was as if I were freezing, I had the jitters so bad. Finally I gave up. I wrapped myself in the soft blue cardigan sweater my mother kept on the knob on the back of the kitchen door. It smelled faintly of soap and vanilla, and in the pocket I found a tissue and a small silver stud in the shape of a scallop shell. I had given her the earrings for her last birthday. I began to cry then, gulping sobs that went on until there was a pincer of pain in my chest. When I stopped I made myself some tea and slumped over my mug, gripping it with both hands for the warmth.

When the tea cooled I got up to reheat it, and noticed the envelope my mother had given me, which I'd slipped on top of the microwave. I slid a nail under the flap and opened it. My mother said she had written a letter for each of the visits we were to take, but inside were only two sheets of paper. On the first were typed directions to upstate New York, car rental information, and a plane ticket taped to it, from San Francisco to New York, for August 18th. The second sheet was a letter, dated six days earlier.

Dear Layla,

I have only a little time left to live. By the time you read this I will be gone. Right now it's comforting to write to you this way – lying in my hospital bed in between your visits.

I know you are hurting, Layla, and I can only hope that I – certainly not a very mystical mother! – can be a kind of spirit with you always. *I know it's especially hard that you, who have never had a father, now lose your mother. It's terrible for me to leave you. It's my main regret, but, as you will learn, I have many.*

I've always tried to be a good parent, but I'm aware of my deficiencies. Many of the problems between us have been my fault, because of things I haven't been able to tell you about, which you can't possibly understand now, but soon will. I can't say more just yet. I know you blame my unconventional life for some of our difficulties, and you are right, although not, perhaps, in the way that you think.

I'm hoping this journey will give you some of what you need. I'll be with you every step of the way through these letters. Darling Layla, please know how much I love you.

Mom

P.S. I can't stress enough how important it is that you go on this trip, and that you follow my instructions exactly.

I had to hold the letter in both hands to stop the trembling. I couldn't remember her ever calling me darling.

As I look back now at that moment, the moment of reading that first letter, what I remember is the roar of air, as if I were being sucked down into a tunnel. I shoved the letter back into the envelope and out of sight, afraid of being engulfed by a grief so huge it would bring down the universe, crushing me with its weight.

O

Finally the clock's hands moved. I picked up the phone, hands shaking. My mother had been estranged from her family, and it had been ages since I'd seen or talked with them.

"Oh Layla, oh my god, oh my god," my grandmother said. I could only squeeze my eyes shut against my tears, not able to talk. "Are you all right, sweetheart?" Her sympathy somehow made things worse.

Everything was a blurry mass of confusion in the days that followed my mother's death. Jenny's mom insisted I stay with them until after the funeral. She made me more meals than I could possibly eat and invited my friends over to watch silly movies. She was regularly on the phone with my mother's younger sister, my Aunt Stacy, talking in whispers.

"You don't have to worry, you'll be fine," she said to me. I must have looked puzzled, because she added, "your mother left you enough – you'll be just fine."

I felt my skin go warm with embarrassment. "Oh. Thanks."

"We'll go over it all another time," she said, and gave my hand a squeeze.

But when it came to the arrangements for my mother's funeral, my grandparents and aunt took charge. They were religious Catholics and insisted on a Mass. My mother was an atheist, but I didn't have the energy to protest. I felt like a block of wood to be moved from church to graveyard to the gathering afterward at my Aunt Stacy's house in Flushing, Queens.

My brain was too foggy to make sense of anything. I expected my mother's funeral to be mobbed by the hoards that had always surrounded her – teachers from Barnard, where she taught Women's Studies, students, friends who were active in all her causes – but my grandparents said it was my mother's wish that the funeral be only for family and old family friends. I wondered if, because she had been estranged from them in life, my mother wanted to let her parents have her all to themselves in death. I was too tired to care.

My mother had never explained what had happened between her and her parents except to say "politics." I could remember visiting my grandparents when I was small, traveling with my mother by subway and bus from Manhattan deep into Queens, a trip that took longer than the visits themselves, because at some point a fight would flare, and my mother would grab my hand and march me out of the apartment. I could remember listening intently for the moment when that would happen, making a game of it. I never understood the arguments, but I could predict by the tone, the gestures, the precise moment my mother would say, "That's it!" and out we'd go.

The morning of the funeral I followed that same route to my grandparents' home. It was the first time I'd gone there without my mother, and I realized, as I stood awkwardly at their door, that it was as if I had inherited her mantle of unease. My grandfather gave me a brusque hug, and I inhaled the scent of his bay-rum aftershave. "Don't be such a stranger," he said, drawing me in.

But I was a stranger.

I rode with my grandparents and aunt to the church. As he got out of the car, my grandfather suddenly turned and kicked the door.

"She made herself a martyr, and for what?"

His anger frightened me. "What do you mean?" I asked. But he just shook his head.

In the church I sat between them, my grandfather's thick, square hand covering my left, my grandmother stroking my right. I sat very still, trying to concentrate. The priest seemed far away, as if seen through the wrong end of a pair of binoculars, and I had to strain to hear. There was a sound like wind through trees that wouldn't go away.

The day stretched on and on, in an endless loop, as we went from the Mass to the cemetery to the gathering afterward at my aunt's brand-new co-op apartment, bland and immaculate, like Aunt Stacy herself. She was trim and petite, with wavy blond hair fluffed like spun sugar, always in the kind of dressy clothes I rarely saw on the Upper West Side, the complete opposite of my gray-haired, hippie mother. As I helped her bring out tidy little sandwiches with the crusts cut off – watercress and cream cheese, duck paté, as if it were High Tea – I almost asked her about their lack of connection. But Stacy seemed too busy filling platters and making coffee to bother.

I went back in to the gathering, but I couldn't sit still. I kept picking up and moving cups and plates even before people had finished eating. I felt as if I were trapped behind glass, cut off and separate. I was relieved when people began to leave, and I could clean up in earnest. I was bringing in a load of dishes when my legs buckled, and I steadied myself against the kitchen wall.

"The daughter's a cold fish," I heard a friend of my aunt's say. "She didn't cry a tear – and that hair!"

My hair? I had added gorgeous mahogany henna to the tips of my hair. I was quite enamored of the effect with my green eyes, of which I was, perhaps, a little vain.

"She's just numb," Stacy said.

But I knew her friend was right. I was cold. I was a block of ice, my breath vaporous as fog, enveloping me like a shroud.

On the subway back to Manhattan I fell asleep, waking up with a jolt at 125th Street. I got out even though it wasn't the right stop, and walked down Broadway. I felt the way I did when I had the flu, head swollen, disoriented. Suddenly I didn't want to go to Jenny's – I wanted to be home.

When I opened the door, the apartment smelled like I'd forgotten to take out the garbage. It seemed so large and empty. I could hear the hum of the refrigerator cycling on and off, and the sound of my upstairs neighbor's heels clicking back and forth from kitchen to hallway. I went from room to room, opening the windows, letting in noise.

I didn't know what to do with myself. I felt something gathering in my chest, a hard pressure against my ribs, and a flutter like the panic I felt when I had to give a presentation in class.

I went into the bathroom to splash cold water on my face. In the mirror my eyes were smudged with liner and my hair was wild, the mahogany tips over-bright against the darker roots. Behind my reflection was my mother's pale yellow chenille bathrobe, limp and worn. The buildup in my chest was unbearable; I grabbed the bathroom scissors and hacked away.

When I was done the mahogany was gone and my head was a mass of short, lethal, spikes.

○

I keep my promises – I like to say it's one of my better traits. So although part of me did not want to go on the trip my mother had planned, I never really considered not going. The other part of me wanted to get away, to be distracted from the reminders, the sadness. And then there was what my mother had hinted in the hospital – that I would learn more about my father.

But in the week after her funeral, as I got everything in order, I fumed. Why had my mother roped me into this? Why did she have to dole out instructions piecemeal as I went along? The whole trip was just a tease, another one of her games, as if I were still a child. My mother had loved puzzles, the daily crossword, Chinese Checkers. Each year for my birthday party when I was little she set up a scavenger hunt in our building. This trip was just an updated version. To get her next clue – next letter – I had to play along. And what was I going to do with all these boring people I was supposed to visit?

At night it was comforting to be with Jenny and her parents. Daytimes, though, I needed to be alone. What I really wanted was to climb in bed and pull the covers over my head. But as soon as I mounded the blankets over myself I felt as if bedbugs were crawling up my skin, and I would find myself jumping back out of bed. I had to keep moving, to work myself to exhaustion so I could collapse into sleep like one of the homeless men I sometimes photographed, bundled up in a heap against the side of our building, out cold.

As I cleaned behind the stove, scrubbed cabinets, reorganized closets, I thought about the apartment. Jenny's parents said that I shouldn't make any decisions just yet, but I couldn't help obsessing. I had wanted an apartment of my own. But if there was one thing I had to agree with my mother about, it was holding on to a rent-controlled apartment. Ours was sprawling and comfortable. My parents and their friends had lived there after graduation, a kind of commune. Our apartment had held zillions of meetings – my mother's seminar classes, her women's group, the building's tenants' association. There were worn parquet floors and shabby rugs and sofas, afternoon light, lots of plants, and no pets because she was allergic. No potpourri, no fancy soaps, no matching towels, and, to appease me, she kept her political posters in her study, except for the peace sign that I let her hang from the living room window, fronting Broadway, after Jenny's cousin's husband was killed in Iraq.

While I was away, Jenny was going to stay in the apartment and keep an eye on it; this would give me time before I got back to figure out where I wanted to live. Jenny would be working at her father's office before starting graduate school in the fall.

"Jesus, what have you done?" she said, coming over near the end of the week to give me a hand.

I touched my hair, embarrassed. "I went to Super Cuts."

"Not your hair, silly," Jenny said. "Your room."

Had I gone overboard? Jenny wore that bewildered look I found so endearing. I could still see in her the small, wispy blond girl she'd been in the third grade, when she was new to my school and we became fast friends. Her anxiety, written all over her delicate, mottled skin, made me feel strong. I smiled.

"I just thought I should make space for you," I said, sitting back down in the middle of the floor, where I had been packing up the last of my things. I couldn't face packing up my mother's possessions, so I'd packed my own. Not just the obvious – winter clothes and textbooks – but books, jewelry, everything. Once I started, I couldn't stop. I had emptied my desk, cleared the top of my bureau, removed all the art supplies from my cabinet. Unlike my mother, who kept so little, I was a hoarder – fabric, old jewelry, buttons that I used for art projects or to decorate the clothes I picked up cheap at the Salvation Army store on 96th Street. I liked mixing the old hippie paisley and tie-dye and velvet with punk-era black. And since I'd started with photography, I had boxes of prints and shoeboxes of cut-up photos I used in montages. I took shots I thought were "edgy": upended trash, grimy subway walls, graffiti.

Jenny sat next to me on the floor.

"You doing O.K.?" she asked softly.

"Sure," I said, keeping my eyes on the carton I was taping shut.

"I loved your mother," she said.

"She loved you, too," I told her, when I could speak. It was true. Jenny got along with my mother almost as well as she did with me. The odd thing was, I didn't even mind – maybe because she never once took my mother's side in our arguments, even when I was in the wrong.

When I was going through my mother's jewelry I found a necklace Jenny had loved, with blue glass balls linked by a gold-filigreed chain. I had planned to give it to her when I left, but now the time felt right.

Jenny opened the package, wrapped with paper I'd hand-painted. Color shot across her face and her eyes welled up. "You can't give me this."

"She would have wanted you to have it. I want you to have it." My voice was gruff with the effort of fighting back my own tears. "Hold your hair up," I ordered. I fixed the clasp and then turned her around. The blue stones matched her eyes. "Perfect."

We hugged; her hair tickled my cheek. We plopped back down amid my cartons, waiting to collect ourselves.

Jenny sneezed. A shaft of sunlight lit the dust motes I had stirred up with the packing. She sneezed again. The silence stretched between us, across the great divide that had opened up between me and everyone else since my mother's death.

"Is there anything I can help with?" Jenny asked.

"I guess help me move these to my mother's room?" A tower of cartons listed against one wall.

"I could stay in there instead of your bedroom while you're gone," she said. My stomach catapulted. I could only shake my head.

"I'm sorry, I understand."

I squeezed her hand.

I've been told that some people can't face reminders of someone who has died. But I couldn't keep away from my mother's things, especially her dresser, where she displayed a collection of little boxes. Some held earrings, some old coins, some were empty. When I was little she would sit me on her lap and let me peek inside – the wooden one with a pine cone etched on top, the green lacquered one painted with unicorns and trees, the hexagonal of ceramic clay with pastel stripes of mint green, cream, and lavender.

I dusted the boxes and put them back on her bureau as reverently as the choir boy had set up the altar at my mother's funeral Mass.

Except for a few things I'd given her – a bit oversized so I could borrow them – there was only one thing I coveted, a black leather jacket. It wasn't her kind of thing at all, and I had been surprised when she had brought it back from a weekend away. Even though I didn't eat red meat or use cosmetics that had been tested on animals, I couldn't bear not to keep the jacket. I told myself I would wear it in mourning for her. Screw political correctness. It looked really great on me.

There was no way I could let anyone stay in my mother's room, not even Jenny. We put my cartons in there and shut the door.

"I'm gonna miss you so much," Jenny said.

"Me too," I said. I poured us both ice tea and flopped down on the sofa.

"Actually..." Jenny hesitated. "I don't want you to feel pressured, but I was talking it over with my father...."

"Full sentences, please."

"Well, he said I could wait to start work. So if you'd like company, for the first couple of weeks? He says they can get a temp to fill in. But I wasn't sure how you'd feel."

"You mean you'd come?"

"You really want me to?"

We grabbed each other and whirled around, as if we were twelve years old again.

"I better go call my dad!"

I watched her leave the room, waiting for the feelings of excitement – or at least relief – to wash over me. But the excitement didn't come. I listened to Jenny's voice on the phone, and a strange, leaden feeling began to settle behind my ribs.

I got up to rinse my glass. On the counter was the manila envelope from my mother. Quietly, so Jenny wouldn't notice, I took it to my room and slipped it into my knapsack.

Chapter 2

Digital camera, check. Cell phone, check. Credit card and cash, check. The car keys were pressed tight in my hand, an extra set in my wallet in case I lost the first.

"We're on our way!" Jenny fairly bounced in her seat.

Suddenly my palms were a little sweaty. "Seat belt," I barked. A city dweller, I hadn't had my driver's license long. I wiped my palms on my snazzy turquoise silk-shantung Capri pants (a major thrift shop bargain) and took a deep breath.

We had dressed to conquer the world – as if we would see some hot guys on the highway. Well, you never know. I was wearing my green cashmere cardigan, to match my eyes. I had packed my mother's soft and fragrant black leather jacket. While I dressed I had imagined myself behind the wheel, shades on, head tilted back. I could almost hear the soundtrack.

But as we rounded onto the West Side Highway at 96th street, the playground with the cement dinosaur where I used to play came into view, and my throat constricted.

I was learning that it would be like this: For only split seconds at a time would I really understand that my mother was gone.

As we drove along the Hudson I saw that all the trees had leafed out while I wasn't looking, and that, too, came as a shock. If I'd been asked, I'd have said that spring had never come, and that the sky had been black and murderous since my mother's death, the air a sooty, smoggy haze. But the sparkle of the Hudson River and the glaze of sunlight on the cars were so bright I lowered the visor.

"Music?" I said, before Jenny could ask me why I was so quiet.

"Leather and lace, baby," Jenny said, popping *Bella Donna* in the CD player, "leather and lace."

I laughed. This had long been our mantra – the old Stevie Nicks song title was what we were going for: Tough, yet feminine. Soon the hard pulse of the music had me lowering my foot to the gas. I'd taken Driver's Ed. I'd passed my drivers' test the very first time. I knew how to do this.

"So," Jenny said, turning down the music, "tell me about these people we're going to be staying with."

"Karen and Ben," I said. Of all the people my mother had wanted to visit, they were the only ones I remembered. What was I going to talk to them about? If my mother were with me, it would have been a trip down memory lane. But with her gone.... Had she been hoping we would reminisce about their glory days in "The Movement"?

I smiled at Jenny, glad to have her along. I always felt awkward around my mother's friends. Some gave me a moment of polite interest before ignoring me. Others, like Karen and Ben, treated me with too much respect – I was, after all, the daughter of my wise and wonderful mother. They'd ask me what I thought about the crisis in the Middle East or the Seattle anti-globalization protests, and I'd feel really stupid.

"They're OK," I said. "Real hippie types." They were outdoorsy, make your own pesto, live gently among the rural rednecks kind of people. My mother used to say how much she admired them – very supportive, she said – but what was there to be supportive of? They had moved to the country with the back-to-the-land hippies in the '70s and actually stayed. My mother found that heroic: I thought it was idiotic. They were keeping the faith for something that, in my opinion, they, like my mother, didn't want to face was long dead.

"Like how?" Jenny asked. "Do they do organic farming and stuff like that?" She sounded excited. I sighed. It was bad enough my mother seemed to think her time was so much better than mine – why did my friends have to think it was cool, too?

"I was only at their house once." I could clearly remember the dark forbidding woods and air thick with mosquitoes. "I was maybe 13." I had been old enough to argue with my mother to let me stay home, but young enough that she insisted on dragging me along. Karen and Ben had two sons, but they were eons older – 16 or 17 – with fiercely sullen faces that barely registered my existence.

The plan had been to go canoeing and camping, but the weather was horrible. When it wasn't raining the sky stayed overcast and the temperature was miserably cold. Karen made big fires and Ben whipped up batch after batch of too-spicy guacamole. The adults sat drinking wine and talking: politics, politics, politics. I wandered on and off the porch, picking up magazines and setting them down. Each time the rain stopped and I put on a jacket to go outside, the sky opened up again. Finally I grabbed a book and climbed into the hammock that was strung between the porch beams.

The more wine the grown-ups drank the louder they got. I was used to political talk – the soft sounds of Yes, Yes, you're so right – and the loud, argumentative sounds – No way! Are you out of your mind? – that didn't mean people were really angry. But the tone of this conversation must have shifted, because something, some sharpness, made me look up.

A skinny woman with frizzy red hair was jabbing her finger in the air at my mother, saying "don't you dare accuse me!" Then she stalked out with a sudden slap of the porch screen door.

For the rest of the weekend there were whispered conferences and people leaving rooms and pairing up to disappear into the rain. Everyone seemed on edge. Karen and my mother sat talking late into the night in the kitchen. When I asked her what was going on, she said, "nothing." I don't know why I bothered. I should have known by then there was only so much she would let me in on.

I thought back to what she had said in the hospital, her hint that I would learn more about my father. I knew I shouldn't get my hopes up. The trip would probably turn out to be a wild goose chase, and I would learn nothing at all.

Jenny began to doze, and I lowered the music. North of Albany the traffic thinned, the Thruway became the Northway, and it went down to two lanes. The road climbed into mountains that formed dark masses on both sides. Signs began to give the mileage for Montreal, and I slowed for exit 30.

"Where are we?" Jenny said, waking up as I took the exit ramp a little wide. I pulled over so we could get coffee at a roadside truck.

"Wow," Jenny said, getting out of the car and twirling in a 360-degree turn. "Will you look at this? It's total wilderness."

The road ahead seemed squeezed between the steel-gray, canyon-like mountains. The quiet, the sense of being overwhelmed, the forbiddingness of the landscape, came back to me from my earlier visit. But I noticed now what I hadn't then: The Adirondacks are beautiful.

I grabbed my camera from my pack on the back seat. I didn't photograph beautiful; I liked to shoot strewn broken bottles, layers of posters juxtaposed on a boarded up construction wall. But the light playing against the dark pines, the billowing white clouds shooting across the sky, were too striking to ignore.

Jenny got behind the wheel even though we didn't have far to go, and I navigated. As we drove the road twisted and turned, and great expanses of mountain unfolded in all directions. The scale was so vast, so unlike anything I knew, that I felt it unlock some tightness in my chest. There were waterfalls and rivers and meadows, and I guessed that whatever lay hidden in the wilderness must be even more dramatic.

The towns were so tiny we were out of them before we knew we were in. "There should be a fork in the road any minute," I said finally, following the hand-drawn map Karen had sent when I'd called to confirm my arrival. We turned onto a dirt road that led through dense woods until we saw a sign saying Berkstein/Rice and a big open meadow with a house set far back. We drove up the driveway.

"They're here!" I heard Ben call out, and saw Karen emerge from the back of the house, wiping her hands on her jeans. She was stockier than I remembered, her hair a cloud of blondish gray. I wondered when she had cut the waist-long braid she used to wear. From the dirt on her jeans I guessed she had been gardening. Ben, loping toward me, was a big scruffy man in overalls with an enormous black beard who always hugged me too hard. Now was no exception.

"Well!" they beamed, holding me at arms' length, just looking at me.

"This is my friend Jenny," I said. When I'd called to ask if it was O.K. to bring a friend, Karen had hesitated a split second before saying, "of course."

"Thanks for having me," Jenny reached out and shook hands.

"Let's take your bags in and get you settled," Ben said. "It's too late for a hike, but we can show you around, at least. We don't always get such great weather. Are you hungry?" I remembered what a talker Ben was, and how his constant good cheer put me off; somehow he always seemed a little too pleased with himself.

"We stopped for lunch," I said. We walked toward the house. It was larger than I remembered, and prettier, with an off-center peak, a wide front porch, and a sunroom facing east.

"It's not quite how I remember it," I said.

"It's been awhile since you were up," Karen said. "We added on a guest bedroom and the sun porch, and we cleared to make the meadow." We followed her inside. The house was a cliché of a country home magazine spread, I thought: exposed beams and bunches of herbs drying in the kitchen near the window seat, pine furniture and a wood-burning stove in the living room, just a shade too cozy for my taste. Karen led me down a hallway to a small bedroom that looked out on the distant mountains. "We put in lots of windows and converted to solar, both active and passive," she said, going on to explain what that meant — something to do with the stone tiles in the living room and panels on the roof — reminding me how earnest she was, how, just like my mother, she was always telling you more than you wanted to know.

"Do you have a letter for me from my mother?" I asked as soon as she took a breath.

"Yes, but she asked that we talk before I give it to you."

"But why?"

"There's just some things she wanted us to explain to you first – O.K.?"

I wanted to argue, but Karen was biting her lip, so I dropped it. What, really, was the point. "I guess," I said.

Over dinner they told us how they baked their own bread and grew their own vegetables and grazed sheep in a far pasture. Cartoons with farmers that I'd watched on TV as a kid came to mind. When they said they were considering keeping bees I started to nudge Jenny under the table, but then I saw she was actually impressed.

"Wow," she said. "I didn't know people could do that."

Karen went on to tell us that she worked at a community center and was heading up a project to get locally made crafts into stores statewide. "Your mother was helping me with that — did you know?" Karen turned to me. I didn't, but I nodded anyhow. "She had great advice on my campaign, too," Ben chimed in. He said he had been elected to the Town Board on a "sustainable economy" platform, whatever that was. "We can't expect folks to resist the lure of development if there's no alternative source of work," he said, staring at us intently, as if he needed our votes.

"And what are you involved in, Layla," Karen asked.

"Besides finishing school and visiting my mother in the hospital?" I said. "Nothing." They were just like my mother, thinking everyone had to be an activist. Was this what the trip was supposed to be about – my political education?

"Of course, sorry," Karen said, and I felt a flicker of shame. "Your mom said you and she went to the antiwar rally in Manhattan this past April. She was so pleased."

"It was awesome," Jenny chimed in eagerly, "really massive."

I bit my lip. I had gone to the rally only because all my friends were going and I didn't want to be left out. But Jenny didn't know that. Her cousin's husband had gotten killed in Iraq; I couldn't let her know I was unsure what I thought. I still worried that Iraq really did have weapons of mass destruction, and even if I was starting to think the invasion had been a mistake, I wasn't in the least convinced protest rallies were going to change anything.

The march had actually been kind of fun, except that I couldn't let go of the worry that I'd run into my mother and she'd embarrass me in front of my friends by chanting slogans at the top of her voice or singing "We Shall Overcome."

"I had a part-time job at a photo lab," I said to change the subject.

"Did you major in photography?"

"Art history." I had picked the major because it was different from my mother's world, her interests. Then I'd discovered photography.

"I may stay on at the lab," I said. "Whatever it takes to pay the rent." I wasn't ready to own up to my desire to do photography. It would be like saying I thought I was special, had talent. I wasn't going to kid myself about an artistic career.

"Gave up on becoming a hairdresser?" Karen grinned. I look down at the table and smoothed the fringe on my placemat. Once, when she was visiting us, Karen asked what I wanted to be when I grew up. My mother had been telling her about my difficulties in school. When my mother insisted that I only had to try harder, to believe in myself, I would feel as if she were standing behind me, pressing my shoulders down, and the sensation of pressure traveled all the way down my back to my feet.

I had stared at Karen's braid, at the way the sun highlighted the fuzzy split ends along its length in a kind of halo, and "hairdresser" popped out.

Karen's mouth dropped open in surprise. After a second she patted my hand. "Why, that's fine honey. Anything you want to do is just fine."

Later I heard her say to my mother, "she'll come into her own, you'll see." The hairdresser comment had embarrassed my mother with one of her feminist friends; I didn't hesitate to bring it up whenever I wanted to needle her.

"So, how long has it been since you were up here?" Ben asked, when the silence went on too long.

"I'm not sure exactly," I said. "There were a bunch of people, and it kept raining, and there was some woman who got pissed at my mother —"

"Oh that weekend!" Ben said, laughing. "Poor you, to be in the middle of that."

"What was it about, anyhow?"

"It was kind of ugly," Ben leaned forward on his elbows. "It had become public that the FBI had infiltrated the student political groups in the early '70s. That woman accused your mother."

"Of being an FBI agent?" Jenny asked, her eyes like round blue marbles.

"It turns out the woman doing the accusing was herself an infiltrator," Karen added. "Your mother suspected it."

"Wow," Jenny said. I suddenly thought of my mother's fear in the hospital of being overheard by the woman in the adjacent bed. Had the morphine shaken loose old memories?

"Yeah, those were pretty hairy times," Ben said, but he looked dreamy, as if he missed them.

"Listen," Karen said, "about tomorrow. Don't take offense at this Jenny, but we need to take Layla off with us. I don't mean to be mysterious. It's just that her mother asked us to keep it private."

"Oh sure, of course," Jenny said, her words rushed. "No problem."

"We'll bring you to a nice place to swim and then drop Layla to meet up with you later, if that's OK?"

"I understand," Jenny said graciously, cutting off the argument I'd been just about to give them. Why couldn't Jenny be privy to whatever they had to say?

We all turned in, but I couldn't get comfortable. I pulled the heavy wool blanket closer around me and made a mess of the bed sheets. After the warmth of the day, the chill of nighttime mountain air took me by surprise. Everything was unfamiliar — the scent of the dried lavender in a bowl on the night table, strange creaks in the house, rustlings from outside.

I got up, closed the window, and got back into bed, but I could still hear the eerie sound of wind high in the trees. I shimmied deep under the covers. I wanted to be home in my own bed, on the 15th floor. I finally drifted off to sleep by imagining that the wind wasn't wind but traffic, the white noise of the cars far down on Broadway.

○

The next morning was sharp and clear enough to cut yourself on. After we dropped Jenny, who whispered "good luck!" as she left the car with a beach chair, Karen and Ben insisted on taking me for what they called an easy hike. The hike left me breathless, and not because of the beauty of the mountains unfolding in all directions. Here they were, people in their 50s, in better shape than I was.

We settled on the granite boulders they told me had been left by glaciers and ate our lunch of tuna and egg salad while I hugged my knees, trying to contain my impatience. In the distance, mountains overlapped each other like the tissue-paper collages I'd done in school.

"We heard from your mother just before she died," Karen said finally. The words, dropped into the peace of the afternoon, seemed to echo against the mountains. "She asked us to tell you a little about your father."

I felt pinpricks on my skin, a curious tingling, even though it was what I had been waiting for. "She never wanted to talk about him," I said. "Not much, anyway."

"She had her reasons, good reasons. I guess she judged that you're old enough now to understand."

I had always hated the phrase, "not old enough to understand." So patronizing, smug. A handy excuse when people have their own reasons for holding back – shame, or sorrow, or anger.

When I didn't respond, Karen said, "You do want to know, don't you?" She and Ben were looking at me with the feigned casualness that masks intensity. I nodded. I felt my body pull into itself, like a turtle. I had always believed two things about my father. I believed he had loved my mother and me. And I believed that my mother didn't want to talk about him because there was something I might not want to hear. I did want to know more, but I didn't want to learn it from them.

"We were all part of SDS in the late '60s, early '70s, Students for a Democratic Society – you knew that, right?" Ben said. "I'm sure you've heard plenty about those days, but no matter how much you've heard, I doubt you could get a sense of what those times felt like – the sense of turmoil, of excitement, of being in the middle of history as it was being made." He paused. My father, I wanted to say. Enough about the '60s, tell me about my father.

"Everyone had friends going off to war. The draft made it very different from today's antiwar movement – more immediate, more personal. A huge number of young people were involved in the Movement, and over time, as the war dragged on, there was less agreement about how to end it, different factions with different ideas about how we could change society. It's so hard to convey..." his voice trailed off. "Anyhow, there was tremendous urgency. We felt we could lead the country to radical transformation only if our line – our theory – was correct. And so we were all in study groups...."

"I'm sorry," I broke in, "but what does this have to do with my father?"

"I'm getting to it," Ben said, looking uncharacteristically uncomfortable. He tugged at the black-and-white-checked bandana he wore around his neck.

"Your father was pretty mainstream. He believed in the cause, in fighting the war and transforming the political life of the United States. He was very committed. But he took a practical approach to politics. He would never have done anything crazy. There were some extreme factions on the Left – the Weatherpeople – but believe me, Layla, that was not our crowd. Your father was not like them. No way would he have had anything to do with them."

A chill went down my spine; what was Ben trying to say? I pulled my jacket on. From nearby came tiny rustles and murmurings of insects, as if the air itself were speaking.

"Look," I said. "Can't you just tell me whatever it is?"

Karen put a hand on Ben's arm. "On April 17th, 1971," she said, "a small group, including your father, staged a protest about the treatment of some Puerto Rican activists who were in jail awaiting trial. One of them, Raul, was a friend and classmate of your father's. Raul's brother learned he was to be taken from the jail to his arraignment, and when. The protest was supposed to be along the route the van was to travel. But some of the group decided to hold up the van, to let Raul escape. There was violence." She paused. "I'm sorry, Layla."

I felt my face become warm, my throat close up.

"What are you telling me?"

Ben and Karen were silent, just looking at me. "Your father's life changed as a result of that situation. He got caught up in something that, well – what matters is that ultimately it meant he wasn't part of your life."

"What do you mean?" my voice croaked. A jolt of fear and fury ripped through me. "What did it have to do with him dying?"

Karen and Ben exchanged glances. "I'm sorry we can't give you more details. The situation is complicated, Layla. There's a lot of history. I'm sure you'll learn more on this trip. You just have to be a bit patient."

"I don't understand!"

Karen gave a big sigh, then went on. "We gave your mother our word to do just as she asked. I'm sorry, I'm sure it's frustrating." Karen's voice was soft and soothing, as if she were talking to an overtired child throwing a tantrum. "She had her reasons."

"What bullshit!" I jumped up and rushed to the edge of the precipice so quickly Karen called out.

I stomped back. "What's all this supposed to mean? Why all the secrecy? Why didn't she tell me? Was she proud of him? Ashamed? Not that it matters. It's all such garbage –"

Ben grabbed me and wrapped his arms around me. He covered my mouth with a bear paw of a hand and rocked me back against him until I stopped fighting.

"It's no way to lose a father, that's for sure," he said finally.

O

But you can't lose something you've never had, can you? Even so, in some peculiar way, I had always felt I knew my father. Like that, I would find myself thinking, when I saw Jenny's father kiss the top of her head, or, not like that, when some man tweaked his daughter's ear.

Ben and Karen dropped me at the nearby swimming hole, but Jenny was nowhere to be seen. I propped myself against a rock to read but couldn't concentrate, so I closed my eyes and listened to the water bubbling around me. The rushing waters of a huge waterfall seemed to keep the bugs at bay. I tried to focus on the heat of the sun on my skin, the music of water over rock, the distant squeals of children, and blot out all thought. But Ben's words kept spinning in my head: "Your father ... very committed ... extreme factions." My mother had told me stories all my life about the antiwar movement, and I'd seen movies about that time. It was easy to imagine the angry young men with raised fists, the police van, the prisoners in handcuffs, uniformed guards.

I sat up, agitated, and put my feet in a little rivulet up to my ankles, which were immediately bombarded by tiny minnows. Near me children were exploring in the mosaic of rocks, poking a stick into the pea-green scum that coated the surface of a small pool. "Dad!" a girl shrieked, cupping something in her hands.

A man separated himself from a group. He had on cutoffs and a multicolored canvas hat and sunglasses: Quintessential, All-American Dad, the kind of dad I would have wanted.

"Please, Dad, please," the little girl was saying. He bent down and released into the water what may have been a frog. The girl's face was contorted with tears, and she began hitting him. "I hate you, I hate you."

I grabbed a fistful of pebbles. I stood up, flung the pebbles into the water, watched the little ripples they caused. I did not want to think of my father as a left-wing politico. I wanted him normal – conventional, even. Right now, I didn't want to think about him at all.

O

The next morning dawned overcast and gloomy, like a bad omen. I woke early and walked along the AuSable River. I had sat up late on the porch with Jenny, telling her everything I had learned, even though Karen had specifically told me not to, then not been able to sleep. Jenny's sympathy was like aloe on sunburn, but of course she had no answers, either.

On the way back from my walk I saw Ben in the garden, a ridiculous rumpled straw hat on his head.

"Dirt on my nose?" he said, looking up, catching my amusement.

I shook my head no.

"I love weeding," Ben said. "A simple exercise in good and evil. Weeds are evil, flowers are good. Unambiguous. As long as you know which ones are the weeds, right?"

It was the first thing he'd said that displayed a lack of total certainty, and I warmed to him despite myself.

"Sit for a minute?" he said, gesturing to a low wooden bench. After a second I sat down, a careful foot away, hunched into my jacket. Dark clouds raced over the mountains so quickly you would swear they were on fast-forward.

"So," Ben said. "How are you doing?"

"O.K.," I said.

He just looked at me.

"I'm fine," I said again.

"I'm sorry you're hurting," he said, and put a hand on my arm to stop my protest. My face burned, and my good feelings for him evaporated. I pulled my jacket hood over my head. How dare he? He had no right to tell me how I was feeling.

He waited, and when I didn't say anything, he went on. "It must be hard to make sense of, whatever your beliefs." He ran his hand through his bushy beard. "I have no idea what life must feel like to someone your age, Layla. No idea how you perceive the world, no idea of your experience. What happened with your father only makes sense in a context. He was trying to make a difference. Ours was a complicated time, an extraordinary time." His voice had quickened, but he must have seen something in my expression, because he sighed. "I'm not explaining this well."

"Yeah, I know all about it," I said dryly. "An incredible natural high."

"I guess I can't expect you to understand."

"Oh, I do. I just don't buy how great you think your experience was."

"What's your generation got that can compare? MySpace?"

"Just about," I said, flip. "That's what we're left with. I'm sure you can't imagine that." Belief systems like his and my mother's were bogus, just something to make you feel better in the face of a senseless universe. I wanted to be free of hypocrisy, to be too smart to get fooled that way.

"What keeps you going?" he said after a moment, as if he really wanted to know.

"The lack of a better alternative," I said. I turned away. I didn't want him to see from my face how lost I often felt, how terrified I was of the world. North Korea had just done nuclear tests. The U.S. was storing plutonium in outer space. Global warming was causing natural disasters everywhere. It was a joke to think some petition or rally was going to make any difference. I tried very hard not to think about any of it.

Ben fell silent, the fight gone out of him. But the victory left a bad taste in my mouth. We headed back to the house, the odors of fresh dirt pungent in the morning dew. It brought to mind the patch of dirt just outside our apartment building's lobby doors, where my mother, on the garden committee, planted marigolds, and I suddenly ached for her.

I went in search of Jenny, desperate to leave. She was in the kitchen helping Karen prepare breakfast. The blueberry pancakes were probably the best I've ever tasted, but they settled like cement in my stomach. The rain began just as we finished eating. Karen and Ben dashed with us to the car with our bags and we hugged in the rain.

"Thanks a lot," I said, sliding behind the wheel. "I really appreciate your putting up with me." It was a slip – I'd meant to thank them for putting me up. I knew I hadn't been much of a guest.

"I hope to see you again sometime," Jenny piped in.

"Keep in touch, O.K.?" Ben said. "Let us know how it goes." They leaned over the car window in their matching Gortex jackets, looking at me with identical expressions of parental concern, rain dripping from their hoods.

"Go inside, you're drowning," I said.

"Take care of yourself," Karen said. She smoothed a piece of hair off my forehead.

"Thanks again." I backed up and out quickly, trying to outrace the lump in my throat.

Once on the main road I pulled over and took out the sealed envelope Karen had given me. Like an animal with a prized bit of food, I had felt an incredible urge to get away from them before opening it.

Jenny leaned over my shoulder as I read.

Darling Layla,

Karen and Ben are such good people and the Adirondacks so spectacular that I wanted to start our journey here. It helps to know they are looking after you.

Enough beating around the bush. You must be angry – or confused? – that I left it to them to tell you the start of what happened with your father. The simple truth is that if I had told you when you were young you would have asked me questions that I wouldn't have wanted to answer. There was danger involved, danger to others that you would have been too young to understand. When I knew I was dying, I wanted to tell you, but couldn't, for important reasons. I know that growing up in a vacuum about your father has been painful, and I have to be honest here Layla, I chose that hurt to you over hurts I would have caused others.

I know I am holding back. You must feel I am toying with you, being mysterious, treating you like a child. I'm sorry. But this I promise: It won't be for much longer, and then you will know everything you need to make your own choices. I have faith that you will forgive me.

I love you,

Mom

I sat back, stunned. What was she talking about? What circumstances, what danger? Why was she being so evasive? How could any of my questions about my father, so long after his death, matter?

"What does she mean?" Jenny whispered.

"I have no idea." I thought of the days while I was in classes and my mother lay in her hospital bed, writing these letters. Whatever game she was playing, I was already sick of it. Sick of the drama and mystery. My mother was so stuck in '60s that she still believed in the dream, the vision, the "Revolution." Whatever she was going on about would have to do with that, I was sure, would turn out to be nothing.

I was sure of this. Because there was nothing in me – no fear, no tingles of presentiment – that vibrated in response to her words. Ultimately, whatever this was about, it would mean the world to her, but mean nothing whatsoever to me.

Chapter 3

$\mathcal{T}$he rain got heavier as we drove through softer, less dramatic countryside than the high peaks where Karen and Ben lived, but had eased to a light drizzle by the time we reached Lake Champlain. Jenny kept up a constant patter in time with the windshield wipers, darting little glances at me as she drove, as if assessing my mood. I made an effort, but "yeah," or "um, guess so," was all I could manage. Maybe it was what I'd learned about my parents, or maybe I was coming down with a cold; my skull was actually sore.

My mother's instructions were to spend a day in Burlington, Vermont, and then head to Massachusetts. On the ferry I got out of the car and stood at the railing, looking back at the Adirondack mountains, just visible through the gray mist. The water, too, was gray, gray with tiny whitecaps ruffled by the light breeze. I stared at the boat's wake as we plowed through the chop, feeling as if I – not the boat – was being pulled against my will, resisting going forward.

At least we would have Burlington. My mother had told me the city was a dump until a socialist mayor, Bernie Sanders, revived it. Now it was a showpiece and Sanders was in Congress. She had said this with pride, but all Jenny and I cared about was that it was supposed to be a fun college town, with tons of restaurants and stores, home of Ben and Jerry's ice cream. For a day at least, I'd put my mother and her secrets out of my mind.

Burlington had a funky waterfront, huge Victorian houses, and a cobblestoned downtown that was closed to cars and thronged with people. I imagined how it would have been to go to college here, biking up the windy streets to class. While Jenny went to find a bathroom I waited for her at a café and sipped a latte. The clothing style here was a punk-country hybrid, heavy black boots and long skirts, nose rings and tattoos. A couple, arms entwined so tightly they stumbled as they walked, sat down next to me. They leaned into each other, laughing. I found myself suddenly standing, wanting to run, like an uninvited guest at a party, badly dressed and without a date.

When Jenny returned we sauntered up the street, wandering in and out of stores. In a thrift shop she popped a funky felt hat on her head Janis Joplin style and struck a pose while I snapped her picture. In a Peace and Justice store we browsed for something to send as a thank you to Karen and Ben. There were Peruvian sweaters and utensils made from coconuts and some pretty handwoven placemats we decided Karen and Ben would love – they were made in Belize by a collective of Mayan Indians. "Sooooo P.C.," I mocked.

Then I spotted a tin box with little indentations – hammered, the sales clerk called it. I cupped it in my palm, curling my fingers around it. My mother's presence was so palpable I was sure that when I turned around I would see her on the other side of the store, looking through the Women's Studies books. I held the box so long my flesh brought the metal to the temperature of my skin.

My mother was not into "things" – as if it were a crime to own more than what was absolutely necessary when people in the world went without – but the little boxes in the collection on her bureau hinted at a softer side of her. She was no longer alive, but I bought the tin box for her just the same.

○

The next morning we set out for the long drive across Vermont and New Hampshire, most of it through forest interspersed with small towns, all looking the same after a while. Jenny and I took turns at the wheel and talked about everything – her uncertainties about whether she really wanted to start graduate school or should take a gap year, my mother's crazy agenda, whatever it was, our friends and what they were up to in the city – until we finally had enough and put on the radio.

We stopped at a diner for lunch; Jenny's phone beeped just as we were paying the bill, and she went outside to take the call. When she came back in her expression was worried.

"Layla, I hope you won't be upset."

"What is it?" I took the keys from her, my turn to drive.

"That was my cousin Cathy. I was thinking maybe, if you wouldn't mind? I'll stay with her in Boston instead of with your mom's friends?"

"I've bored you to death with all of this," I got in behind the wheel and closed the door, a little more emphatically than I meant to.

"No, you haven't, really. It's not that at all."

"I'm sorry. It's just a lot, you know?"

"Layla, look, you can check my messages. I called Cathy ages ago." She tilted her phone toward me. I glanced over at the list of calls and shrugged.

"I'll come with you if you'd rather – just say the word."

"No, really, it's OK. You haven't seen her in forever. We can all meet up."

"Exactly," she said, and stuck a post-it with Cathy's number on the glove compartment for me.

But the second I dropped Jenny at her cousin's in Jamaica Plain, I felt bereft. It would be so much easier having her along. I could remember nothing my mother might have told me about Lenny and Letitia, the couple I was to stay with. Still, they sounded nice on the phone when I called to confirm my arrival time, and as I drove into Cambridge I saw it was the kind of place that fit my mothers' friends – old houses, tall trees, bicycles everywhere. It spelled family, comfortable, hip family, we're all liberal professionals here.

A mocha-skinned male about my own age answered the door. He, at least, remembered his manners. I mostly gawked. He was drop-dead gorgeous. Suddenly I wasn't so sad Jenny wasn't along.

"You must be Layla," he said, "come on in." His voice, low and husky, surprised me, too, with its pronounced Boston accent. "Mom, Dad!" he yelled.

He drew me into a foyer whose walls were covered floor to ceiling with framed prints. A smiling black woman came toward me, followed by a reedy, fair-haired man, their contrasting skin tones explaining the luscious shade of their son's.

"Welcome," the woman kissed me on both cheeks. She was small and somewhat plump, meticulously dressed and made up. "I'm Letitia, you've met my son Trent, and this is my husband, Lenny."

"You remind me very much of your father," Lenny said. He was as pale as his wife was dark, with soft, tired-looking eyes.

"I do?" No one had ever said this before.

"But I never met your mother – maybe you resemble her, too," Lenny was quick to add. I was taken aback. He had never met my mother? What was I doing here, then?

"You must be exhausted. Come on in." Letitia said. "We were just relaxing before dinner. Trent, bring Layla's bags."

Trent, who had been leaning against the doorjamb, moved at the same time I did, and we nearly collided.

"Sorry," we both said. I looked into his dark eyes and then quickly away. He was a serious type, with close-cropped hair and studious glasses. I was glad I'd cut off my henna dye job – I had a sense it wouldn't have been his style.

I followed them into the living room, which had nooks and alcoves, a built-in bookcase, and a bay window with a cushioned seat. It was painted the palest green, like new leaves in springtime.

"Wow," I said.

Letitia smiled. "It was a bit cramped when the kids were

small, but now Justine is married and Trent is moving out, so it's manageable again."

"Where are you moving?" I asked Trent.

"Just off-campus," he said.

"Trent is starting a PhD in history at Harvard," Letitia said.

"Oh," I said.

"And yourself?" Lenny asked. "What are your plans?"

"This cross-country trip, then job hunting in the fall." I told them about my part-time job, the photography club. They told me which museums and exhibits I simply mustn't miss. I was aware how differently I was talking to them than I had to Karen and Ben – no edgy defensiveness here. Amazing what the presence of a really hot guy can do.

"With everything digital now, do you even learn developing?" Lenny asked.

"The teacher of the photography club thought it was still important. I like it – it's pretty cool." For a moment I was in the darkroom, apron covering my clothes, trying not to breathe as I stood over the tub full of chemicals.

"I've been thinking of buying a new camera," Trent said. "Maybe you could help?"

"Sure," I said, and took a sip of water so fast I nearly choked.

We had dinner around a large table in the kitchen, which was crammed with books and journals, reminding me of home, except that dinner times at home were just my mother and me, or, more often than not, just me, because she was out so much. Lenny and Letitia were both lawyers, and they were talkers, their words skipping over and around each other. "Imagine growing up with them," Trent turned to me at one point. "I could never win an argument."

"Oh you!" Letitia said, brushing his cheek with the back of her hand. He smiled, and my skin felt warm, as if it were my cheek she'd caressed.

After dessert, as if from a cue from his parents, Trent disappeared upstairs and Lenny and Letitia brought me into the living room. Suddenly I had no interest in finding out any more about my father. They settled me on the couch with masses of cushions and asked if I'd like a glass of Amaretto. I didn't, but I said yes; I had the uneasy feeling I was going to need it.

"We figured you'd like to talk right away," Letitia said. "We'll fill you in on what we can and then leave it to you what we can help you with." I felt myself fidget under their steady gaze. I sure wouldn't have wanted to be on the other side of a witness stand from either of them.

"My mother never told me anything, then she sends me on this trip – ." I stopped myself mid-sentence. "Thanks." I took a nervous sip of the liqueur and coughed. It sent a burning sensation down my throat.

"It's a long story," Letitia said. "Your mother wrote that by the time you got here you would know a little about what happened?" She waited for me to nod. "She and I met in college. Even though I was a couple of years older than she was and graduated earlier, we remained friends. After the incident with your father, she turned to me. She needed a lawyer. I was fresh out of law school."

"I'm confused," I said. "What did she need a lawyer for?"

Letitia hesitated. "Well, to clear your father's name."

"I don't understand." I tried to relax back into the couch cushions but immediately felt myself stiffen forward again.

"A guard was killed," Letitia said.

"Killed? I just thought there was some rock throwing. I didn't think someone got killed!"

Letitia's forehead wrinkled. "Your father was blamed. The others involved named him as the shooter."

"What?" My fingers clutched the edge of the couch, as if it were a boat that I was in danger of falling off.

"Your mother believed he had been wrongly accused," Lenny interjected quickly. "That's why she contacted Letitia."

I just stared at them. I couldn't take in what I was hearing.

"We kept a file from that time," Letitia said. "Mostly newspaper clippings. I think it's best to just give it to you to go through. Then we can talk some more."

They looked uncomfortable. I had the feeling they wanted to get rid of me, wanted to let the newspapers fill me in on the full horror of whatever my father – my parents – had been involved in.

Lenny left the room and returned with a large accordion-pleated file tied with a string. He held it until he had accompanied me to the guest room on the second floor, then placed it carefully on a bureau. I could hear music from down the hall, something I didn't recognize.

"Whenever you're ready, we'll answer any questions we can," Lenny said. "Sleep tight."

I stood at the door, not moving. I didn't know if I felt relieved to be left alone with whatever was in the file or upset that they had dumped it on me. The insistent bass from down the hall drew me; I wanted to knock on Trent's door and ask to hang out with him. I wanted to get away from the certainty of more to upset me. Instead I closed the door, put the thick file on the bed, and went to the window. The fresh air cooled my damp face. It was a sultry night, and I could hear cars, and muted laughter, and even crickets. There was a strong scent of roses, and of the honeysuckle that grew up the side of their house.

I sat on the bed and propped myself up against the pillows, put the folder next to me on the cotton bedspread. I drummed my fingers on the brown cardboard cover, then shoved the file away. I stared at it for a few minutes and then took a deep breath and pulled it onto my lap and untied the cord. Despite the coolness, my palms were sweating.

I spilled the contents on the bed. The folders were all labeled by date. I found the earliest, April 17, 1971. Inside were news-paper clippings.

"Shooting in the Bronx," said *The New York Times*. "Two Wounded in Jail Break," said the *Post*. "Peaceful Protest Turns

Violent," said *Newsday*. The photographs showed clusters of men with long hair or large Afros and very young faces, bodies on the ground, police with fierce, angry expressions. I read through all the clippings for April 17th. Although they said more or less what Karen and Ben had told me, there was no mention of my father, and only the guard's death was reported. Had my father had a gun? Could he have pulled the trigger? I had never touched a gun, never even seen more than a glimpse of a handle poking from a policeman's holster.

I put the clippings back into the file. Tomorrow, I thought. I'd deal with it better tomorrow.

I slipped into bed but couldn't fall asleep, still seeing the faces from the photos, the grainy expressions frozen for all time. Young, so very young. To have been involved in such a thing – such a terrible thing – when they were barely older than I was. It was unimaginable.

So young, so young, so young; the words played over and over in my mind. How old had my father been? I was tired, and when I tried to figure backward, the numbers swirled me toward sleep. April 22nd,1971. I was struggling with an incongruity, something that didn't add up. I sat up abruptly. I realized I had been assuming the incident was connected to my father's death. But Karen and Ben, I realized, had never said that. They had said I had lost him. I wasn't born until 1983, 12 years later, and he supposedly died soon after my birth.

I got back up, turned on the light, and pulled out the next file folder, even though my head was throbbing, my eyes burning. The clippings from the next day only rehashed the incident. Then I flipped to the next file and felt my stomach drop to my knees. There was a fuzzy photo of a solemn-faced man I wouldn't have known was my father and the headline: Shooter Flees. The paper shook in my fingers. According to the clipping, my father had run away.

O

The next morning I found Lenny alone in the kitchen. I stood a moment to try and control myself. I was furious, so furious my body was actually vibrating with anger, though at least the anger had cleared my mind.

"I need to know." I said to Lenny. "Did my father do this? How and when did he die? And why has it been kept such a big mystery?"

Lenny shoveled shredded wheat into his mouth as he considered my questions. He was dressed in a white shirt and a red tie, his jacket hanging on the doorknob. A lock of his pale blond hair fell over one eye. It made him look guilty, I thought, or at least apologetic.

"I'm sorry, Layla. I can't quite answer that."

"This is so unfair!"

"It is unfair, Layla, but –"

"Look, I know it's not your fault that my mother set this whole thing up this way, but I don't care what she told you to tell me. I really need to know. I have a right to know." It wasn't his fault, but he was here and my mother wasn't – I needed to shout at somebody.

"Layla, I didn't mean I wouldn't tell you – I meant I don't actually know. And from what you read in the clippings, maybe you can understand that there are things that can only be hinted at?"

I was too frustrated to think. "I don't know what you're talking about."

Lenny put his hands together, tip to tip, and leaned forward, like a lecturer at a podium. "Let's say, for the sake of argument, that I had helped your father rob a bank. I couldn't own up to that, right?"

Lenny just looked at me measuringly, waiting for me to put it together.

I pulled up a chair, scraping it too hard on the floor, and plunked myself into it. Lenny had said that he had never met my mother. It was Letitia who had known her. So his involvement would have been through Letitia.

"When did you and Letitia meet?" I asked.

Lenny nodded, smiling slightly, as if pleased with a key witness. "The winter of 1971. We met in a café near court. At the point when your mother needed help, we were at the early stages of our relationship, and no one – not friends, family, no one – knew about us. Interracial romances were something of a rarity back then. So there was no link. Letitia knew she could ask me for anything."

"I see," I said slowly. He was suggesting that he had helped my father – maybe even hidden him – after he ran away. But then why not just tell me? I knew it would have been a crime, maybe even landed him in jail, at the time. But now? I glanced up. He was an important lawyer. Could it ruin his career even now, so many years later? Was that what he meant by "things that can only be hinted at?"

The clippings had described the trial of two other defendants who had gotten heavy sentences. According to the papers, my father had remained missing for the duration of the trial. That was all I knew.

"We each can see only a small piece of the picture," Lenny said.

I felt my face get hot. Why was he spouting this nonsense? I started to snap back when it dawned on me that he might be telling me the exact truth. He wiped his mouth with a napkin, regarding me silently over his coffee cup. Karen and Ben had been members of the study group my father belonged to before the incident. Lenny had secretly helped my father after. So maybe everyone, and not just me, had been kept in the dark. Maybe each of them was connected to what happened with my father, but to only a piece of it. Could this be the point of my mother's plan? In a flash I glimpsed the design of the trip I was on – the careful sequencing of visits, the timing of the letters. Was I being told a story, and for some reason I couldn't yet understand, each person I would meet knew only a piece of the truth?

"Can you at least tell me how he died?" I said. "My mother said he was in a car crash. Was there one?"

"Layla, I'm sorry to say this again, but I really can't tell you."

"Can't, or won't?"

"A little bit of both. Your mother –"

"I don't believe this," I cut him off.

"I really am sorry. I know it's terribly frustrating, and a lot to take in." Lenny stood. "Look, I'm running late for work. We'll talk more later, O.K.?" Then, just as I was about to argue some more, he took the wind out of my sails.

"Trent's going to chauffeur you around today."

All I could do was nod. As angry and upset as I was, my heart leapt.

The pale yellow walls of the kitchen seemed to shimmer when Trent walked in a few minutes later – clean white T-shirt, still-damp hair, skin polished like in a magazine ad. He looked a little nerdy, but in a cool way, with his long face and high cheekbones and small-framed glasses. I wanted to touch that skin, it looked so silky.

"It's really nice of you to show me around," I said, in case he was thinking of backing out.

"I'm looking forward to it," he said. Amazingly he did seem eager. "You ever been to Boston before?"

I hadn't. We discussed where to go and set off. I was trying to figure out what I could talk to him about when he startled me by asking how I felt.

"What do you mean?"

"Learning about your father."

"You know about it?"

"Just what's public," he said, earnestly. "Don't worry, my parents wouldn't say much. I hope you don't think I'm being too nosy." He held the door open for me to pass. Outside was a clear, cool day, the shadows knife-edge perfect.

"I can't understand why my mother didn't just tell me."

"Well, it'd be a pretty upsetting thing for a little kid, I guess."

"But what about when I got older? I mean, let's face it, it's ancient history. Instead she sends me on this trip. At each place I get instructions about where I'm going next. And she seems to have told everyone I'm visiting exactly what, and what not, they're allowed to tell me."

"That is odd."

Trent ran a hand over his jaw, as if testing for stubble. "Maybe she wanted you to be with people who could be supportive when you learned the truth."

"Strangers?" I started to say, but I didn't want to be insulting. "Maybe." Suddenly I thought of my grandparents – both sets of grandparents. They must have conspired with my mother to say nothing. Was all this at the root of the "politics" that came between her and her parents?

An odd thought popped into my mind. I carried my mother's last name, not my father's. "He gave you your first, I get to give you your second," my mother, the true feminist, had explained. But maybe that, too, had been a lie. Maybe she had been ashamed.

"It feels so weird, like a movie," I sighed. "Somebody else's life."

"Well, those times were as dramatic as any movie," Trent said. "God, what I'd give to have been part of all that."

"What?" I said, taken aback.

"They had such an impact on history. Their lives were so much more intense. The antiwar movement these days doesn't come close."

"Yeah, but back then you could have been drafted! That sure didn't rock." I was so tired of how everyone hyped the '60s – the Beatles, the clothes – thinking everything about those times was so much better.

My tone was dryly snotty, but Trent just laughed. "True enough. But if we still had the draft, there'd be more of a movement now."

As I looked at his deep brown, slightly slanted eyes, the lovely planes of his cheeks, I found myself nodding.

"We could go to the Museum of Fine Arts," he was saying as we arrived at the bus stop, "but it's such a pretty day, I thought I'd first show you Beacon Hill and some Revolutionary War sites. Faneuil Hall, the Paul Revere House, the Old State House. The State House is my favorite – though it reminds me why I shouldn't romanticize protestors. Five of them – including a black guy, Crispus Attucks, were killed by the redcoats in the Boston massacre of 1770."

"Is that your field," I asked. "The Revolution?"

Trent laughed. "Yes, but not that one. I'm much more interested in this century – the Civil Rights Movement, the '60s, the history of social movements, which ones succeed and which ones fail. I'm so lucky to have activists for parents."

Lucky, I thought. Lucky was not the word I would have used.

"Primary sources," he went on. "To have direct access to such a transformative time." He fairly wiggled in his excitement. "And to have parents who care, who do something about problems, who make sacrifices."

I was silent. Sacrifices? It was possible my own father might have sacrificed someone else's life.

"It's so good to get to talk to someone who has the same background," Trent was still talking. "I was so excited when I heard you were coming."

The air got suddenly heavy, the shimmer zapped from the day. What a jerk I was. I'd totally misunderstood. I'd thought he was interested in me.

"You probably would have loved to watch *Salt of the Earth* with my mother," I said.

"That would have been great," he said, missing my sarcasm entirely. I kicked at a pebble. Couldn't I have something of my own? Did I always have to feel that I didn't measure up, that I couldn't escape my mother's shadow?

"Layla? Are you O.K.?"

I just shook my head.

"I've been insensitive," he said. "I've been so eager to talk about all this that I forgot it might be too painful. I'm so sorry."

"It's OK," I began. Then, as if his words called them forth, tears bloomed. If I'd tried to calculate something to snag his interest, I couldn't have done better. He gently put his arms around me and patted my back. Then he held my hand lightly for the rest of the day.

Like the sun coming back out after a storm, I was suddenly happy. And as the day went on, I found myself willing to at least think about ideas I usually brushed off, ideas like my mother's but sounding so much better coming from Trent. Was I a phony, just trying to get him to like me? Or was I more my mother's daughter in my beliefs than I liked to think? I don't know. Maybe it was just that I wanted to keep Trent's eyes fixed on my face.

And so as we walked, he mostly talked and I mostly listened. He told me how it felt to be biracial. He said he felt black in school in Boston but white when he was around street kids, so different from him, the son of professionals. "I went through my black nationalist phase, but I really couldn't buy it, and I went through my black street phase, but I didn't fit in. And of course with leftists for parents, it's hard to rebel, right? It's the downside of sharing your parents' values. For me, music's the only arena to rebel in," he shrugged, smiling.

"I never thought about it like that," I said. "But my mother and I weren't as close in our values as I guess you and your parents are."

"Like what?" he asked. "What did you disagree about?" We settled on a bench in the Public Garden. The leaves on the trees were so bright they looked just hatched.

"Well, Cuba – she always made excuses for Castro – and the death penalty. It bothered her that I thought it was justified in certain situations." Even to me, this sounded pretty lame.

"But the war? Abortion rights, civil rights, the environment?"

"Well yeah, we agreed on those." Funny, but I'd never thought of my conflicts with my mother in terms of rebelling against a rebel. I'd become so frustrated by our arguments, the way the issues between us seemed hard to put a finger on, to become thin as ash. Something about her know-it-all-ness? Had I butted up against her just to butt up against her?

"Maybe it was that she was kind of rigid," I said, thinking aloud. "She didn't want me to have a MySpace page, she barely let me download anything, she was afraid of viruses and privacy and all that. Plus," I turned to him, eager now that I thought of something, "she was upset with my photographs. I like to take pictures of homeless people, drunks. Stuff that's real. She called them exploitative."

"Will you show me some of your photographs?"

"Well, maybe," I hesitated. I felt a warm tingly glow. "O.K. But you have to let me photograph you." The words popped out of my mouth before I could censor them.

"No!" he groaned, covering his face, laughing.

"Yes," I said, feeling as bold as if I had just jumped on a table to shimmy in a room full of strangers.

We started walking again. "I'm sure you and your mother would have worked things out between you," he said, serious again.

I felt a pang. That would never be possible now. "Do you ever feel like the politics are too dominant?" I asked him. "That other things get sacrificed?"

"It sounds like you've felt that way," he said. "What was it you think your mother may have sacrificed?"

Me, I thought, but was too embarrassed to say. How could my little problems compete with women's rights or nuclear disarmament? "Well, she never had time for relationships, you know, with men," I said. "And we were always short of money...." I trailed off. I sounded so petty.

I expected a lecture, but he surprised me again.

"I understand. It was different for me. I mean, my parents do a lot of pro bono work, but they still make decent money. I'm wondering, though. Maybe what you're thinking had to do with your mother's activism had more to do with being raised by a single parent?"

"I never thought of that," I said slowly. My mother was so competent; it hadn't crossed my mind that she found anything difficult. "She never complained about it being hard."

"She probably didn't want you to feel like a burden."

His words stung. As if he sensed it, he brushed my cheek with the back of his hand, a gesture just like his mother's to him the night before.

We got on the T to go back. I was suddenly exhausted, feeling the effects of having been up half the night, and rested my head on his shoulder. "You said you're interested in which social movements are successful," I said. "Does that mean you think our parents were successful?"

"Yeah, right – what's success?" he straightened slightly. "Well, the Movement died, but it did bring attention to the war, the ills of capitalism. And many of those activists, like our parents, stayed active. That's one of the things I'm interested in – how they keep up their energy and commitment over time." He turned, tapped the inside of my wrist with a finger. "Hey. This peace group I'm involved with is having a rally next week. It would be fun to do together."

A flame of excitement shot through me. For a moment I imagined it. I imagined leading a demonstration with Trent, escaping teargas, reading statements to the press. I imagined being a heroine. For a moment I was in the '60s, just like my parents, and, for a second, I got it.

Then I was in the here and now, and in a brazen mood unlike my normal self, I was tracing the silky smooth skin of Trent's arm with a finger.

○

That night I went to an outdoor concert with Jenny and her cousin Cathy. I'd been about to ask Trent if he wanted to come when he mentioned he was going to a ballgame with a friend and apologized for not having an extra ticket for me. "But save tomorrow night for me, O.K.?" I nodded. I couldn't get him off my mind all night: I was so comfortable with him it was positively weird.

The next morning, when I walked into the kitchen I saw my mother's head bent over her morning *Times*, her pencil poised above the crossword. I must have made some sound, because she looked up. It was Letitia, of course.

"Did I startle you?" she said. "I get up early," she went on, as if apologizing for being there.

"No – I thought – ." I just shook my head. My mother's hair was brown going gray. How could I have thought Letitia's black hair was hers?

"Come, sit, have some coffee. When the kids were small I used to sneak down before they were up. I had tons of legal work to do but I did these instead. My addiction. My guilty little secret." She smiled.

"My mother's too," I smiled back. "Among others," I added.

The smile disappeared from Letitia's face. I felt my own grow hot under her scrutiny, and turned away to fill up a mug. "Do I sound like a bitch?" I finally asked, when she still said nothing.

"Uh-uh," she shook her head. "It's not that. I was just thinking how peculiar it must seem to you. How confused and upset you must be."

"All this secrecy. It all seems so, so.... overblown."

"I guess, for now, you just have to trust her," Letitia said. She shrugged, gave a rueful smile. I was tired of being told to trust, to be patient. I wanted answers. But I couldn't think of anything to say that wouldn't be rude. I felt Letitia's eyes on me, an appraising look laced with sympathy.

"Trust that there's a reason for this plan of hers," she continued. "I'm not sure what your mother had in mind, but what I do know is that she always had your best interests at heart. Realize that there could still be –" she seemed to be struggling for the exact word " – consequences. You understand?"

Consequences? To whom? "Not really," I said. "Does it have to be such a big mystery?"

"We've told you everything we can." Her voice trailed off. She looked as if she was going to say something more, but just shrugged and shook her head. "Try not to worry, Layla." She surprised me then, placed her hands on my shoulders and kissed my forehead. She did a half twirl to the counter and pulled on an apron, as if seized by a manic energy. "I'm in the mood to whip up some French toast, how does that sound?"

She wouldn't let me help, so I just watched her, the smooth way she moved around the kitchen. She seemed so comfortable with herself. She conveyed warmth, serenity, security, and I found myself leaning toward her, like an undernourished plant to the sun. I wanted to be in that circle of light, warmed by it. I wanted, I realized, to be hugged.

Letitia tilted her head at me and smiled, and I noticed for the first time that she had a dimple in her cheek, just like her son's.

○

That night, Lenny and Letitia went out with friends. Trent and I borrowed candles from the downstairs mantle and closed the door to his room. We drank an inexpensive bottle of wine too quickly. Then I posed him in all sorts of silly ways and took pictures, until we fell giggling on the bed. His face was close to mine and I traced the dimple in his cheek with a finger. He pulled me to him and held me so tightly I could feel how fast his heart beat. We made love, and I was full of a desperate energy, so desperate that, had it not been so sweet, I would have felt embarrassed afterward.

We talked then, he leaning up against the headboard, me leaning up against him. "I wish you didn't have to leave so soon," he said. He stroked my hair, and in the mirror opposite I could see just the top of my head and his long, slender fingers.

"Me too," I said.

"Want to hear some music?" He jumped up. "What do you like? Probably that emo stuff, like all the females your age."

"Ha!" I said, "and you probably like rap, like all the males your age."

"OK, now this is serious. If you don't like indie rock I may have to throw you out of my room."

"But I do, I do!" I cried. "Don't banish me."

"How about Black Mountain?" I had never heard of them.

"OK, then, sit still and just listen."

"They are pretty amazing," I said after a couple of cuts.

"I'll burn you some CDs before you leave." He kissed my shoulder, and a shiver went from my head to the soles of my feet. "I'll come visit you in New York once you're back, if you like." I felt a spurt of happiness, chased by trepidation.

"Trent," I hesitated. Was I crazy? I didn't want to sabotage myself, but I needed to get this out. "You know I'm not like you when it comes to politics." I felt his breath on my neck, but he didn't say anything. Why did I feel I had to be so honest? "I'm not an activist. I mean, I go to rallies against the war, and to concerts for good causes, but –"

"Are you giving me the brush off?"

"Of course not. I've never clicked with anyone like this," I mumbled into his arm.

"Other things are important, too." He turned me toward him, drew my eyebrows with his finger. "Besides, I'm not sure that you don't share my values, exactly."

"What other things?" I asked, ignoring the last part.

"Well," he drawled, his finger running down my throat, making me swallow doubletime, "you have a good heart, and I like your sense of humor," his finger was in my armpit now, tickling me. "I like that it embarrasses you that you're so pretty. And you're passionate – not just like this," he said, his hand grazing my leg. "I like that you're full of feeling – about whatever – music, photography."

"I guess I just worry that you don't really know me."

His arms around me tightened. "Of course not. But I want to. O.K. to leave it at that for now?"

"OK," I said. But later, unable to sleep, I couldn't help but wonder if he had thrown a gloss over me, like a magic cape spun from my left-wing pedigree. And I couldn't quite trust my own feelings, either. What if I was drawn to him because he was exotic? Being around boys always felt strained. How could I trust something that felt this easy?

I woke up edgy from half-remembered dreams. Confronting me, on the bureau, was my mother's envelope; Lenny had given it to me, but I hadn't wanted to open it the night before. I hadn't wanted to spoil the evening.

I said my goodbyes, hugging Lenny, Letitia, and Trent in turn and then doing another round, ending with Trent, before I finally got myself out the door. Trent pressed a piece of paper into my hand – his contact info. I slipped it into my organizer, like a pressed rose.

On my way to pick up Jenny in Jamaica Plain, I knew I had to say goodbye to her, too.

We sat side by side on the stoop. I had not yet read my mother's letter except to glance at the instructions about where to go next – a motel near San Francisco – and the dates I was booked in.

"It's clear across to California," I said. "You need to get to your job."

"Are you sure? Are you really really sure?"

"Yes," I said emphatically. I didn't want to give voice to the uneasiness I was beginning to feel. But something made me hold back from telling her what I'd learned from Letitia and Lenny, and something was telling me the rest of the trip was something I had to do on my own.

"I'll miss you so much," I said. My eyes filled. She put her hand over mine.

"Love you," she said.

"Love you, too."

Once on the highway, I needed all my concentration to navigate the thick clog of highway traffic. At some point I became aware of sirens behind me; the snarling wail raised the hairs on the back of my neck. In the rearview mirror I saw lights twirling madly, an ambulance thundering toward me, loudly honking cars out of its way. Suddenly I was back in the hospital, running down the corridor to my mother, heart pounding. I pulled over to the side of the road. The ambulance passed me like a shot, still honking.

The traffic had thinned without my noticing. Up ahead was something white in the road. For a second I thought it was a garment somehow escaped from the ambulance. But it was just a roll of toilet paper. It skittered along the ground, unraveling into a long streamer. With a gust of wind, it broke into several pieces, flutters of white floating up, like a flock of birds leaving the ground all at once. I began to giggle, and then, abruptly, to cry.

It shouldn't be so easy for what was solid to dissipate just like that. To unravel in seconds, just like that.

Chapter 4

Looking back from the other end of this summer, I can see that Trent and Cambridge were a turning point. Something inside me had shifted slightly, a shift in perspective, a slight softening, perhaps. I think of what my mother said to me just before she died: Try and let go of your anger, Layla. I still have some of that out-of-temper child in me. But I like to think that there is also the beginning of the wiser woman I will someday become.

Did I sense that shift? I was unsettled by how quickly things had happened between Trent and me. In a way he had given me a new story of myself, and I wondered if that was part of why I found him so seductive. His openness seemed to draw things from me I'd never voiced aloud. It felt good to fling myself at something, to feel daring and reckless, as exhilarating as standing, toes curled over the edge of a diving board, and letting myself fall into a deep pool of water. But now, alone with my thoughts as I drove, I felt queasy. I kept thinking, why did I tell him that? I felt like an egg cracked open, yolk trembling.

Just the thought of his coming to visit me in New York gave me a rush down to my fingertips, and I could feel my face heat up. I tucked the thought close, to sustain me in the weeks ahead. But I didn't yet sense that his presence in my life, the way he looked at things, had made me think a little differently, too. He had turned me ever so slightly in a different direction, realigned me the way a magnet does metal filings. He had set me up for what was to come.

I did sense that I was headed straight into the heart of my journey, into the real center, the long lonely stretches, the unfamiliar terrain, the dust and heat of summer. I learned that there's a rhythm to driving long distances, a rhythm and a mood, and I felt a strange sadness as I passed the outskirts of towns and cities I never stopped to see, at the sameness of the McDonald's and the Mobil gas stations that fool you into thinking you've seen everything, when you've seen nothing at all. Just off the road there might be a woman who could become a friend, or an old man with a story to tell, or a river whose grassy banks could alter the course of your life. But I would never know, because my eyes were on the asphalt and one hand gripped the wheel while the other held coffee in a nonrecyclable Styrofoam cup, and I was feeling smug with my growing confidence in myself, my big city sophistication that I wasn't yet sophisticated enough to know had no value whatsoever.

I remember the sheer hugeness of the country, how much was nearly empty, and how 80 feels like 40 when the road is flat and straight. I remember heat that shimmered in little pools on the blacktop and then vanished, heat that pooled in my armpits the instant I stepped out of the car, and the way my moods shifted every two-and-a-half minutes with the song on the radio. But most of all I remember the eerie sound of emptiness, like a heartbeat of silence, as I stood next to the car on the highway to take a stretch, just me and the sun and the heat, and the big sky and me, and a faint trill of bird song on a faint rush of wind.

My mother's letter read:

> Darling Layla,
> Bear with me just a little longer. Lean on those around you for support, like strong trees with welcoming branches. Know I love you.
> Mom

This was it? She keeps from me my own history, and she offers me trees and branches?

According to her instructions I had eight days to make it to the motel in Oakland. She had indicated no designated places along the way, so I could stop when and where I wanted. But I took nine days instead, and so I missed a chance, a chance that perhaps would have changed the way everything has turned out. Perhaps.

I knew nothing of the middle of the country. The cities, towns, and states were just words from grade-school geography, words that matched the products I had drawn on maps: potatoes for Idaho, steak for Nebraska. I decided to travel on Route 80 the whole way, a straight shot. I didn't stay for the Fire Department barbecues or the ooze-ball tournament. I didn't detour to check out the road race and I didn't stop for the wild blueberry pie. I made it from Boston to Buffalo the first day, to Chicago the second, and to just past Des Moines the third, traveling close to 10 hours a day. Route 80 was like a tightrope connecting me to the west coast; I was a little afraid that if I stepped off I'd fall into an abyss and never find my way back.

I was amazed at the flatness of the land in the middle of the country opening out before me like a vast undulating blanket. Des Moines to Omaha, Omaha to North Platte. I'd never seen grasses like this, rippling in the breeze as far as the eye could see, the sun glinting and shimmering like the sheen of gold thread in a lustrous silk moiré. It was hypnotic, and I kept rubbing my eyes, afraid I'd drift off.

As the hours passed I found myself relaxing to the hum of the motor and the swish of the cars. I found I liked the anonymity of the road, the mystery, the sense that, although you are part of this metallic stream, no one knows who you are or what you're like other than what can be gleaned from the size and make and color of your car, the way you pass and speed and signal. And I discovered the best thing of all: You can sing to your heart's content.

Even at home alone I was too self-conscious to really let loose; I didn't have a good voice, and I was sure the neighbors would hear me through the walls. But a car on a highway is a soundproof vocal chamber. I put Sarah McLaughlin in the CD player and sang along until I could match every inflection, every tremble, in her voice. It felt great. I played all my rock CDs, everything upbeat, singing until I tired, avoiding anything slow or sad that might make me cry. My Derek and the Dominos tape, which my mother had played for me every year on my birthday, I kept zipped into an inside pocket of my backpack.

I checked in to cheap motels with crappy TV reception each night. And after a few days I was tired, bored, and lonely.

Which, of course, explains that extra day.

I had been afraid of the one rite of passage I was sure would befall me – the flat tire, the breakdown. It was a breakdown, but it wasn't mine.

She was standing by the side of the road beside a beat-up old blue Chevy. I slowed. I knew not to pick up hitchhikers, but this wasn't some psychotic guy hiding a machete. This was a woman, and an amazing-looking one at that. She was very tall and slender, with blond hair that hung to her waist and then some. She was dressed in a halter T-shirt and cargo shorts – cut down from pants, with frayed edges – that showed off her tanned legs and arms. And muscles! They were the kind you get roping cattle or white-water rafting, I thought. Something they did in the West.

"Hi," I said, pulling over. "Need help?"

"I broke down," she said. "Where are you headed?"

"Cheyenne or thereabouts," I said. "I figure I'll make it there tomorrow morning. Or I can take you to a nearby garage if you like."

"I'm ditching the car. Can I just hitch a ride?"

"Sure," I said. I was surprised she'd just leave the car, but it wasn't my business.

She pulled off her canvas backpack and threw it in my back seat, held out her hand. "Heather." Then she turned and shouted, "Peewee!" and from the grasses by the side of the road emerged a small boy. He had wheat-blond hair flattened by sweat and a splatter of freckles across his nose and cheeks. "It's hard hitching with a kid," she explained, and I realized she'd purposely hidden him.

We plopped the boy in the back and strapped him in. Heather slid in the front and flipped her hair behind her shoulder with the back of her hand in a graceful, practiced gesture. I suddenly wished I hadn't chopped off all of mine, and I found myself imitating her movement with my hand, storing it for the future.

"So," I said, "where to?"

"I'm headed back to Colorado – Cheyenne's not far from the border, so that will get me close. You really should come to Colorado."

"I've got a timetable to keep to," I said. "So where in Colorado do you live?"

"Nowhere at the moment. I've been living with Tyler's dad. We broke up. I was thinking I'd go to Boulder. I got a friend plays in a band. There's a big music festival happening. I'm gonna camp there while I figure out what to do."

Music festival. The words were like a chocolate shake on a hot day. Boulder wasn't so far south, I thought. Just a little tether off my Route 80 tightrope.

"It's gonna be great, you should check it out." She began beating a little rhythm with her forefinger on the dashboard.

"Who's playing?" I asked.

"Oh, everyone. Nickel Creek, Arcade Fire, tons of others. My friend's band is In Tune. They're good."

I took a swig from my water bottle. "Well, maybe," I said.

"Cool," she said, unsurprised, as if she'd known I would.

As we drove Heather talked a blue streak, but she was sparing with any actual facts. She said she was going to get her old job back at a mountaineering club in Estes Park. I admired how sure of herself she was, as if she knew that life would always give her what she wanted, that things would always work out.

At the outskirts of Cheyenne we found a motel. There was just one room available, with a king-sized bed, so Tyler slept in the middle. He had the sweetest little boy smell after his bath, of lemon soap and fresh-cut grass. I woke up in the night and found him curled up against me, his airy snore like blowing bubbles.

"So, do you think you'll stay in Boulder, now that you and your husband broke up?" I asked Heather the next morning as we ate a huge breakfast at a truck stop diner. It felt refreshing to get away from my problems.

"My ex-boyfriend, you mean," Heather said. "Good-for-nothing creep. I don't know. Leaving was kind of an impulse. I just wish I could have seen his face when he noticed his car was gone."

"The car was his?"

She laughed. "You could say we broke up when I walked out with Peewee and the car."

"Does he have legal rights to your son?" I noticed I was crumbling my toast into little pebbles, and stopped.

"Hey, don't go getting all prissy on me," she said.

"Sorry."

"Tyler's all mine, no need to worry."

I sighed. It was not my problem. Still, I looked at Tyler, and my stomach knotted.

We were back in the car, already seeing signs for Boulder, when she asked for a favor. I felt something sink inside me, a feeling like, uh-oh, I should have known, but I had no idea what, exactly, I feared.

"Sure, I guess," I said.

"I want to stop a minute at my mom's. It's on the way."

She directed me to a housing development and into the driveway of a small house. "I'll just be a minute," she said. "Peewee, come and say hi to grandma."

I watched them go inside, turned on the radio. I should try to be more like her, I thought, carefree, easy. A real free spirit. I sighed. Somehow, without the long blond hair, I couldn't picture it. I twirled the radio dial. Just as I was starting to get edgy, there was a burst of shouting from the house, the door was flung open, and Heather was hurtling to the car, Tyler running on little legs to keep up. A big woman was framed in the doorway. She shouted, "don't think you can fool me again!" and slammed the door.

Heather flung open the back door, shoved Tyler in. "She's such a bitch," Heather breathed.

"I used to fight with my mother, too," I said.

"You'd think she'd want to spend a little time with her grandson."

"You wanted to leave Tyler?" I asked.

"We're only talking a few days, until I get myself settled," she said.

I started to say how much fun the festival would be for Tyler, but checked myself. I could understand it might be hard for her to look for a place to live with him in tow.

"You ever make a big effin' mistake in your life?" Heather said, as I headed back to the highway.

"Well, not really yet, I guess," I said. "I'm only 22."

Heather threw back her head and guffawed. "That's good, that's really good." She couldn't stop laughing. "I'm 25. I was 17 when I had Tyler, not that I don't love him to death, right Peewee?" I glanced back again at Tyler. He was staring out the window, expressionless.

At the festival we parked in a huge field crowded with cars. "Guess I'll go pitch the tent," Heather said. "Want to stay with Layla?" she asked Tyler. He said no before I had time to react. "He doesn't really know you," she said to me apologetically, as if I would have wanted to mind her son.

I felt enormous relief as soon as they were out of sight and made my way to the area of the music tents, standing on the fringes. My mood lifted with the crowds jumping up and down, half-naked in the heat, and the music, clear and wild and perfect. I took out my camera and began shooting. It occurred to me that I could use this trip for my own, rather than my mother's, purposes – my photography; it amazed me the thought hadn't crossed my mind, it was so obvious, and I laughed.

I didn't see Heather again until her friends' band was playing. I saw her dancing like a whirling dervish in front of the stage. She was so loose, so oblivious. Tyler was standing alone on the outskirts of the tent, watching his mother and looking lost; I grabbed him and swung him around.

Suddenly I was knocked into, hard, and stumbled to my knees. Over me stood a rail-thin man with a long cowboy mustache and ferocious, angry eyes.

"Daddy!" Tyler grabbed the man's legs. The man scooped him up. I stood up, stupid, not knowing what to do.

"Hey," I said, as he started to walk away, "you can't just take him."

"Who are you, anyway?" he asked me.

"Nobody," I said. "I just gave them a ride."

"What did she tell you?" he asked. He leaned back a little, his weight on one leg, as if suddenly he had all the time in world.

"Nothing much," I said, unsure. "Just that you two broke up."

"She's been cheating on me," he said. He pointed. "The drummer."

"Oh," I said.

"She's a piece of work, all right." Again he started to walk away.

"Wait – " I started again. "She said you had no legal rights – "

He turned back to me. "What are you, a lawyer? She walked out on me, took my son, you're telling me what I can and can't do?"

I breathed out; I felt my fists open and close.

"No, I'm sorry," I said. "But please, just go talk to her. For Tyler's sake?"

"She's left him for weeks at a time with her mother, her friends. You're lucky you didn't end up with him."

"She loves him," I said, wanting it to be true.

"She likes the power it gives her over me," he said, "that's it."

But to my surprise, he started toward Heather. She turned. Go to him, I thought, go! But instead she turned her back. Tyler's father glanced at me and shrugged, as if to say, "see?" He hoisted Tyler to his shoulders and strode away. I watched, shaken. When I looked again at Heather, she was back in front of the stage, dancing.

O

I arrived at the Ho-Hum motel in Oakland, California, a full day late, though I'd tried to make up the time. I was shaken by the experience with Heather. I never felt I mattered as much to my mother as her politics or even, sometimes, her students, but she would never have left me. Face to face with true indifference shocked me to the core. And my confidence in myself was thrown, too. I'd been taken in by Heather, accepted what was on the surface. Clearly I wasn't as clear-eyed as I'd thought.

It was late afternoon and I was as kinked as a pretzel from the drive. I unpacked my bathing suit for a swim.

The motel pool fronted the road, so close I jumped each time I heard a car, but it was ringed with flowering bushes, and the water was as warm and soothing as warm milk. The sun twinkled and zigzagged on the pool's aquamarine surface like in the David Hockney paintings I'd seen at the Met. I swam a few laps and then settled into a chaise, thinking about Trent, drifting into a soft, dreamy mood, a velvety golden mood I've always thought of as Californian.

The tap on my shoulder startled me. The desk clerk handed me an Express envelope. "Forgot to give this to you," he said. "Been here a couple of days."

I struggled to sit up, suddenly anxious and alert. I recognized my mother's handwriting, yet the postmark said San Diego. Who could have mailed this? I ripped it open. Inside a short note was paper-clipped to yet another sealed envelope.

Layla,

I should have burned these, but I couldn't bring myself to.

Mom

What now? More clippings? I pulled out a few sheets of paper as worn and thin as an old Chambray shirt. Letters. I flipped through quickly; they were all addressed to my mother. The first was dated 1971.

Dear Audrey,

What joy in having the luxury to write to you! First off, I am safe and sound; be reassured on that point! Happy? As happy as I can be under the circumstances and away from you. I keep you in my heart always, I talk to you in my mind between our talks, I keep the date of the next time I will see you fixed like a star on the horizon to comfort me.

The place where I'm living has much to recommend it. There are tall trees, very tall, and the communities are tight, the tradition tough. Can you guess? Here people judge you by how hard you work, by the kind of silence you keep. It suits me fine, though it's too far from you.

Love as always

There was a mark, perhaps an initial, that I couldn't make out. Could the letter have been from my father? It didn't sound like the kind of thing a man who had just run away from a shooting would write.

The next letter, dated 8 months later, was clearly in the same hand.

Dear Audrey,

The goblins of depression have got me in their grip. I hate to write to you when I'm like this, but you've said I should, and I'm listening to you, as always! I'm in one of those moods where *my life feels claustrophobic and worthless, where I yearn for normalcy, where every woman reminds me that I'm not with you, every man seems a threat for your attentions, every child the child I cannot have. I'm useless these days, Audrey. I need to hear that this isn't how I will always feel.*

Again the enigmatic doodle at the end, even though the letter simply trailed off. Was this my father? Had he been writing from jail? Who was the child he could not have? If these were from my father, why had my mother never shown them to me? The next letter was dated 1993.

Darling Audrey,

GOD, I could shout with ecstasy! I swear I will hold on to our three days together and make them last until we are together again.

And thank you, thank you, thank you for figuring out a way for me to see her. They were playing in the schoolyard, I was craning my neck to keep my eye on her among all the children, afraid one of the teachers would think I was a letch and report me, when like a miracle the ball she was chasing came zooming toward the fence. I've never run so fast. I made as if I thought the ball was going to come through the fence and I was going to catch it. All I wanted was to come face to face with her. We made it to the same spot at the same time, she on her side of the fence, me on mine, and she snatched at the ball as if she thought I could magically get it. She looked at me, face red with exertion or confusion or accusation – my paranoia, no doubt? – and I just stared at her. I couldn't help it, even at the risk of unnerving and frightening her. "Great catch," I said, and tried to smile in a winning, nonthreatening way.

"But I didn't catch it," she said.

"A great try is as great as a great catch," I said. She just stared at me for a long moment, then turned and ran away. There was something in her stare, Audrey, I don't know how to express it,

and I'm sure you'll think I'm being fanciful. But it was as if she knew who I was – or somehow knew that she was important to me. I wonder if she mentioned it to you? I really feel as if something meaningful passed between us.

I put down the letter. The memory was sharp and immediate: the dusty school yard, the hard, white ball, the stare from a strange man, a stare that had thrilled and terrified me in its intensity.

There were a few more letters. Later I would read them slowly and carefully, plumbing them for details, but that afternoon, by the side of the pool, I simply rushed through them all.

The last paper in the pack was a short note from my mother.

If you want to see him, go straight to the address below. He'll be there until the 15th. You'll have another opportunity later on if you change your mind.

It would be best if you burn all of these.

And so it was in this way, alone, 3,000 miles from home, shivering in a wet bathing suit by the side of a pool at the Ho-Hum motel, the late afternoon light fracturing my vision, that I learned my father was alive. He was not dead. He was not in jail. He was still, apparently, a fugitive. I raced to the car and pulled out my map. I stood out in the parking lot in my towel, studying the map, calculating and recalculating, trying to make the impossible, possible. He was a day's drive away. I could not get there in time. I bit down into the wet cloth to cut off a sob.

Of course, I don't know if, had I arrived at the motel on schedule, I would have chosen to meet my father anyway. Maybe I would have chickened out. Maybe I would have decided to give myself more time to get used to the idea that he was alive and waited for the second chance she mentioned. I can never know.

I didn't sleep that night, questions buzzing in my brain like mosquitoes, incessant, maddening. It was excruciating to be given these mere droplets of information, not enough to satisfy but enough to keep me hooked. Had my father ever faced the murder charge? Had he been to prison and escaped, or had he been on the run all this time? Had he been in the U.S. throughout my childhood, or had he been in some other country – Mexico, Canada, Europe? And why why why had I been kept in the dark?

I awoke late the next morning, groggy with exhaustion. I drove to San Francisco, put the car in a garage, and called the friend of my mother's I was to stay with next, Philip Logan, leaving a message saying I'd arrive that evening. I couldn't face anyone just yet. Like a mechanical wind-up toy, I began to walk. I walked from one end of Market to the other. I walked all along the Embarcadero and through Golden Gate Park. I walked up steep hills to Buena Vista and through Haight Ashbury and the Mission district. I walked and I walked and I walked. I felt as if I was plowing through some thick soup or colorless gel, and everything felt as weird as in a dream – the glimpses of water, the sugar-coated pastel confections of San Francisco's houses. My thoughts were so chaotic I could not take anything in.

By the time I arrived at Philip Logan's home it was after 10. My mind was burning like an overheated engine and my body ached so I could barely stand. Philip answered the door when I rang, took one look at me, and said, "Dear God." He fed me spicy chili and sent me to bed.

The next morning my calves and thighs still ached from walking up and down all those hills, but I felt a little more like myself.

I slowly went downstairs to where I could hear clatter and a male voice singing. "Welllll," Philip drawled when he noticed me standing uncertainly in the doorframe. My mother wrote that he was an old college friend, but there was something about him that made him seemed younger. His face was lined and craggy, but he was athletic-looking and clean-shaven with shaggy brown hair, a lock of which was flopping over one eye. He wore jeans and a magenta T-shirt, a leather belt with an elaborate buckle in the shape of a peace symbol, and a silver bracelet that, on him, somehow didn't look ridiculous.

He fed me an enormous breakfast and chatted away while I ate, beaming like a parent at the vast quantities I put away.

"Been having a rough time of it, eh?" he said, hopping on a bar stool and straddling it.

Somehow his air of familiarity didn't bother me. Something about him put me at ease. He was like a Peter Pan, different from the serious adults I knew.

"It's been like one knockdown punch after the other, and now I find out my father's not dead after all. So yeah, I guess you could say I'm having a rough time," I said.

"Well, that's what I'm here for, to help you through this, your mom's special emissary, your guide to past and future, to understanding and acceptance." He grinned in a way that let me know he was only half-joking. "Your mom said you'd show up today if you chose not to see him just yet. I gather you decided not to?"

"It wasn't a choice," I said, "I blew the timing."

"Can't buy it," he said, "everything's a choice."

"That's a load of crap."

"We won't argue the point," he said. "Point is, here you are, and here I am, at your service."

"Your service has been great, so far," I said, smiling. "By the way, do you have a letter for me from my mother?"

"She wanted me to wait until we'd talked."

"She's been parceling out information like it's gold, like I can't handle it."

"Hey," he shrugged, "I'm just the messenger. As far as I'm concerned, it's yours." He left the room and returned a moment later with a manila envelope and put it in front of me.

But now that I had it, I hesitated.

"It's just so frustrating. I don't understand any of this."

"Well maybe I can help. Fire away. What do you want to know?"

His openness caught me off-guard. "Everything, I guess. Whatever you're willing to tell me."

"I'll tell you anything and everything, including the story of my life. As you might have suspected, I like to talk." His blue eyes were eager.

"I want to know what's going on. What my father did. What this is all about."

"I don't know anything about what's going on now," Philip said. "But I'll tell you everything I can about what happened back then."

"I already know about the demonstration and the shooting – what was in the papers. But that's about it."

"So you know your father went underground. Well, he was never caught. He's still a fugitive."

Hearing the words out loud made them more real, and I felt the air cut off from my chest. The words sank into me like heavy stones, cold and hard. "Can you at least tell me what he's like?" I said. I picked up the saltshaker in the form of a yellow duck and ran my fingers over the cool ceramic.

"Is like?" Philip said. "Sorry. I haven't laid eyes on him in over 30 years. I'm sorry, Layla. I don't know what he'd be like now. I don't know what all this may have done to him."

I was so disappointed I couldn't speak. I carefully placed the duck back on the table. After a moment Philip said, "but hasn't your mother told you about him? I mean about their lives, what kind of person your dad was?"

"Only the politics," I said. My mother had told me about what motivated my father and her – about the children who were killed in Alabama churches and Vietnam, about burning crosses and burning bras. But at some point I hadn't wanted to know any more. I resented their history. It was almost as if I suspected that something about those times, the Movement, had taken my father from me.

"Your parents were the real McCoy – in it for the principles," Philip said. "I admired them tremendously. Still do."

It was my father's personality I wanted to know about, what he was like to be around, the kinds of jokes he told, but I didn't know how to express it.

"Your father stayed with me after the shooting," Philip went on.

I was shocked. "Why are you willing to – you know – actually say it?" Everyone else had been so cagey.

"I'm the open type. And I've always liked living dangerously. I'll take a chance on you."

"What?" I said, not getting it. Then I felt my face burn. "Is that what this secrecy's been about? People have been afraid of me? Afraid I'd go to the police?"

"You can't blame people for being careful. How do you think your father has remained in hiding all these years? How do you think your mother managed the communications?"

I had only just learned my father was alive. I hadn't yet gotten around to those other kinds of questions. I couldn't begin to imagine.

"After he went underground I helped him and your mother stay in touch. I would receive an occasional letter from your mother – through an anonymous intermediary. She set it up so that none of us who helps them knows any more than is strictly necessary for us to know. That way none of us could ever implicate anyone else. We're all protected."

I thought of what Lenny had said: We only know what we know. "But then how were you able to harbor my father? Didn't the police check all his friends?"

"Of course. But I wasn't a friend." He grinned at my confusion. "Your mom was one smart cookie, but I guess you know that. As far as dealing with me was concerned, she was brilliant. See, I had been her boyfriend – she dumped me for your dad. And, well, there was a lot of rancor and animosity on my part. Forget what you've heard about those times – about free love and all that crap. I was jealous and carried on and the point is everyone knew it. So your mom figured no one would ever think of me when they thought about where your father would go. Hell, most people had no idea where I was. I had split for the coast, as we say."

"Why did she trust you, then?"

He looked embarrassed. "I'd left to make her feel bad – you know the routine, now that I'm gone you'll see you really love me kind of crap. She knew I'd do anything to prove myself, show her that my political commitment was as deep as your father's. Shit, it's embarrassing to admit what a jerk I was, but she was the love of my life. Anyhow, she knew me all too well, knew it was the excitement and the hint of danger that was what really drew me to the Left. But she also knew I had integrity. So I was perfect for her purposes. I wasn't going to win her, but I could be a hero and have her eternally grateful to me. It wasn't a bad role, considering." He gave me an utterly charming grin and got up to get us more coffee. I thought how appealing he was, and wondered about my father, and why my mother had preferred him.

"So," Philip said, handing me my cup, "she ever mention me to you?"

O

Upstairs in my room, I took out my mother's letter. It was marked "after San Francisco," but I didn't care. This time, at least, there was a full page of writing.

Dear Layla,

I had so wanted to show you San Francisco, to explore with you all its nooks and crannies. It's my favorite city besides New York. Have you fallen in love with it as I did?

I hope you liked Philip. You might have found him too hippy-dippy. He always was more of a counterculture than a political person. *The Movement split along those lines – the ones who thought that lifestyle issues were most important, and the ones, like your father and me, who were more concerned with changing the government. Philip has a heart of gold, as I am sure you've discovered for yourself.*

I'm stalling, here, Layla. But you've probably sensed that. I'm stalling because I'm scared. Have you realized that by now? Have you figured out that I'm a coward? Fear has governed my life, fear, and the desire to protect you from fear.

It was a choice we made, and only you can say whether we made the right one where it concerns you. We didn't want you to bear the stigma. We wanted you to have a normal life.

You always wondered why my parents and I were so at odds. They thought it was irresponsible of me to become pregnant, to be, in essence, a single mother, to bear a child by a fugitive. In many ways, of course, they were right. I've always known what I was depriving you of, and the burden of that choice – of deciding what would be best for you, for all of us – has in some ways crippled me.

I didn't want you crushed under that kind of burden, Layla. I feared your judgment, then and now. It's your decision what role, if any, you want to play. And it's up to you whether you want to have a father.

You are no longer a small child who can't understand how serious all this is, who might, by accident, jeopardize someone's life.

All my love, Mom

I felt my heart hammering in my chest and my whole body felt hot, as if I'd just run a race. *You are no longer a small child who might, by accident, jeopardize someone's life.* My own mother hadn't felt she could trust me! In fact, even now, she wasn't sure she could. Because she still wrote nothing about my father, where he was, what he was like, what his circumstances were.

I ran charging down the stairs. Philip looked up in alarm. "Excuses!" I said. "That's all I get. She says she wanted to protect me – she was only protecting herself!"

"Well it's a pretty complicated situation." He made a little apologetic gesture with his hands.

"Nobody was thinking about me." I didn't give him a chance to answer. "I'm going for a walk."

Once outside, I realized I had no idea of the neighborhood. So I walked in squares. I walked three blocks in one direction, made a right, walked three more, made a right, and circled back. The second time around, when I passed a flower shop, I bought a small bunch of some exotic-looking flowers.

Philip looked unperturbed by my outburst and uncommonly pleased by the flowers.

"She was thinking of you," he said, as he trimmed the stalks and filled a lump of an obviously handmade vase with water. "But that doesn't mean she made the right decisions."

"She says the burden of decision-making crippled her. Well, so why didn't she share it then?"

Philip scratched at the back of his neck. "I understand how you feel," he said. "But she couldn't talk about this stuff when you were little. Think about it."

"I haven't been little for a long time," I said.

He looked me up and down. "True." Neither of us said anything. "I guess that's what she's trying to do now," he finally said. "With this summer. You know, most parents in this situation would probably have told you partial truths, or made up stories to string you along. But that's not your mother. I can see her deciding that keeping completely mum was the best way to go. She was a very tough person. I guess, in a way, you could say she could be very hard."

I just stared at Philip. It felt strange – and gratifying – for an adult to side with me against my mother. "Of course," he said, "it had to be tough on her too."

I've always been fascinated by what adults want to pass on to the next generation. They seem to be so intense about getting their message across, even though they pay lip service to the fact that we have to find our own way, make our own mistakes. What's interesting is not so much what they say as what it tells you about them – their fears and anxieties, their failures and hurts.

What my mother had always emphasized was moral responsibility and consequences. "Layla, what you do now may affect the rest of your life." How many times had she said that? "I don't care what decision you make as long as you think it through, as long as you really own it." I had felt she was trying to take the spontaneity out of my life. But maybe she had really been talking about herself and my father, the choices she had made.

In the days I spent in San Francisco with Philip, he didn't hesitate to pass on the gems of his wisdom, either, though his advice was 180-degrees different from my mother's. "Security's not what it's cracked up to be, Layla. You can worry about that later in life. What's important at your age is freedom, risk-taking, being alive to the moment. Agree?"

"Sounds good," I said. We were in Golden Gate Park and he hopped up on a bench, walking one foot in front of the other as if it were a balance beam. I grabbed my camera and snapped away: the goofy grin on his face, his arms flung wide. He plopped down next to me and hunched over, hands dangling between his legs. "Layla, I wish I had more information to give you. I don't know anything about your father. I'm not even sure why your mother wanted you to visit me."

"You've told me more than everyone else combined!" I exclaimed.

He tousled my head. "I can't imagine how all this must sit with you. When I was coming of age the country was torn apart by war. Not like with Iraq now – it was much more divisive. Families weren't speaking to each other. But for me it's all mixed together. I can't separate how I experienced that time – whether it was the politics then or the fact that I was growing up. Testing my wings, so to speak."

"Getting laid, you mean," I said.

He laughed. "That was certainly part of it. But I'm talking about something else – the sense of momentousness, of incredible possibility. I know you probably hate hearing this, and I'm sure some of it must be what everyone feels as they come of age, but that time was truly different. It was a cultural explosion, a total upheaval." He threw his arms out wide in a grand gesture. "Oh, Layla, I live in an agony of nostalgia sometimes. It's like having been a child star – you've had your peak experiences early and nothing that comes after ever quite measures up. Sad, really. People like your Mom managed to keep the faith and move on, but honestly, I don't know how they managed it. I can't stop trying to hang on."

I stared at him. I didn't know what to say. Nostalgia was not an emotion in my repertoire. There was nothing in my experience that could compare with his.

Sometimes, with my friends or at a concert, I'd feel a little rush of joy or pleasure, and a few times I thought maybe I was in love, but in my heart of hearts I had to admit that – until Trent – I was still waiting for those peak experiences. I'd been afraid that I'd never know that intensity. Suddenly I realized why it had bugged me so much when my mother went on and on about those times.

"But it was pretty bleak, too," Philip was saying. "Charred bodies on the news, protestors beaten up. It's not the same with Iraq – after what happened with Vietnam, they know to keep those images from the news. Shit, they won't even show the funerals. It makes this war less real. Even so, we felt powerful."

"I don't think my generation feels at all powerful," I said. The world seemed way beyond my reach or control, beyond anyone's, as endlessly unfathomable as the galaxies. My friends had gotten on the antiwar bandwagon, but even so, I didn't think many of them really thought it would have much effect. I suspected many of them sported peace T-shirts just to seem cool.

Philip jumped back on the bench and made a sweeping gesture that encompassed the wide expanse in front of us where people lay sunning on bright colored towels. "Imagine a giant party, one with a zillion people who all feel just like you about something important. You're all joined together in this noble enterprise. Whew!" he pretended to wipe the perspiration off his brow.

"Yeah, I've seen the movie," I said.

"Heady stuff," he went on, ignoring me. "I don't know how I handled it, quite frankly." He grinned. "Of course, some of my friends say I didn't. Lots of little lost brain cells from dropping too much LSD." He turned to me. "You and your friends do hallucinogens?"

"Just weed."

"Hmm," he said, sitting down again and leaning his head back with his face in the sun. "Boy, I'd love a joint right now."

I laughed, enjoying him. During my stay we talked more, yet as the days passed, I somehow couldn't bring myself to ask him what I most wanted to know.

"What do you say we go to Sausalito?" Philip said the third day I was there. He had time to sightsee with me because he was self-employed, an accountant.

"I get a kick out of helping people get around the government," he told me. "I mean, the corporations get tax breaks, the rich have loopholes. Who's to figure the angles for the rest of us? Plus – and I know it'll sound strange coming from an accountant – I'm not into money." I laughed at that, because his lack of a materialistic streak was quite apparent from his clothes and his home, borderline threadbare. "I work hard around tax time, and play the rest of the year."

The little community of crowded makeshift houseboats and the long-haired, tie-dyed inhabitants made me feel I'd gone back in time to my mother's world. There, standing next to the pier looking over the water, the words popped out.

"Could he really have done it, Philip?" I said.

"Who?" He turned to look at me. "Do what?"

I stared at him. I couldn't ask. I couldn't say, is my father a murderer?

Philip stared back at me. "Oh. Well, I can't guarantee it, Layla, but I don't think so."

"Why would he have run if he weren't guilty?" I asked.

"Guilty or not, he would have been crucified," Philip said. "The times had really changed by then. Things had gotten ugly. The Panthers, the Weatherpeople – the government was out for blood. And the others involved got very heavy sentences, remember."

I was silent. Guilt, crucifixion, blood, incarceration: How had these words entered my life?

"He had to have been terrified," Philip was saying. "Or maybe he was waiting until he was vindicated. Or he may have thought that by going underground he could be of more use to society – continue his political work. There are any number of reasons, I guess." When I didn't respond, he went on. "It was a war then, and I don't mean Vietnam. I mean it was Us Against Them. Us against the State. That might sound paranoid to you, but the FBI did infiltrate everywhere. The country spied on its own people. It's all public record now."

I was silent, a little afraid. Maybe I should forget all this, I thought, just walk away. Choices, my mother always said. As long as you own them. Did I want to meet this father, this man who might have killed? A man who had chosen the life of a fugitive over that of being my father? Or if not, could I live with what it would mean to turn away from him forever?

It was getting late; shadows lengthened on the docks and a breeze picked up, ruffling the water, flapping the flags on the houseboats. As we drove back over the bridge I watched the sun sink into the Pacific; it was a fiery red ball, and it melted into streams of color that saturated the water, a blue cloth soaking up blood.

Chapter 5

Jenny? Jenny, it's me."

Her shriek pierced my ears. "It's you! Oh my God, I can't believe it, oh my God, is it really you?"

I laughed, something hard and tight uncoiling in my chest. "It's so good to hear your voice," I said. Suddenly I wanted to cry. I wanted my own home, my own life, my own friends.

"I know, I know. I have a calendar with the days crossed off 'til you're back. How are you? I loved the photos you sent from that festival, you lucky thing. Why haven't you e-mailed? How are you?"

"I'm fine. Well, not so fine. It's been kinda crazy." I hesitated. Though I longed to tell her everything, I found myself holding back. "I'll explain when I see you. How are you? How's everybody? Tell me!"

Jenny rushed through all the news at breakneck speed and I listened, but it all felt so distant, as if my life was a very long time ago.

"One more thing" Jenny said after a pause.

"What? Tell me."

"Layla, I hope you won't be upset."

"What now?" I said, ungraciously. I was tired of people telling me things and hoping I wouldn't be upset.

"Promise you're not going to get mad at me, I didn't think you would, or – ."

"Jenn-y!"

"Promise first."

"All right!"

"I've been going out with Steve." It took me a second to grasp what she was talking about, that's how far I had traveled from my old life. Steve, my ex-boyfriend.

"But that's great" I said.

"Are you sure?"

"Of course! I can see you together. I'm surprised I didn't think of it myself. Besides, you know how I feel about Trent."

We talked for a few more minutes, and then I said I'd better go. We were both silent, not wanting to break the connection.

"Where are you headed next?"

"Oregon." My mother's letter had included directions and a hand-drawn map to a resort on a lake. "It's supposed to be pretty."

"Your voice sounds funny. Are you sure you're O.K.?" Jen said.

"Yeah, it's just – " I hesitated, but I couldn't help myself. "It's just I've been learning more heavy stuff about my parents. Shocking, actually."

"Shocking? Your mother?"

"Well, more my father."

"Wow. Like what?"

"You're going to flip out," I said, stalling. To tell Jenny was to make it real in a deeper way. "It turns out he was involved in a violent crime."

"Oh my God. What happened?"

"It was a sort of civil rights thing." Suddenly I felt scared. "You can't say anything about this to anyone, O.K.?"

"O.K., I promise, but Layla, you're making me nervous."

"It's just a long story, kind of complicated. I'd rather tell you in person, that's all. I don't like talking on the phone."

"You?" Jenny mocked me. "Give me a break."

"I love you," I said.

"I love you, too," she said.

It was a minute before I could bear to turn off my cell phone.

Although I was to return to Philip's a few days before my flight home in a few weeks, I wanted to do something special for him before leaving this time around. Cooking was the one thing my mother and I had enjoyed doing together, one thing that had been fraught with no significance whatsoever. So I shopped and prepared all day, and made one of my tried and true dinners: braised chicken with figs and apricots, garlic mashed potatoes, salad with pine nuts and goat cheese, and for dessert, ice cream with fudge sauce.

I arranged flowers and found in the cabinet under the sink two candlesticks with the stubs of vanilla-scented candles. When everything was ready Philip came downstairs wearing a loose peasant-style shirt, a silly smile plastered on his face. His slight build and longish hair made him look like an aging rock star – Paul McCartney, maybe – and as I watched him I thought again how incongruous was the notion of him as my mother's boyfriend. For a left-winger she was pretty straight, whereas to imagine him with a flower in his hair wasn't such a stretch.

I lit the candles and dished up the meal. Philip praised it extravagantly. "Oh," he kept exclaiming, "oh. The lucky man who snags you!"

"Enough, already!"

"By the way," he said, as we were polishing off dessert, "I have something to show you. While you were cooking today I went through some boxes that I had stored in the attic. I found all sorts of things."

We took our coffee into the living room. Philip dragged two wooden milk cartons in front of the couch. "Most of it doesn't pertain to your father," he said, "but it's stuff I kept from that time. Just say if it bores you – I'm sure your mother had tons like it." He was removing old magazines and papers, a tin of something that rattled, a shoe box.

"She didn't keep much at all," I said. It had always angered me that my mother had so little to show me, especially pertaining to my father. I had thought it mean-spirited and hard-hearted of her. I settled on the couch with my legs tucked under me, and Philip began to hand me things. There were posters and bumper stickers: War Is Not Healthy for Children and Other Living Things; Make Peace, Not Bombs. There were leaflets and newsletters: *The Berkeley Barb, The Guardian, Off Our Backs.*

I picked up the tin. Inside were metal buttons, their edges and backs rusting. Most were for specific antiwar marches, and a few small buttons had only acronyms printed on them – SDS, SNCC, Student MOBE. One had a black eagle on a red and white background that Philip said was in support of the farm workers' union, and one read simply, "Give a damn," in white on black.

There was the green armband with "Marshall" and the black silk one Philip said he wore after the Kent State shooting. There were frivolous things, too. Old psychedelic posters, a broken strobe light, a roach clip. Handling these artifacts gave me a peculiar feeling. I had always thought of the '60s as a little bit exciting, a little bit dangerous, a lot self-indulgence, but these objects conveyed something different. They seemed innocent and pure, the words and sentiments earnest and hopeful, somehow. I've never been an abstract thinker like my mother; I liked things tactile, concrete – like photography. Taking pictures helped me see more clearly. So when I touched the cheap silk, and sniffed the musty smell and felt the brittleness of the yellow newsletters, the history snapped into focus the way it hadn't before. And it suddenly seemed sad that all that youth and vibrancy and hope was gone, that even today, with another war on and so many other important causes, most people were preoccupied with homes and children and mortgages, and not with changing the world. The thought was such an odd one for apathetic me that I felt almost light-headed.

"What's in the shoe box?" I asked. Birkenstock was written on the side.

"Oh, right." Philip pulled out piles of loose snapshots. I slid next to him to view them under the light.

"A May Day rally," he said, passing one. "You can appreciate how we activists got so burnt out – we were going to demonstrations every week. You felt guilty if you weren't protesting." I flipped through the photos. They were faded and blurry, yet somehow, maybe because of that raw quality, I could practically hear the rock music, smell the incense. Interesting contradiction, I thought, and filed it away for my own picture taking.

"Check this out," Philip said. It was a picture of a couple, arms entwined.

"Some hat!" I said. Big and floppy, it completely obscured its wearer's face.

"That's your Mom," Philip said, "and that's me," he pointed to the skinny boy with bell-bottoms and waist-long hair.

"No way!"

"Afraid so. Here. I saved the best 'til last." He handed me a photo, a bit out of focus, of a young man with curly dark hair and a red bandana, his fingers in a solemn V for peace.

"Your father," Philip said.

My throat clutched. I stared at the picture.

"My mother had only a high school graduation picture and a few snapshots from his childhood," I told Philip. "None of their wedding."

"We all destroyed whatever pictures we had of him," Philip said. "To make it harder for the FBI. I don't know how I missed this one back then. Lucky, huh? Keep it, it's yours."

The man in the photo seemed so young, way too young to be an outlaw.

"Layla, check this out." He pulled from the bottom of the shoebox a funny-looking glass tube with colored lumps, like buds, on the side.

"What is it?"

"A kind of bong."

"I've got some pot." I jumped up. "Be right back. We can try this thing out." Jenny had given me a joint when we parted, but

I had hesitated to smoke it, a little afraid of whatever feelings it might unleash. What the hell, I thought. It would be the perfect way to end the visit.

I handed the joint to Philip. "It's not a tab of acid, but I know you appreciate the thought."

"To the '60s," Philip said. He placed the joint in the hole on the side of the glass tube and demonstrated how to inhale while keeping a finger over the end. The smoke entered my lungs in a whoosh.

"Whoa!" I said.

"Isn't it great?" he said. "Totally eliminates the burning."

"Works faster, too," I said, resting my head back against the couch.

"Thanks for dinner, Layla," Philip said.

"Thanks for being – you know."

"Please," he waved away my gratitude.

Philip swung his feet up on one of the cartons, and moved them to make room for mine. "I was with your mother the first time she got stoned," he said. "It was at a party. She was disappointed – no visions, no hallucinations, no colors. She was so funny, absolutely convinced it had no effect on her at all. Then when we're driving home she's panicking, telling me to slow down, the cops are gonna pick us up. 'Yeah,' I laugh at her, 'for going too slow.' She couldn't believe when I showed her the speedometer said we were only doing 40!"

I smiled and felt my mouth grow wide, elastic. I was the Cheshire cat, floating, floating up to the ceiling, looking down at Philip. I laughed. My laugh sounded like a tinkle, like clear bells in a light breeze. I laughed again, just to hear the sound.

"It's a strange drug, isn't it?" he said. "So subtle. You almost have to learn how to feel it. But like sex, everyone remembers their first time. That thrill of the transgressive…." He threw his arm back along the top of the couch, accidentally brushing my shoulder.

A shiver ran down my back; the spot where his arm had touched me seemed to pulsate.

"Jesus this stuff is strong," Philip said. "Or maybe I'm getting old."

"You're not at all old," I said. His hair gleamed in the lamplight, and the lines radiating from the corners of his eyes were full of humor. I was feeling good, I realized. I hadn't known when I would be able to feel so good again.

"How about a little music," he said. "Should we stay in the past? Some Crosby Stills Nash and Young? Led Zeppelin? Or something contemporary?"

"You pick," I managed to say, trying to peel my tongue from the roof of my mouth.

A minute later the opening sounds of "Layla" swelled and reverberated in the room, and I was momentarily stricken. My song. I closed my eyes, breathed deeply, afraid I would cry. I felt the bass tickle the bottom of my feet, and the mournful piano and guitar at the end of the song raised the hairs on the back of my neck.

"To you, Layla," Philip said, lifting his wine glass.

I looked at him. I saw vulnerability and need in the corners of his mouth, the droop of his eyelids. I touched his wrist. He looked at me, startled, but didn't say anything. I let my finger rest on his pulse. He removed it and clasped my hand in both of his, restraining me. With my other hand I touched his cheek. I heard his breathing quicken, but his jaw was rigid under my hand.

"I just want – ." He lifted my hand away, but gently. "I just want to make you feel good," I whispered. He shook his head, and his eyes closed briefly. "Pretend I'm my mother," I said. The words horrified me and I felt the blood rush to my face.

He cupped my chin tightly, and I thought for a second that he would kiss me. "It's just the dope talking."

"No, it's not," I said, defiant, humiliated.

"Layla, I could be –."

"Stop!" I said. I didn't want to hear him say it. I glared at him, but I couldn't maintain it. My gaze slid to the floor, like a slow leak.

"Layla, Layla, sweetheart." He gripped my shoulder, but I shrugged his hand away. "I would never be able to forgive myself."

The CD came to an end with a sudden click. The silence was deafening. I stood up, fists clenched. I had an awful desire to say something searing, wounding. Anything to make myself feel better.

"It wasn't the dope," I said. I didn't know what it was, but I knew it wasn't the dope.

I walked out of the room. Suddenly I was crashing. I could feel it rushing toward me: a tidal wave of misery. What had come over me? What had I done? I should have known I couldn't handle a joint so soon after my mother's death. I thought of Trent. How could I?

"You're every bit as tough as she was, you know," Philip said from behind me. "You're not as different as you think."

○

It was the worst gloom yet, the gloomy gloom I felt leaving San Francisco for Oregon. And nothing helped. Thinking, not thinking, music, no music. I wanted to smash windows or cry for a week. I wanted to abandon the car and take an instant flight home. I wanted to drive off a cliff or slam into a wall. I wanted to drown in the ocean or burn up like a crisp.

The coast road was supposed to be even more dramatic north of San Francisco than south, but the fog socked in so thick I didn't get much of a chance to see. Keeping to the road soon required all my attention, and the concentration helped take my mind off my blue funk.

I had slunk out early, before Philip was awake, unable to face him, though I had left him a note of apology and thanks propped up against the microwave. It was a truly awful thing I had done. What if he hadn't stopped me? How far would it have gone?

I rushed out, stumbled on his doorstep, and fell to the concrete, scraping my knee. I let the blood pool up. The sting was satisfying in a sick way; I deserved to be hurt. I wanted to feel the pain.

I tried to blot out what had occurred and focus on the road, the trip, my father. I didn't know what to expect of this next stop on the itinerary – there was no contact person, just the resort's address. Would this bring me closer to the second chance my mother had said I would have to meet him?

At some point it occurred to me that driving in such fog might be dangerous, so I pulled over and figured out an inland route. Along the way I came upon a vineyard with an outdoor café, where I ordered a cheese sampler. The waiter suggested a pinot noir, but I asked for a ginger ale instead. While I waited I pulled out my mother's last letter to reread. I had destroyed none of the letters as she had ordered – not hers, not my father's letters to her, not the newspaper clippings Letitia and Lenny had given me – and I wasn't sure I would. At the very least, until I decided whether my father would ever be anything other than a fiction to me, I wanted to keep what I had of him.

The waiter slid a plate in front of me. *I feared your judgment, then and now. I've always known what I was depriving you of, and the burden of that choice – of deciding what would be best for you, for all of us – has in some ways crippled me…. It's your decision what role, if any, you want to play. And it's up to you now whether you want to have a father.*

I stared down at purple-black grapes, thin white crackers, oozing Brie. I took a nibble but the creamy cheese clogged my throat and suddenly I wasn't hungry. What did she mean, she feared my judgment? My mother had always seemed so strong, so powerful. I had felt that my opinions, my point of view, mattered little. I rubbed my thumb hard along the glass and it sounded a tiny squeak of resistance. I pressed harder as if to test its strength, as if I wanted it to shatter in my hand.

I tilted my glass, watched the liquid move right, then left. The ginger ale was a pale gold, picking up a hint of green from nearby bushes, and with the movement of my hand, tiny bubbles lined the perimeter, then evaporated. *And it's up to you now whether you want to have a father.*

I lifted the glass up to my eyes. This close, my focus shifted to the glass itself – solid, transparent, with a sheen of reflections. It seemed no longer just a vessel for the liquid. Vessel, I thought. Vestal virgins. I imagined young girls in white dresses carrying chalices up long stairs to an altar. *And it's up to you now whether you want to have a father.* She was passing me, like a chalice, to him.

My father was alive. My father was alive, and my mother was dead. Alive, dead, alive, dead, the thought a seesaw: One side up only if the other side is down. My father was alive and my mother was dead.

I was home, my mother framed by the kitchen doorway. I had wanted to sleep out all night to get tickets for a concert. I was 16, into my first girl group, the Wreckers. The lead singer's voice cracked on high notes in a way that pierced my heart. But my mother said no, absolutely no, not a chance in hell, end of discussion.

"You're so unfair!" I yelled. "I can't believe you can be so mean. I bet my father would never have been like this. I wish he were alive and it was you who was dead."

For a fraction of a moment I was huge with power. My mother's eyes widened and her face went white with shock, her features flat. Her hand flew to her chest as if she couldn't get her breath, as if she had been hit from behind and her body was registering the blow. I had stolen the air from my mother's body.

She said absolutely nothing. I wanted to take back what I had said, wanted to bridge the enormous distance that was lengthening the kitchen between us with each fraction of a second, but I was incapable of movement. It seemed forever that she just stood there, frozen, her back to the doorway. Then she left the room.

I didn't know what to do. This fight was unlike any we'd ever had. My rages were regular and predictable, and I often said unforgivable things. But no matter what my outburst, my mother's face usually registered only brief distress, a momentary darkening like the sun obscured by a cloud, a flick of annoyance as from a pesky fly. Then she would force me to sit down and talk through whatever the issue was between us.

My mother didn't come back. I waited and I waited and I waited. I remember putting away the groceries, and still she didn't return. I know I cleaned and tidied the kitchen, because I used a new cleanser, one whose too-sweet floral scent has sickened me ever since. I made sandwiches and decorated the plate with a silly paper flower. Still she didn't return. I listened to the ticking of the clock in the silence, a maddening "hist," "hist." She was not coming back.

I walked down the hall to her room, the light casting disturbing shadows on the walls. I stood outside her door, holding the plate of sandwiches, afraid to hear her sobbing. But there was no sound at all coming from behind her door. Could she have left the apartment without my knowing? I stared at the tiny cracks in the door's off-white paint. The silence was interminable. Then, in my mind's eye, I saw the curtain flapping, the open window. "Ma!" I cried out. There was no answer. I opened the door, but in my terror I could not at first make sense of the blur of pattern and shape before me. It seemed eons before the room resolved into something I could comprehend: My mother lay on top of her bed, curled up in a fetal position, snoring gently.

I placed the sandwiches by the side of her bed and tiptoed from the room. On the kitchen table I left a note that said, "I'm sorry." In the morning when I got up she was already gone. Her note to me said, "Do what you want."

Now there was a miasma before my eyes, a blur of color and wet. I watched a tear fall into the last of the ginger ale, then drank it down. As I left the café, voices bubbled like a stream over mossy rocks and the air seemed fuzzy, almost visible, the light suspended in charged raindrops. I put my head on my arms on the steering wheel and cried until I fell asleep.

When I awoke it felt much later, though the clock said only 15 minutes had passed. I turned on the ignition but didn't drive away; I watched people going and coming from their cars. What kinds of lives were they going to? What kinds of plans did they have for their evenings, their kids, their vacations, their futures?

I could do what I wanted, too. No one was making me do anything. My mother was dead. She wouldn't know or care if I did or didn't do as I had promised. It was me I had to answer to, no one else. Just me.

I edged the car slowly out of the parking lot. I could turn in the car and fly back to New York. I could drive all the way back if I wanted. I went the few miles to the highway and came to a stop. Right or left? North as planned? Keep going, or leave for home? Cars whipped by while I idled mine. Seconds passed, minutes. Rain began to fall, first lightly, then heavily. I would go the same direction as the first red car I saw, I thought. Let fate decide. The first red car I spotted headed south. I stepped on the gas and turned north, toward the dark northwoods forest.

O

In the first of my father's letters to my mother he had talked about tall trees and people who valued hard work. Had he been writing about Oregon? Was that why my mother was sending me to the bungalow colony?

It was Hansel and Gretel territory, those woods. Redwood and pine blocking out the sky they were so tall, widely spaced, stately, as deep and hushed a forest as a forest can be. Kramer's Cottages were on a lake on the fringes of national forest, and when I got out of the car, the slam of the door reverberated in the silence. There were a thousand sounds to that silence – the tiny pings of water dripping from leaves, soft rustlings, the sigh of the wind, the fluty calls of birds. The scent of moist humus and damp wood and pine was intense, the air heavy with moisture from the rain that had just ended.

I put on my backpack and followed a sign through the trees for Kramer's. The dirt path dead-ended at the lake, the water gray-blue under the sullen sky.

There were eight or ten cabins and a main lodge spaced out along the waterfront. The bungalows were small and rustic, no doubt smelling of damp and mold. If I were running away, it would be the perfect place. Inside the office, a woman of maybe 45, with a blond ponytail and a pencil behind each ear, was seated at a counter, a book open in front of her.

"Hi," I said. "My name's Layla James. I have reservations for a cabin."

"You're the girl from New York, right? I'm Christine. I went to school in New York eons ago. I loved it."

Christine took me to the last cabin along the shore. "The walking paths are clearly marked, but I'm afraid it's going to rain again." At the cabin Christine showed me the propane tank, which powered the refrigerator, stove, and lights, and we went out back to gather kindling and logs from a basket under the eaves. "On a day like today you might want a fire." Mist was rising off the lake and a damp chill permeated everything.

"So, how's the Big Apple?" Christine asked, as we stood looking out at the lake. "Every year I say I'm going to visit, but when my vacation comes around I find myself back here. My parents can use the help, and I find I'm addicted to the place. I spent all my summers here, growing up."

Dark pines fringed the lake, and a float with brightly colored markers, rowboats, and canoes bobbed on the water. With the sun out it would be far more appealing, I thought.

"This is so peaceful," I said.

"Sometimes I found it dull, but mostly I enjoyed all the comings and goings. There are people from all over the country. Some return every year – it's like a family reunion. Well, I'll leave you to get settled. Let me know if you need anything. And join us at the lodge for dinner if you don't want to cook. It's a limited menu, and we eat family side, but you won't go away hungry."

"Thanks, I'll be fine," I said, though in truth I had to fight the urge to ask her not to leave.

"O.K. then."

I watched her walk off, her footsteps soundless on the pine needles. If I were right, and my father had stayed here after he ran away, Christine might even have been here. I calculated backward. She would have been a teenager. What if she'd actually met him? I took out the photo Philip had given me and brought it under the table light, trying to see if I bore any resemblance to him. I couldn't tell – it was taken from too great a distance. I wondered if I had gotten my green eyes from him. My mother's eyes were a murky hazel that could have led to anything.

I put away my things. On this dreary day in the middle of nowhere, what was I to do with myself? What had my mother intended? A bookshelf held an assortment of titles appropriate for a camp – *Moby Dick* and *Treasure Island* and *Jane Eyre*. I made a fire, boiled water for tea, and got under an afghan with a Nancy Drew.

Dinner was three families, a dog, Christine, and her parents.

"We've been coming to this colony so long you could say we've watched Christine grow up," one man said. "She was one petulant teenager."

"It was hard on her," his wife said, "all the young kids, no one her age."

"There were all the lifeguards, though," Christine said. "Every summer there was some boy I'd manage to get a crush on." She looked dreamy a minute. "I think I remember every cute boy that ever stayed here."

After dinner I waylaid Christine. "Do you have a minute?"

"Sure, what's up?"

"You said you remember all the cute guys who ever stayed here. Do you remember one with green eyes like mine? He would have been maybe 5 foot 10, slender? 1972?"

"Thirty-plus years! What was his name?"

"John," I said, but then I realized I had no idea what name he might have been using. "But he had nicknames. I know he stayed here, because he sent my mother a letter. He and my mother split up soon after I was born, and I never got to know him."

"How awful!" Christine said. She gestured to a little nook with a table and benches and sat down heavily. "I'm so sorry!"

"Yeah, well, so I was hoping maybe he's one of the boys you remember, and you could tell me about him." I handed Christine the photograph of my father. We sat face to face across the scarred and lacquered table. The seats were covered in a dark corduroy, and I ran my hand back and forth against the nap as I waited.

Christine twirled her ponytail with a finger as she stared. "Wait a minute," she said. She covered my father's hair and squinted. "Oh my god, I was crazy about this guy. But his name was Peter."

"That's his middle name!" I said. I was surprised how easily the lie came.

"It's hard to be positive, because the guy I'm remembering had a crew cut – which was unusual, come to think of it. All the guys had long hair back then. But I'm pretty sure this is him!"

If the man she was remembering was my father, I thought, it would make sense that he would have cut off all his hair when he ran away.

"And he did have green eyes, come to think of it."

We were silent a moment. "Can you tell me more about him?" I asked.

"Well, he was pretty quiet, but with a really warm smile. I was young – maybe 14, moody and miserable, but he didn't dismiss me like most older boys did. He was in his early 20s – well you know that. Anyhow, he was really sweet." Christine's expression softened. "He used to sit by himself, incredibly still, just looking out at the lake. He let me hang around, didn't make me feel like a stupid teeny-bopper – you know how flattering that is at that age. But this isn't telling you a thing about him. It's amazing how self-centered my memory is. What I remember isn't really about him but about me – how he made me feel."

"It tells me a little what kind of person he was," I said. I had trouble forming the words. My throat hurt, as if I had scalded the lining. Why couldn't I have been the girl my father had been so attentive to?

Christine nodded eagerly. "You're right. He was simply a really nice guy – you know," she wiggled her fingers to indicate quote marks, "sensitive." She paused. "Wait – there is something! He came from New York, I remember that now! I remember it bothered him that it was so obvious – he was embarrassed about having a New York accent. He kept trying to say, 'fer sure,' like a Californian."

Or trying to keep his identity hidden?

"So maybe it was your dad." Christine fell silent. I traced a groove in the table top, noticing the cuts and gouges that marred its surface, only partly camouflaged by the gloss of shellac.

"How long did he stay?"

"Not long, a few weeks. He was vague about where he was headed." She thought a minute. "Maybe I haven't forgotten what he told me about himself so much as that he didn't tell me much. I was so happy to have the attention I may not have noticed. I know we sat and talked all the time, but it was general talk. It was so wonderful for me – someone who listened, who took what I thought and felt seriously. It mattered quite a lot." Christine suddenly looked almost teary. She recovered herself with a laugh. "Also, his reserve was very attractive – it made him a bit myste-rious, which only enhanced his appeal, of course. I thought maybe he was avoiding the draft and was on his way to Canada. We're so close to the border. I decided that must have been it when he didn't send me a postcard."

"That reminds me," I suddenly remembered, "did a letter come for me here?"

"No, sorry. But mail takes a little longer up here sometimes."

I was immediately anxious. If my mother mailed it before she died, it should have arrived long before. Without it I had no way of knowing where I was to go next, no idea whom to contact. No way for the second chance to meet my father.

"It should have been mailed a while ago. It should have gotten here."

"I'll take another look, I promise," Christine said.

I walked back on the pine-needled path to my cabin. It was pitch dark, no moon, no stars, and I had forgotten to bring a flashlight. I found my way by the lights showing dimly through the curtains in the other cabins, and when mine loomed up out of the darkness it gave me a start.

I opened the door to an even darker dark; I hadn't thought to leave matches handy and it took me a few minutes to get the gas lamps lit. I made another fire, wrapped myself back up in the afghan, and tried to read, but couldn't concentrate. The wind was moaning through the trees, a front coming through.

I played over the conversation with Christine in my mind. There had been no mention of her in the letter my father had sent my mother. But even if he had told my mother about Christine, it was pretty farfetched that my mother would have expected her to be here or to remember him. So why was I here? It seemed she had me retracing my father's steps after he ran away. But why? In the Adirondacks, Boston, and San Francisco her friends had taken me under wing, but there was no one here she'd set up to further enlighten me.

I awoke during the night from a dream and sat up in bed, trying to shake off a sense of dread. There was a strange light in the room. The wind had swept the sky clear of clouds, and each object in the room was clearly visible in the moonlight.

I tried my usual method of concentrating on sounds, the way I did at home, but there was no comforting gurgle of cars on Broadway, just wind whooshing, branches squeaking as they rubbed against each other, other sounds I couldn't identify –

maybe nocturnal animals rustling about, the kinds of animals that didn't dare show their faces in daylight.

I got out of bed and pulled the window curtain aside. The moon was full and bright; it cast pools of light and shadow on the bare ground that was like a swath around the cabin before the woods began. I stared at the deeper dark between the trees, feeling as if someone or something would emerge.

My skin tingled all over. What if my father were out there? What if that's why my mother sent me here? Could he be walking among the cabins, looking for me? I pulled a sweater over my nightgown and stepped just outside the door.

I heard what might have been the screech of an owl, or something scarier. Above me clouds raced across the sky and stars clotted in all the dark patches where the clouds were not. I thought of my father, on the run, 22 years old. How many times had he awoken in the night, heart racing from nightmares? How many times had he heard noises and slammed to the floor, sure the FBI was sneaking up on him, guns drawn? Guilty or not, framed or not, he must have been terrified.

Finally I went back to bed. I didn't think I would be able to sleep but when I awoke it was morning, a clear sunny day noisy with bird song and children's voices echoing from the water. I got up, went to the cabin door, and stood blinking in the sunlight, free of the night's unease.

Then I noticed the package that was propped up against the doorjamb.

Chapter 6

The package had a forlorn look, leaning against the wooden planks of the bungalow, a bit saggy, as if it couldn't hold itself up, was tired of its journey. It was manila, the kind with padding like compressed vacuum cleaner crud, worn, as if recycled one too many times, stabbed by too many staples.

So there had been someone outside the night before! I stared at the trees opposite; the branches moved only slightly in the breeze, a shimmer of light and dark. Everything was still. I looked down at the pine-needle-strewn dirt around the cabin, but there were no discernable footprints other than the distinctive marks of my own sneakers.

I crouched down, and my fear evaporated. The package had been mailed to me care of Kramer's Cottages. Christine must have brought it over early.

But the postmark was from Nevada. And the label had been printed in capital letters in blue ink – not my mother's hand. Who then? Not Philip or Trent or Jenny – none of them knew where I was. Probably my mother left the material in someone else's care, with instructions to mail it on a certain date, like the envelope that had come to me at the motel from San Diego. I yanked open the package, spewing packing dust, and pulled out a spiral notebook. It was worn, with a red cardboard cover that said "narrow ruled." Narrow ruled was my own preference, too.

Inside, clipped to the first page, was a note.

Until we meet –

There was no signature.

I became aware of a hum, a horsefly or mosquito or a crowd of them. I leaned against the door. A breeze lifted the tree branches, and I noticed that even pine needles can shimmy in the wind and how close to black the color of dark green can be. My father might not have been outside my cabin the night before, but I could almost feel the heat of his physical presence. My face was damp. I lifted up the hem of my sweatshirt, blotted my skin, and stood a moment, face pressed into cloth.

I went back inside and made a cup of tea. I stared at the notebook, feeling curiosity and a kind of trapped panic so intertwined I couldn't begin to separate them. I took a few sips of tea and then picked up the notebook. I held it so lightly, so afraid to really take hold of it, that it began to slip from my fingers.

The first page was empty except for the words: *Mass Communications – Professor Lerner, Winter, January 1970*. I did the mental calculation: 15 months before the date my father may have shot the prison guard and gone into hiding.

The next page was dense with cryptic notes. *Frankfurt School – Adorno, e.g., – mass media/culture is the enemy. Focused on production – people consume in the same way that products are produced. de Certeau: consumption is production. TV messages, etc. We need to locate instances of where people subvert the uses intended. Also, where revolution is not possible, how do people survive? Historical process – moments of containment and then moments when action breaks through again.* This was asterisked.

The notes went on for pages, pages dulled by age, a few stuck together where coffee or hot chocolate had spilled. Interspersed with the class notes were reading assignments, doodles, and my father's little injunctions to himself.

I ran my finger over the metal spine of the notebook. It was somewhat mashed; my father's fingers had rebent the metal spiral to fit it back into the holes. The oil from his skin was absorbed into the fabric of the paper, paper worn as soft as cloth washed over and over again. His was a fairly heavy hand, the impression of his marks on one page often showing through to the next. But all of these were only glimmers, slight clues.

I turned pages mechanically, skimming the class notes, hoping for more. Then my mother's name leapt off a page. I realized my father had begun using the notebook as a sort of diary. I turned back until I found the first entry.

Jan. 9 I'm sitting on the floor in a corner of the student lounge, trying to make sense of what's been happening to me. I should be studying or doing research for one of my term papers – gotta hand in an outline for Mass. Comm. in a couple of days – but I've been going through so many changes that I've decided to keep a kind of political journal. I've been reading Marcuse and Marx and C. Wright Mills and my head is completely blown. It's like my entire conception of the world has been turned upside down and I'm freaking out or something.

I never realized how the military industrial complex is dominating – ruining – our country completely and the rest of the world, too. I've been against the war in Vietnam, of course, but I saw it as separate. Now I get that the war is an inevitable extension of the whole thing.

The campus is in complete upheaval. I can't just sit back and do nothing. If you're not part of the solution you're part of the problem. I've been talking with some of my frat brothers, but even Tom says bullshit like he's got too much homework to get involved. I hate how distant I'm beginning to feel from my friends. This new awareness on my part, I guess you could say my politicization, is making a big separation between us, and it makes me feel really sad.

It's embarrassing to even put it down on paper, but the truth is I feel I've experienced a transformation, the way people describe a religious conversion. Where will it all lead?

I teased out a fleck of paper still stuck in the spine. Where would it all lead? It would lead to violence, to his running away, to separation from my mother. To his never knowing his own daughter. I jumped up, banging my knee. I hobbled up and down the room despite the pain. He had given me this piece of himself, like a flower pressed between the covers of a book, and I had begun to like him. I had forgotten why I hadn't had a father to begin with.

January 27 I'm beginning to get to know this really cool girl – I mean woman – in my Mass Comm. class. Her name is Audrey James, and she's incredibly brilliant and serious. She always participates in class discussions, always says thought-provoking things. Today we talked a bit after class and I asked her if she had time to go to the caf and get some hot chocolate or something. She was explaining to me Lenin's concept of the vanguard and why it isn't necessarily elitist. Anyhow, we went, and we ended up talking so much we both cut our next classes.

Feb. 14 Valentine's Day. I have to admit I'm thinking about Audrey as much as politics. But it's all mixed up together, because if I'm honest, she's a large part of me getting so serious. I want to measure up. I'm trying to cram as much into this dumb head of mine as possible. I can't tell if she likes me as a friend or a boyfriend and I'm too much of a wimp to ask. Keep waiting to read the signs. I haven't seen any evidence of a boyfriend and she never mentions anyone. But she's so pretty and terrific I can't understand how she wouldn't be with someone.

The next few entries detailed plans for a teach-in and my father's ideas for reaching apathetic students. One page had only a list of meetings and discussion topics and dates for leafleting. All over the margins was my mother's name, written in a variety of styles: block caps with hollow centers, block caps with shading, ornate cap and lowercase with long spirally tendrils.

March 1 Audrey and I have gotten closer, though we haven't dated or anything. I am so psyched, because we're going together to the march on Washington next Saturday. We're going down on the student bus with lots of others, of course, but I'm picking her up, so it's a date, really.

Audrey told me that she did have a boyfriend, a guy named Philip, but they broke up a little while ago. She has decided she really wants to devote her life to social change, and he doesn't.

I winced for Philip, for how my mother had dismissed him from her life. Not serious enough, not committed enough. I saw him in Golden Gate Park, walking the bench, arms outstretched like a tightrope walker.

March 4 The march was incredible, beyond anything I could have expected. The weather was shitty – cold and wet – but the spirit was so righteous. There were buses from all over the country – even California! You could see thousands and thousands of people no matter where you looked, everyone chanting and singing. The organizers weren't prepared for so many, and everything was a little disorganized. The line of marchers was so long we didn't make it to the Washington monument until two hours after speeches began. Maybe it was good, because I think I would have frozen to death. Audrey is either warmer blooded than me, or she had on Long-Johns or something, because she seemed to have no problem. I was trying not to show how miserably cold I was, but I guess she noticed my lips were blue, because she cuddled up to me, put her arm around my waist.

I thought I'd die!

The rally wasn't over until late, and when we went to the church where we were supposed to be put up for the night, it was already full. Finally they found us a really nice couple who had volunteered to take in protesters. It was so cool. Audrey and I had the living room to ourselves and we sat up talking a little while, but we were so exhausted we basically crashed. The next morning it was sunny and beautiful and we went to a neat little café for breakfast. It was so exciting to wake up in the morning with a girl — I mean, woman — in the room with me.

We held hands the whole way home on the bus.

I was with them on the bus, breathing the stale, stuffy air, seeing the streaks of light out the window as the bus sped through the night, rain falling lightly, feeling the ache throughout my body from having stayed up too late talking.

April 10 At the top of the page my father had written: THINGS I LOVE, followed by a list, each introduced with a tiny asterisk.

❋ The way she works her upper lip with her thumb and forefinger when she's concentrating

❋ The way she folds her arms around her legs and rests her chin on her knees when she's content

❋ The little wisps on the back of her neck when she wears her hair in a ponytail

I felt a sharp sting in my chest. *The way she works her upper lip....* I saw her bent over her books as she concentrated on the next day's teaching plan. *The way she wraps her arms around her knees....* I saw her at the kitchen table in the mornings, her coffee mug resting on her knees, her face turning pink from the liquid's heat.

I yanked on a sweatshirt and ran out of the cabin, bolting up the pathway, my sneakers slipping on the matted pine needles. My mother had been returned to me and then lost again in one swift, cruel moment by my father's words.

After a few minutes I had to stop and stood panting to catch my breath, then continued around the lake, walking now. This stranger had as intimate a knowledge of my mother as I did. The very same images that spoke to me had spoken to him. But it was worse than that. He had something more. Not just her emotional life but the very thing I'd always scorned – her political life. Politics had always seemed dry and dull and boring, but in my father's journal it seemed almost as enthralling as Trent found it.

My early childhood had been filled with demonstrations and meeting halls, conferences and workshops. I remembered faces bending down to smile or touch my hair, comments on how I'd grown. Now, like bubbles adhering to bubbles, words from my father's journal attached in my mind to words from my childhood. Socialism, apathy, mass movement – words that fit into the jigsaw of my mother's life. I could remember how excitement flared in rooms where politics was debated. I had been warmed by the welcoming skin of bodies pressed close in solidarity. I'd arranged the pretty colored papers on the card tables outside conferences while my mother explained to people what the words on the leaflets meant. During meetings I'd played with other children in church back rooms while politically correct men did the childcare. I'd rubbed my cheek against unfamiliar cloth, sniffed the scent of unfamiliar bodies, as I snuggled to sleep on piled-up coats on someone's bed. But as I got older I began to feel left out. I would sometimes come home to find people I didn't know in the living room, serious faces that looked up when I entered, the sudden hush as a topic was halted. Sometimes I sat listening as I did my homework. Once or twice my mother asked me to leave. She said it nicely, gently, kissing me so that I wouldn't act up in front of her friends. I would go, face burning. Banished. It was how I learned – over and over and over again – that the twosome of my mother and me was false. That special place I thought was mine was instead usurped by this other, this thing called politics. I had not gotten to know and experience it as my father had, as my own discovery and on an equal footing with my mother. And so over time I turned my back on what had turned its back on me.

I didn't stop walking until I had made the complete circle around the lake. Slowly, limp with sweat, I returned to the cabin, not knowing what else to do. The notebook lay where I had dropped it on the floor.

April 12 How can someone I've only known for a few months mean more to me than anyone or anything? How is this possible? Yet I know she will be the center of my life forever.

"It's how I feel when I'm with you," she tells me when I ask why she loves me. "I like the self I am with you. And you're so good – fundamentally good. That's important to me."

Philip was warm and funny and giving, yet my mother had chosen my father, whose earnestness seemed both endearing and embarrassing. What had she meant by saying she liked the self she was with him? Was it the same self as the self she was with me?

April 14 THE FIRST TIME!!

The words were circled and surrounded with little hearts. I winced. The next page was torn out. Had my father not wanted me to read about the joys of sex with my mother – or had he been unable to bear them now himself? I thought of how I had gushed about Trent to Jenny and felt heat rise to my face.

May 30 I had a fight with my father last night where we came within a few inches of hitting each other. It was awful.

We were discussing Kent State. I can't believe that National Guardsmen firing on unarmed students is something he can accept. He thinks it was unfortunate but that the students must have provoked it.

I was trying not to get too worked up, was just explaining calmly how bankrupt I think the system is, but then he interrupts me and says, "that girl you've been seeing so much of, she's another hippie protestor?"

"*Audrey is an activist,*" I said. "*Neither of us believes in the system.*"

"*Listen to the words he uses!*" my mother said. "*You sound like a robot – you sound like someone is brainwashing you.*" I tried not to rise to the bait. "*You'd rather we just go along like sheep with this country's policies?*" I said.

"*What's wrong with peaceful change within the system?*" my father said.

"*Genocide, racism, sexism – it's all institutionalized,*" I said.

"*Commie crap!*" he was shouting now.

"*What do that girl's parents say?*" my mother said.

"*She's not 'that girl,'*" I snapped. "*Her name's Audrey.*"

"*Don't you dare speak to your mother that way,*" my father said.

It went from bad to worse. I guess it was their bringing Audrey into it that made me snap. But all our friends are having political arguments at home, too. It's like the whole country is undergoing a huge identity crisis.

I have to summon the guts to apologize. My parents and I haven't spoken, can't even look at each other. I've felt sick about it all day.

My father's parents lived in Florida and I'd seen them only a few times in my life. Did they blame my mother for what happened to their son? I remembered the last time they visited us. When my mother left the room to prepare lunch they seemed to relax a little. They asked me questions about school, and at some point my grandfather took from his pocket cellophane-wrapped peppermints, red-and-white striped, and handed one to my grandmother and one to me. We all put them in our mouths at the same time and smiled at each other through the saliva. I can never see those candies without thinking of them. Later, when my mother walked them to the door after the visit, her voice was sharp in answer to a question I didn't hear. "She knows that her father is dead, that's what she knows." I had thought at the time that it was a peculiar thing to say.

There was only one more entry in my father's notebook, in which he wrote about his excitement to be graduating, doing what he called "Movement work" over the summer. He and my mother were getting married and then going to live with a few other activists; he talked about moving into an Upper West Side apartment, the apartment in which I grew up. I turned over the last page, finding it hard to believe there was nothing more. Something had been written in pencil, and erased. I couldn't decipher it.

At the back of the notebook, taped securely, was an envelope with my name on it in my mother's hand. I couldn't face it right now. I closed the covers, rested the notebook on my lap. Why had my father sent me the notebook? Why hadn't he written to me directly? What had he wanted me to learn? Proof that he had been earnest and well-meaning? That he had loved my mother deeply? That she was the reason for what happened, the woman to win by feats of political bravery – was that it? Or was it just to let me know he was human, a real person with fears, angers, longings?

I looked up, surprised to see how late it had gotten. The day had somehow escaped me. It was getting dark and I was hungry. I thought of the big dining room at the lodge, Christine and the other guests in a convivial cluster, and I knew I couldn't join them. I roused myself to start a fire, heat a bowl of soup.

My parents had built their entire lives around a set of convictions. Had it been worth it to them, to lose each other, for my father to lose me? What would it be like to know so clearly what you believe, and to believe in it so fiercely? I remembered discussions with my mother as we sat eating at the kitchen table, the hanging Tiffany lamp casting a circle of light over the dinner plates. She would tell me about "current events" and I would fidget, feeling a deep well of resistance, as if I knew on some level how much such commitment could cost. I remember my mother turning away, biting her lip.

She had finally stopped trying. She had barely reacted when I told her I wasn't going to take even one Woman's Studies class, her subject. But displeasure – or was it sadness? – tugged at the muscles in her face, and she suddenly looked old.

It changed a little when Jenny's cousin's husband died in Iraq; we had a few tentative conversations about the war. I still didn't want to discuss anything with her, though. She would have all the answers, and I didn't want to hear them.

O

That night, for the first time since she died, I dreamed about my mother. We were walking through Riverside Park with the cherry trees in bloom. In the dream I knew my mother had cancer, but she seemed unaware. She was lighthearted, fairly skipping amidst the pink petals that wafted all over her and the ground. A feeling of dread built up in me, anticipating the pain of her death, and as the walk went on, sorrow built in my chest, and I wanted desperately to cry. I awoke with the same pressure, a longing for release, but it did not come.

I spent two more days at Kramers' Cottages, days of humid, buggy, sleepy numbness. With the weather turned hot, I went to the lake. I would wrap my lunch and a book and towel into a plastic bag inside another plastic bag fashioned into a makeshift knapsack and swim out to the float. I swam and dozed and then dozed some more. It was as if I hadn't slept in a month, I was so tired.

My brain did not want to work. I couldn't seem to think about my father and whether or not I wanted to meet him. I couldn't seem to think about my future after the summer was over. We were too deep in the woods to get a cell phone signal, and I couldn't even summon the energy to take a picture or to e-mail Jenny or Trent on the computer in Christine's office. So I fell asleep in the sun and awakened stunned and sweaty from the sleep and the sun and swam around the float until I grew tired and began the process again.

In between naps I turned to Nancy Drew. I had read the series the summer I turned thirteen, in the grip of a different kind of lethargy, the mood swings I didn't realize had to do with hormones. I would lie on my bed, windows wide open to capture the breeze, reading mysteries. With Nancy Drew I discovered the fun of peeling a mystery like a flower, petal by petal, until the core is revealed.

Now, on the float on the lake, I tore through Nancy Drew, finishing the three books that were in my cabin and hunting up another two in the lodge, which I sneaked out. I had been embarrassed to be reading them at thirteen; I was doubly embarrassed now. On the float I turned from one side to the other as my muscles cramped, hiding the book in my towel if anyone approached. Nancy had adventures just as good as any boy's, and she was the one with all the smarts. Nancy was swift and sure, clever and confident, full of what the books called pluck. She didn't waste time on silly moods; she didn't have moods. In Nancy's world, evil could always be named and understood, and it could be overcome by common sense and truth and justice. Truth and justice were always clear and obvious, too.

I liked the scenes where Nancy talked over the case with her debonair dad. I noted the tender hand her father put on her arm as she went off to fight the bad guys, the I-have-confidence-in-you-but-be-careful partings. Nancy and her father were such pals. Maybe I could be like Nancy, and solve the crime my father was accused of, exonerating him. Like mine, Nancy's mother was no longer alive.

I procrastinated in reading my mother's letter until the night before I was due to leave. I knew that sometime within the next few weeks must be the second chance she had mentioned to meet my father, and I flirted with the idea of missing that one too. I stared at the pattern of marks and stains on the cover of my father's notebook, so familiar by now I could see them with my eyes closed. Then I opened to the back, where my mother's letter was taped.

Dear Layla,

Assuming you are in Cabin 10, as I requested, you are staying where I stayed once when I came to be with your father after he left New York.

The room went blank for a moment. Then the couch came into focus, the red-plaid throw, the raggedy cushions. They might have snuggled together on that couch. I looked away, to the rocker where I had sat reading, to the fireplace whose warmth had comforted me. The flames cast long shadows on the walls, gleamed off a pair of brass candlesticks I had removed from the mantle and placed on the little coffee table. Had they curled up in front of the fire, the light casting a sheen over their skin, glittering their hair?

It was soon after your father went underground. We kept in touch through an elaborate system, and I was so desperate to see him that we took the chance.

I stared at the bed, the narrow, comfy bed. Had they lain there in each other's arms, terrified and desperate, making terrified, desperate love? I could see them; he, with his newly shorn hair, looking thin and pale, she, eyes too bright with nervous excitement. I thought of myself in Trent's bedroom, his arms encircling me. I wanted to think of my mother as a mother, not a woman. I remembered how she twisted the hair at the top of her head into a ridiculous little swirl, like soft ice cream, of the lines that had puckered the sides of her mouth, creased the corners of her eyes. A mother, not a woman. I didn't want to think of her running her hands along a man's skin – not my father's, not any man's. I did not want to imagine their coupling.

It was so risky it gives me the willies to think of even now. But I couldn't bear to be separated from him.

I needed to move. The room was no longer mine. I got up and left my parents together, her letter leaning on his notebook. Outside the shadows had lengthened and the sky was a light strip of dusky haze above the forest. A fog had begun to creep through the trees, to roll across the lake, a fog that could obscure many things. I imagined my mother sneaking through the forest to find my father, her heart beating so hard it hurt, her sweat stinging as she stood frozen, hearing someone walking up the path, someone who might see her. Perhaps she glanced in the lighted windows of the lodge, where Christine and her family were gathered, Christine, whom she would have to make sure never caught a glimpse of her. My mother had been foolhardy to meet my father, but daring and brave as well.

Where my mother had sureness, I had confusion, where she had certainty, I had ambivalence.

I felt as if I had lost my mother not once, but twice. Lost her because she was dead, and lost her because I had lost the chance to know her truly when she was alive. I had already lost my father once, because he had run away. I would lose him a second time, too, if I couldn't summon the courage to meet him.

I wrapped my arms around myself, cupped my elbows in my hands. My mother had belonged to my father before she had belonged to me; they belonged to each other more profoundly than I could hope to compete with. I felt something let go inside of me, felt the struggle to matter so much to either of them slip from my body and into the night. I felt more alone than ever.

But the aloneness felt different now – it wasn't frightening or even sad, but strange and deep like the forest, dark and vast and immutable. I squeezed myself tight against the damp fog. I felt real to myself. I looked up, wanting to see the stars, but the sky was a dense black cipher. But even if I couldn't see the stars, I knew they were there, somewhere deep in the folds of the universe.

Chapter 7

Leaving the northwest woods was like letting go of a depression. The sky seemed to lift higher, the light to become brighter. I had awoken that last morning at Kramer's with the voices of my parents in my head: my mother, my past; my father, who might be in my future – and realized I needed my present.

Trent's voice on the phone sounded husky with surprise; I had been afraid there'd be coolness, a how-can-I-get-her-off-my-back-I-wish-I'd-never-met-her tone. I had begun to convince myself I'd made up everything between us.

"I'm so happy you called!" he said. "I've been thinking about you."

"Good thoughts?" I asked.

"You know it," he said. I felt a blush creep over my face.

"How've you been?" I asked.

"Great. We moved into the apartment; my friends and I threw a party."

I was silent, realizing how little a part of his life I was, a cold knot in my stomach. But what he said next thawed it. "I've been telling everyone about you."

He was sounding shy, like someone who had been having hopeful fantasies about a person he'd just met. It was hard for me to believe the someone was me.

"Really?" I said, my voice going up in pitch. "Like what?"

We went on in that vein for a few more minutes. My insides were bursting with effervescence, as if I had downed a can of soda way too fast.

"So tell me, how's the quest going?"

"Oh, frustrating," I said. The urge to talk it over was so strong I was practically hopping from one foot to the other – but uneasiness held me back.

"Where are you off to next?" he was asking.

"Southern California," I said. Included in my mother's letter had been directions to visit her friend Nina. "Only call her if you don't want to meet him," she wrote. "If you do want to, just show up." Nina would know how to contact my father, would work out all the details.

I hadn't called. Yet.

"How was San Francisco?"

I coughed, and squeaked out a "fine." My finger began a staccato tapping against my phone as if it had a mind of its own. I had managed to forget the episode with Philip, and now my face burned.

"So get your ass back to the east coast soon, O.K.?"

I pressed the phone against my cheek for a moment before snapping it shut, as if to hold on to the warmth in his voice.

I had plenty of time to think as I drove down the coast. I thought about how strange it was that Trent seemed so real to me, when we had only just met. I thought about my parents, how young they had been when they got involved, and wondered if they had felt ready, or if circumstances had forced them to grow up faster. And I wondered if I would meet my father or if I would chicken out at the last moment. Would I recognize him from the photo? Would he have stayed youthful like Philip, or would his face have fleshed out, his neck and jaw thickened? Would his hair still be dark? Would he even have hair? I had been imagining my father as the age he was in the photo. It was easier to think of him as young and naïve, not as a middle-aged man. Not, definitely not, as a killer.

I didn't have to go through with it. It was not too late. Yet the questions nagged, and only he would have the answers. Why did he run? Did he do what he was accused of? Why this crazy scavenger hunt? And the thing that hurt the most: Why didn't you live with us? Why didn't you ever get in touch with me?

The weather cleared by the time I reached California. This time, as I drove down Highway 1, the surf and the cliffs were huge and magnificent. The driving was exhilarating, too – scary enough to command all my attention, as if specially designed to divert my anxiety. Near Big Sur I stopped overnight at a bungalow colony that hugged the hillside, and by the next day, as I continued south, the coast became less spectacular but more accessible, and I got out of the car several times to stretch my legs.

But soon I had to swing east to Bakersfield and Tehachapi and then north, a meandering route that skirted the Sierra Nevada Mountains, heading toward the Nevada border. Hours later I reached a tiny speck of a town called Lone Pine, passed a gas station and a church, made the next three rights, and stopped at the fourth house on the left, all as instructed.

Nina Fisher had been in my mother's women's group in college – that was about all I could remember being told about her. Because she couldn't have counted on the exact time of my arrival, it was unlikely my father was waiting for me; still, I couldn't get out of the car. I sat locked into the seat belt and rubbed my hand along the wheel, which was covered with beige imitation leather. I was playing with a strand of the plastic when a knock on the car startled me. A woman I vaguely recognized was peering in. I rolled down the window.

"Layla?"

I nodded, my face flushing, as if she had caught me hot-wiring the car.

"I'm Nina, do you want to come in?"

I nodded. She was small and compact, and held herself stiffly. I slowly got out, finding it difficult to breathe, as if the air was too thick.

"You weren't sure you were in the right place?" she asked as she led me up the short path.

"I didn't see the number," I mumbled, looking away from the mailbox where it was clearly displayed. The neighborhood was modest, tiny stucco houses with small lawns and beat-up cars. It was quiet, no people around at all, and a dry wind blew, carrying dust and an intoxicating scent I didn't recognize.

Nina held the door open for me. I looked at her, hoping she would understand my unspoken question, but she merely swung the door back and forth, unnerving me with her silence. She seemed impatient, as if she wanted to get me inside before saying anything, although there was clearly no one around who could possibly overhear us. I took a deep breath and stepped in, feeling my stomach plummet.

No one was inside. There was the kind of silence that told me I could relax. When I got my bearings I noticed that the place was totally bare.

"Have you just moved in?" I asked.

Nina seemed to hesitate. She had a broad face with small features and a sprinkling of freckles all over, and wore an open-necked chambray shirt from which poked a thin silver chain with a hammered peace sign.

"No," she said finally. "This isn't my place."

"It's not?" I was confused.

"We'll only stay here tonight, and then I'll take you into the desert."

"I'm sorry?"

Nina gave me a searching look. "Why don't you come into the kitchen."

I found her brusqueness off-putting. I'll just get back in the car, I thought. I'll ask for the bathroom and then I'll just walk out. Instead I followed her, watching as she poured water into a kettle and rummaged in the cabinets for tea bags, humming under her breath as if I weren't there.

"Here you go," she said finally, handing me a cup, nudging me into a metal folding chair. I sipped, waiting. My lemon zinger tasted stale, as if the tea bags had been in the house for some time.

Nina studied me under very straight, very dark brows. "What are you expecting?" she said bluntly.

I went hot with anxiety, not sure how much I should say. I had grown accustomed to everyone knowing more than I did about my parents, about what had happened, what I was in the middle of.

"I thought you were going to arrange a meeting?" I said.

Her face cleared. "You had me worried there – I thought we had our signals seriously crossed. I guess your mother didn't explain? This is a safe house, a place to decamp before the desert. He's nearby, in a settlement, and that's where we're headed."

"What? Why? Why couldn't he just meet us here?" I was totally flummoxed.

"Don't know. Your mother didn't say. Sorry. I guess this is difficult for you."

"That's an understatement," I said, bristling from her impersonal, almost cold, manner.

"We'll head out tomorrow," Nina went on. "I've got a week's vacation to give us enough time to get there and back."

"A week? How far is it?"

She threw back her head and laughed, her face relaxing into friendliness for the first time. "I hope you're in good shape."

I sometimes think the body has its own mind, independent of the one controlling our conscious thoughts. I was so focused on meeting my father that when Nina said it would be days, I was seething with frustration. Or so I thought. My body had a different perspective. Nina brought me into the living room, which looked as if it had been furnished from Salvation Army castoffs, and I sagged into the skimpy couch, felt myself meld into the fabric. I watched as she laid out clothing and equipment on the floor, dividing everything into two piles as she regaled me with information about the challenges of desert backpacking.

Gradually my brain got the message from my body: Waiting was O.K. I didn't mind being let off the hook and putting myself in Nina's hands.

Once we set out there would be no turning back.

Nina had tents and tarps, food and first aid, moleskin in case of blisters, and adhesive tape for emergency repairs. She checked my hiking shoes and pronounced them suitable, surveyed my clothing and lent me a few things.

"I know you're not experienced, but don't worry," she said, smiling. "The walking part will be relatively easy, as desert hiking goes – all valley."

I thought of how I had been shamed on that small Adirondack mountain with Karen and Ben, and hoped my swimming at Kramer's had gotten me into better shape.

"Desert conditions are extreme, so you have to be careful," she was saying. "The key things are to keep the sand from burning through the soles of your shoes and, of course, to have enough liquid. But no need to worry. I've stashed some water on the route and we'll be carrying plenty. I know survival skills – like how to condense water into a can. And despite what you've probably heard, snakes and scorpions really pose no danger. If we stay out of their way, they'll stay out of ours."

Snakes? Scorpions? My mother had formulated a fucking gauntlet for me, I thought. "Why can't we just drive?" I asked.

Nina spread a map over the coffee table. "The town we're in here is at the corner of this little corridor of land between these two national parks." She ran her finger up a smudge of yellow between the beige of Death Valley and the green of Inyo National Forest. "Here's the settlement." She pointed to a penciled red X. "There is a dirt road in, but park roads are patrolled. So by walking this corridor between the parks, we avoid most people, who prefer roads and running water."

Roads and running water sounded good to me. "You really think, after all this time...?" The word "patrolled" reverberated.

"Being careful has worked so far. No need to change the script, right? Besides," she smiled, making the sprinkling of freckles across her nose dance, "those were your mother's orders."

The way she said it made me look at her. Had she, too, found my mother a little overbearing? I suddenly remembered something my mother had said about her when we were planning the trip, and it reassured me now: "I'd trust Nina with my life."

"You and my mother were close?" I asked.

Nina looked up from tightening the cinches around a sleeping bag. "Do you miss her something terrible?" she asked.

Her abruptness startled me into truth. "Yes," I said, "when it gets through."

"I guess you still don't really believe it," she said.

"I guess," I said.

"I lost someone, too," Nina said. "A year ago. There are still days when I turn to tell her something. But what's almost worse is I think I'm starting to forget a little. Maybe that's part of the healing, but I hate it. What I want is to hold on to her hereness, do you know what I mean? For her to be so much a part of my present that I don't have to try and remember. I'm not sure how to do that and let her go too."

I felt my eyes sting. I saw my mother, pale and thin in her hospital bed. I had been trying hard to force memories of her from my mind, because it hurt so. It hadn't occurred to me that time might erase them completely, and I'd be left with nothing.

We rose before dawn and donned our packs at the door. At the edge of town we confronted a flat sandy plain with low mountains in the far distance. I was not reassured to be told it was Last Chance Range. Nina took out the topographical map, explaining that in the desert it was crucial to know exactly where you were at all times. "There are often only very minimal reference points, and so you have to calculate exactly how much distance you've covered," she said. "You may find the desert boring, especially at first. This is all sagebrush country, the southernmost bit of what's called the Great Basin, what was left after a huge lake evaporated eons ago. It's got a subtle beauty I love. Of course, your aesthetic may be quite different."

My aesthetic. As if it were my aesthetic I was concerned about. I thought of myself as a city girl; I used to joke that I would die without concrete under my feet. It was a posture of course, like only wearing black. But now, facing this flat desert plain, pockmocked with bits of green and gray, I was surprised by the dullness of it.

Still, there was something about the whole expedition that appealed to me once I got used to the idea that I was going to be walking for days with what felt like a mountain on my back. I decided to try to enjoy it. If nothing else, it would make a good story to tell my friends when I got back.

The early morning air was cool and fresh, and there was that distinctive scent. Nina said it was creosote and sagebrush, and pointed out a grey treelike shrub. "It'll get a little dunelike up ahead," she reassured me. "The interesting thing is how after a while you start to see all the variations in the sand and the vegetation. Like the way you can see so many more stars out at night if you're away from a town and there are no lights from buildings and street lamps to compete."

We walked and took a break and walked again. As the day drew on, the sounds of early morning birds gave way to silence, the coolness to increasingly intense heat. We stripped down to our sleeveless T-shirts, slathered on more sunscreen, gulped from our water bottles. I got to know Nina's jaunty walk, the way her arms slanted from her sides as she propelled herself along.

And she was right about the landscape – soon the beiges showed white and coral and even blue, the land to undulate into low dunes. Suddenly I wanted to take pictures, to try to capture those sensual textures and subtle colors. Nina waited patiently as I snapped, staring off into space, as still as a rabbit.

Around 11 o'clock we stopped. "Come see," Nina said. Amazingly, at the base of a small pile of rocks, there was a tiny trickle of water. Nina yanked her boots and socks off. I was suddenly aware of the throbbing and prickling of my skin. We sat side by side, taking turns dipping our feet – the trickle wasn't big enough for both of us at once – into the coolness.

"I used to backpack with Sue, the woman I was involved with, mainly the Mojave and Joshua Tree," Nina said, drying off her feet. "Now I usually hike alone. It's a little scary, but it gives me something I don't get otherwise, something I guess I'd have to call spiritual." I searched for a glimmer of the spiritual in her dark brows, square jaw. She worked as a social worker at a shelter for battered women, she had told me. I imagined she would need that "something spiritual" to face the broken teeth and shattered lives she must see day after day.

"Someday I'd love to hike the entire Pacific Crest Trail," she was saying. "That goes from the Mexican border all the way up to Oregon."

I shook my head. Just getting through these few days would be more than enough for me.

I helped Nina construct a shelter from a tarp and fiberglass poles threaded with shock cord. Then we spread a groundcloth underneath the tarp and crawled into the shade. Like the other creatures of the desert, snakes and insects and birds and squirrels, we would rest during the hottest part of each day.

"So," Nina said, passing me a baggie of dried fruit and nuts, "you found your mother a bit tough?"

"Well, maybe, in a way. I mean...."

"It's O.K., I know you loved her. But I can understand how it might have been hard being your mother's daughter."

"How do you mean?"

"Understand that she was one of my best friends," Nina said, crunching meditatively on a cashew. "But she was hard to take sometimes. So fucking smart, I guess? So serious and sure of herself?" She suddenly looked alarmed. "I'm sorry, I don't mean to put your mother down in any way."

"It's O.K.!" I said, perhaps too eagerly.

Nina burst out laughing. "Your mother was something, that's for sure," she said, her voice full of the admiration I was accustomed to. "But it's hard living with a paragon, isn't it? And sometimes you need a mother more than a heroine, am I right?"

I slept for several hours and woke up disoriented, the sun low on the horizon, shadows beginning to creep across the valley. Nina was nearby, reading. It was 4:30. We packed everything up and walked for another few hours to a site Nina had previously selected, a small space between a mesquite tree and some low boulders. It was important to set up camp before it got dark, she said, to get everything done while we could see. To make sure we weren't, for instance, pitching the tent on a rattler's home.

Nina gave me a quick lesson in camping basics, a running commentary as I handed her things and she showed me how to put up the small tent, assemble a tiny stove that didn't look big enough to cook a cup of coffee, and dig a pit to use as a latrine. In another hole we buried a metal canteen of water for the return trip, in case the little trickle in which we had dipped our feet dried up. Then we prepared dinner – cold soup, freeze-dried spaghetti and meatballs, carrot sticks, fudge brownies. I couldn't believe how delicious it tasted.

"Once I had a package of beef stew left over after a camping trip," Nina said. "I made it at home, but it was revolting. It's extraordinary what a difference being so seriously ravenous makes."

As the sun began to set, ribbons of color suffused the sky in a flamboyant light show. Coolness descended rapidly, and soon we needed sweaters and a fire. "The temperature difference in the desert is more extreme than anywhere," Nina said. "Sometimes as much as 80 degrees in the same day."

I leaned back against the boulders. The sky was now black, with the stars layered so densely that I felt if I kept looking, I would be sucked up and lost forever. How did Nina camp out here alone?

"Tell me more about the settlement," I said. We had stayed off the topic of my father all day. "Is it some sort of secret community?"

"Secret?" Nina said. "Not at all. Even within wilderness areas every road and feature is mapped. People see the unfamiliar car, the smoke from a chimney. It's much easier to get lost in a crowded city."

"Then why all this?" I asked.

"Oh, I was talking permanent. For short-term disappearance a place like the settlement is perfect. It's a very transient community mixed in with a small core of year-rounders and an anti-establishment culture. As long as you act cooperatively with the others, no questions are asked. It's run by a bunch of hippies and is frequented by all sorts – old countercultural types and Hell's Angels and assorted weirdoes. Even ordinary people."

"Sounds pretty unappealing."

"It's actually kind of fun. Your mother and I planned to take you even before she knew she was dying and had to rejigger the trip for you alone."

"So this isn't where my father lives?"

"I doubt it, but I don't know. Your mother never talked about him. She must have wanted to sometimes, but she never did. You know how incredibly self-disciplined she was. She said it was best if those of us who help them know nothing about his life at all. For everyone's protection."

We put out the fire and got into the tent, having first double-bagged and hung the food from a tree Nina said was a small oak. The tent was small, but I was glad of Nina's proximity. She had told me that many desert creatures are nocturnal and asked if I wanted to stay up to watch them, but I said I'd pass. With every slight noise I imagined snakes and spiders and coyotes; I thought I'd never fall asleep.

And indeed I slept badly, too cold and then too hot. I had the dream again about my mother, and I awoke from the sound of my own whimpering, my cheeks wet. I longed to put my hand on Nina's arm or rest against her, but I was afraid to awaken her, afraid of what she might think. And so I lay motionless on my back, my arms crossed over my chest like a corpse, listening to the early morning birds. There were so many of them! I was amazed they could exist in such a harsh environment. And I thought how people, like birds, could adapt to trying circumstances. I hated the thought of all that accommodation.

O

It took us another day of walking until, at dusk, we reached the settlement, campfires already beginning to be lit. We were in the Saline Valley, on Bureau of Land Management land.

"Government land?" I was surprised.

Nina laughed. "Ironic, no? There's a complicated political dance going on. The Bureau of Land Management allows the trespass occupancy, because by having years of uninterrupted use they can lobby to keep the roads open. Environmentalists want to close the roads so the entire area can be added to Death Valley National Park."

We stood on a slight rise overlooking the settlement. It seemed to be mostly a campground, the tents interspersed among a large stand of willows and cottonwoods. "See what I mean," Nina said, as we watched a group of women in long skirts and men in leather vests. "It's like a cross between a hippie commune and a frontier town of the Old West." A teenager with flaming orange hair slouched past, hands in pockets so deep they were at his knees.

We hoisted our packs. "First things first," Nina said, "let's get cleaned up." The settlement was in a bona-fide geothermal resource area; people came from far and wide to bask in the hot tubs. After two days of drinking and washing with only the water we had carried, I had a finer appreciation of geothermal.

I felt the stares as we walked down the dirt path, very conscious of my matted hair and sweaty skin. Though there was no one at the hot tubs, I felt embarrassed shedding my clothes and sliding into the hot bubbling water. Still, it felt so good I gave a long sigh and leaned back. When I opened my eyes the sun's rays were striking the multicolor rock face of the Last Chance Range that rose in layers from the soft desert in the distance.

"The year-round residents have developed governing rules for everything from garbage removal and hot tub cleaning to running a school for the kids," Nina was saying, just as a group of men approached, all with long hair and an abundance of tattoos. They stripped and slipped naked into the adjacent hot tub. A jolt of horror shot through me. The last thing I wanted was to meet my father for the first time naked in a hot tub.

Nina was talking. I watched her mouth moving and the dying light dancing on the bubbling water, but I had gone deaf. It had finally hit: any minute, any hour, now. The word "dread" came into my mind, and it became a drumbeat: dread, dread, dread. I found myself sinking even lower in the water. This wasn't a story, an adventure. This was my life, my one true life, and I was on the cusp of something momentous. It isn't often we know ahead of time that a person we are going to meet is going to change our lives forever. But I could know with certainty that even if we had little to say to one another, even if we never met again, what happened between my father and me would matter.

Dinner was a communal potluck, but I could barely eat. Later in my stay I would notice the cactus garden and the cleverness of the solar electric system, the interpersonal dynamics among the colonists. But that night I was too tense to be aware of much except the dreamy light that bathed everything in a rosy haze and heightened my sense of unreality. After dinner I grabbed Nina's wrist as she lifted her wine glass to her mouth and said, "we have to talk."

"Sure," she said. I released her wrist. She stood up, holding her glass, and led me to one of the flat boulders that served as benches. "What's up?"

"What's up? What do you mean, what's up? You haven't told me a thing. Where is he? When do I meet him?"

"Sorry, Layla, I thought I said. Tomorrow. He must be coming from the mountains. All I know is I'm to take you to a place just a few miles away."

"Miles?" I croaked. I couldn't believe it. I was shaking. "This is totally ridiculous."

"I don't know why. Maybe where he judged would be most comfortable."

"For him, maybe." Was this some sort of Outward Bound for the spirit, a test of how much they could put me through before I cracked? I wanted to howl, to turn and leave. I was thoroughly trapped.

○

In the morning I dressed quickly and was ready before Nina. We were mostly silent as we walked; I was too anxious and pissed off to talk.

We were on a well-traveled trail, ascending toward the mountain range, and as we walked the air became slightly cooler, the sagebrush slightly taller. Here and there was a juniper tree around which Nina tied a small length of red tape.

"I'm turning back now, Layla," Nina said after we'd walked about an hour, and I felt a clutch in my stomach. Somehow I hadn't expected this. "He'll be up ahead, at that outcrop. You have enough food and water, and he'll have plenty. I don't know if he'll come back with you, but you can't miss the trail – you saw me mark it."

I stared at her, swallowed, anger chased away by fear. I was 6 years old again, my mother abandoning me at school. "O.K." I managed.

"You'll be fine," she said, pulling the visor of my cap down over my eyes. "Good luck."

I watched Nina's retreating figure until she disappeared. Then I started slowly toward the rock outcrop.

The small canyon was no more than a story high and perhaps a block or so in length. There were several thin trees, which I knew by now signaled a water source; sometimes a small pool could be found several feet deep and siphoned off with a rubber tube, Nina had told me. I fingered my canteen. Even though I had everything I needed, I was intensely nervous.

I walked in and around the canyon, but there was nothing, no one. I climbed up, dislodging small stones, surprised by delicate yellow flowers. I settled in the shade of a slight ledge near the summit from which I could see almost 360 degrees around. I was surrounded by a vast empty space, dun colored and undulating, the mountain range blocking my vision in one direction, the settlement a hazy green smear in the distance. The bird song had died off, and I was aware of the roar of the silence, a kind of hum that seemed to build into a crescendo of absence. I felt an urge to shout, just to shatter that terrifying emptiness.

I looked at my watch. Only twenty minutes had passed since Nina left. I took a swig of water from my bottle. I wasn't sure how long I could hold out before panicking and heading back.

So I devised a game. I would focus on one thing – a plant, a shadow, a distant peak – and try to watch it steadily for an entire minute. When I was absolutely sure the minute had passed, I would check my watch to see how close I had come. But even in my best attempt, only forty seconds had passed. It was clear I didn't have it in me to be a Zen master.

By the time a half-hour had gone by I was limp from tension. I climbed back down the canyon and circled the perimeter again, half-afraid I would find no one, half-afraid I would. Once I thought I saw movement, but it was only the shimmer of heat on the face of the rock. I went back to my lookout perch to gulp some more water and think what to do. I began to sing softly to calm myself. The sense of letdown and anticlimax was so overpowering I felt almost faint.

Just then something caught my eye. Close to where I was sitting was a tiny beige lizard, completely still. How long had it been there? I couldn't restrain the impulse to pick it up, although it squirmed in fright as I pried it from the rock. I loved the feel of its dry skin as I ran my finger down its back, the soft plumpness of its underbelly pulsating in my palm. Holding it was deeply satisfying. I pressed it to my cheek, ran its smooth cool belly across my hot lips.

"Layla?"

With a shriek I leapt up, dropping the lizard, and stumbled as I tried not to stomp it underfoot. Watching me, a few feet away, was a man. There was no doubt who he was. I was staring into eyes so like mine as to be completely unnerving.

This was how it came to be that the first words I ever said to my father were, "Fuck you."

His expression seemed to waver between amusement and wariness.

"Did you have to scare me like that?"

"I'm sorry," he said, and touched my arm. I drew back, and he removed his hand. I stared at him. He was of medium height and build, bearded, his dark curly hair a trifle too long and shot with gray. In shorts, T-shirt, and khaki vest with many pockets, he looked more Sierra Club than anything, and more composed than he had any right to be. His eyes on mine were steady and sure, as if taking my measure. It made me angry, and yet I felt myself falter, go still, a snake under the gaze of a charmer.

He let out his breath. "I'm your father, Layla," he said, "I can't tell you what it means to me to meet you."

I could only turn away from the emotion in his voice. I felt flushed with a kind of burning heat – anger, confusion, sorrow?

"I'm surprised you got here before me," he said. "I've set up on the other side. Let's go sit down there – it'll be cooler."

I followed him back down and around to the side of the canyon facing the mountain range, pins and needles running a scale up and down my body. He had created a small encampment under a tarp, and we sat down, crosslegged, facing one another. The laces of my hiking boots had come undone. I gripped them, but my hands were so shaky I didn't attempt to retie them.

"This must be very strange and awkward for you," he said finally.

"And it isn't for you?" I said.

"Of course. I've been more than just a bit of a wreck about it all. But at least I've been calling the shots, more or less."

"You," I asked, "or my mother?" I hated how in control he seemed.

He ran his hand over his beard.

"Look, Layla, I get that you're angry. I don't blame you. I'm not even asking for your understanding when I say that this is hard for me, too. Just some acknowledgment, I guess."

"It's a bit of a stretch to ask me to worry about your feelings," I said.

He grimaced. "You're right. Of course it is. And I'm willing to bear up under any abuse you want to heap on me. But that's really the best I can do."

I nearly choked. "After everything, that's the best you can do?" I tried to jump up, but I couldn't untangle myself from my crosslegged position.

"What I mean is that I can try, I can do my best, but it can never be enough, I know that."

I yanked at my shoelaces. "That's just too easy," I finally managed.

"I can't pretend to make up for the harm that's been done to you. You were deprived of a father. You were lied to. All I meant was that I recognize there is no repairing that kind of harm. That there's nothing in the world can be done about that now."

"God, can't you even say you're sorry?" I grabbed a fistful of sand and flung it at the ground.

He backed up, as if alarmed. "Sorry? What I feel goes so far beyond sorry. Layla, I owe you the most profound apology any human being can offer another. I should have said that from the first."

Despite my anger, I felt tears welling up. I mashed the shoelaces into a ball in my hand and then smoothed them out again.

"Layla," he said. "We can start from today. That's all we have. Will you try and do that?"

I looked away, somehow ashamed. The shade from the tarp formed a circle around us. Beyond I saw what appeared to be shallow pools of water. Nina had explained that mirages are not figments of overheated imaginations or of underquenched bodies but are true optical illusions from the heat shimmering on the sand. As if in response to those shimmers, I felt my body begin to quiver.

"I don't know who you are," I heard myself say.

"Do you want to?" he asked.

The seconds passed. My heartbeats were separate distinct thumps against my chest. "I'm here," I finally said. "That's as much as I'm sure of."

"Fair enough," he said. We fell silent, and I became aware of how hot it was. I took a swig of water and wiped the sweat from my upper lip. He took a pink grapefruit from his pack and cut it open with a Swiss Army knife, skewered a piece with the knife tip, and offered it to me. My teeth met metal as I slid the grapefruit section into my mouth.

"I read the notebook you sent, but I still don't know what happened," I finally managed. "I don't know what you did or why, I don't know what's been going on." I heard the shakiness in my voice and stopped to catch my breath. "Why didn't you ever contact me? Why wasn't I told you were alive?"

"I'm a fugitive, Layla. It was too risky to have any contact. When you were little, your mother and I thought it would be better all around if you thought I was dead. Look, it's all very complicated, and you've every right to know everything. I give you my word that I will tell you. But would it be O.K. with you if we get to know each other a little bit first?" He skewered another section of grapefruit for me, then popped one in his own mouth.

He ran his hand over his beard as he waited for my response. There were little age lines radiating from the corners of his eyes, lines that made him seem warm and full of humor, somehow. I wondered if my eyes would take on that aspect with age, or if my mean-spiritedness would manifest itself instead. I sighed, nodded, my mouth full of the grapefruit's sour sweetness.

And so he told me about himself, and the morning stretched into midday and midday stretched into afternoon. He told me about his childhood in Queens and his life up to his college years, the part I knew. He told me about his time since, how he was 6 months here, 6 months there, only gradually staying a year or more in any one place. After the first year as a fugitive he had gotten fake ID and bought a trailer. "There's a whole culture of trailer parks, a kind of invisible visible life – it's the underbelly of America," he said. He supported himself with all sorts of odd jobs – in restaurant kitchens, gas stations – the kind of work that paid next to nothing but where the employers didn't ask questions. And, all through the years, he continued to see my mother.

I was taken aback. "How? When?"

"We could only chance it three or four times a year. We sometimes used conferences as a cover."

I had realized, of course, that they had to have seen each other after he became a fugitive, since she had gotten pregnant with me. But it shocked me that it had been ongoing. Three or four times a year? She had not only kept her past secret from me, I thought, but her present as well. I felt almost weak with anger. I thought of all the weekends when she had gone away and left me in a neighbor's care. Of all the times she must have lied about what she was really doing, where she was really going.

"It's your turn now, Layla," my father said. "Though I have the advantage – I know it won't seem like much, but I've been connected to you all along through your mother. She sent me pictures, report cards, videos. But I don't know, for instance, if you still hate Brussels sprouts," his voice was light now, teasing.

I recoiled. "That makes me feel really weird." I looked away. Had she told him all the awful things I had said and done over the years, about all my petty vices, my shames? I looked down, noticed my shoelaces again, and this time yanked them into compact tight bows.

"I'm sorry, it must feel like having a stranger spying on you, stripping you of your privacy. But you're my only daughter, only child. It's probably hard for you to believe this, but I do love you."

"No," I said. "You can't say that, you're not entitled to say that." He had broken the fragile connection, as delicate as a spider's tender filament, that we had been making.

"I don't mean to push you," he said.

The light on the mountains was sharper now, and there was a slight breeze carrying the scent of creosote.

"Shouldn't we be getting back?" I said.

"Right," he said.

And so this time it was my father I followed through the desert. I concentrated on my footing, on the snake curled up under a bush, the flower in a crevice. I watched the sun lowering toward the horizon, the blue of the afternoon sky deepen. After an hour I was exhausted. My nerves were on fire and my eyeballs burned. But I didn't have any idea what I felt. Didn't know what I wanted to feel.

At the outskirts of the settlement we both stopped, as if we both felt the need to say something.

"Why here?" I asked. "Why this settlement?"

"I feel very safe here. I often camp in Last Chance all summer – it's very beautiful. I'd have loved to have shown it to you, but it's a difficult climb." He fell silent, and looked away. "I guess it's because no other place seemed right. I couldn't imagine talking to you in a coffee shop or hotel room. Somehow I thought that here, in the wild, far away from everything, we'd be able to be very real with each other."

I started to say something sarcastic, then didn't. He turned back to me, his eyes fixed on mine. And this time I couldn't look away.

Chapter 8

Nina was waiting for us at the outskirts of the settlement. She and my father stopped short a few feet from each other, then she bounced up on tippy toes high enough for the kiss he planted on her cheek. After a second he gave her a brusque hug, a peppy hug, the kind that goes with a burst of emotion you need to discharge.

"It's good to see you, Nina," he said.

"It's good to see you, too—"

"Jim," my father interrupted quickly. Jim was the name my father said he was using now.

I watched as they appraised each other for a moment, smiling with their heads tilted to the same side, and told each other how good they looked, how little they had aged.

"I should put up my tent," my father said. "Meet you for dinner?" he lay his hand on my shoulder. I could still feel the pressure even after he removed it.

"So," Nina said, as we stood watching him walk off. "How did it go?"

It was a question I couldn't begin to consider. "O.K., I guess." I didn't want to talk about it. "You and he haven't seen each other?"

"Not since he went underground," Nina said. "I never knew him well."

"You don't like him, do you?" I asked. There was something in her tone.

"Whoa," Nina laughed. "Where did that come from?" When I just shrugged, she went on. "At the time I resented him a little, that's all. After he came along, I didn't see as much of your mother as I would have liked, especially after they started living together."

"Were you lovers?" I burst out before I knew I was going to.

"Me and your dad?" she said.

"My mother and you!" The thought had been nipping at the edges of my mind.

"Your mother and me?" she repeated, as if the very idea surprised her. "No, not at all." She paused, then grinned. "She wasn't my type."

I didn't believe her, and she saw it in my face. "Seriously, Layla, we weren't. Your mother wasn't so inclined. And I was just as glad, really. Lovers come and go; friends last. We were roommates, and active in the Women's Movement together. We had a strong bond, but it wasn't sexual."

"Then why be angry with my father?"

"Oh, I wasn't angry, really. She just had less time for me, that was all." At my look she grinned again. "O.K., so maybe I was a wee bit jealous. Look, it's all ages ago. He's been through a lot."

I grunted.

"Do you think you'll be able to cut him some slack?" she asked.

I was taken aback. "I don't know. Do you think he deserves it?"

"That's not my call."

I looked down, kicked at the sand with my toe.

"Well, give it time."

But I didn't know what kind of time we had, what kind of time I wanted.

I headed down the path to the hot tubs, feeling slick with sweat, gritty. All around was activity – kids spinning frisbees, three girls about my age sitting in a circle playing recorders. A breeze had picked up, and from the hot tub I watched the sand being teased and scalloped by the wind until my eyes stung. I returned to the tent and lay down, telling myself I would rest for only a moment. Voices and birds wove a textured music that lulled me to sleep from which I awoke, befuddled, with Nina telling me to come to dinner, my father was saving us seats.

The long picnic tables in the open-air dining area were festive with candles, and the clearing was strung with solar lights, tiny pinpricks of gold, magenta, navy. It was a mixed crowd, some middle-aged or older, some younger than I was. I spotted my father. There was a big space at the end of the table between him and the next person, presumably the space he was saving for us, but it made him seem solitary, and a little sad. That afternoon he had seemed wiry and athletic, but now he was a little stooped, and the streaks of gray in his hair looked faded, not the sparkly silver they had been in the sunlight.

There were bowls of steamed vegetables, quinoa, and grilled slabs of tofu in barbeque sauce, but I just picked at the food and helped myself to wine. The setting and people were so unreal I felt caught in some strange dream. There was a woman who had just returned from a month tending rare birds in a 300-foot tree in Venezuela, a bungie-jumper, two bikers, a watercolor artist. There was a greasy-haired guy who vied with me for the wine bottle and a scientist who had created a wildlife refuge for the fringed-toed lizard in the Coachella Valley. Like me, my father, too, was mostly silent.

As we finished eating, the sound of an airplane became audible and a cheer went up. "What is it?" I asked.

"Come on," my father said, and we jogged after everyone else to where the plane was landing on the hard-packed sand of an alkaline flat. The pilot, a large man with a handlebar mustache, stepped out to another cheer. "It's Ice Cream Ike," my father explained. "Once a week he flies in. It's like the coming of the Messiah."

Tubs of ice cream – the politically correct Ben and Jerry's, of course – were unloaded and carried to the tables. I saw my father heading for the New York Superfudge Chunk. It was my favorite, too. I scooped up Cherry Garcia instead.

We took our bowls and walked along the perimeter of the settlement to sit and watch the fading sunset, our backs against a boulder.

"You don't talk about yourself much, do you?" my father said, after a moment. "Or is it me?"

"There's not a lot to say," I said. The light was seeping rapidly from the sky now, and palm leaf shadows played across his face. He stared at me. I looked down into my empty ice cream bowl. I suddenly felt like the bowl – filled with air or, at most, a sweet concoction with no nutritional value whatsoever.

"How about this," he said. "I'll ask questions and try to guess the answers. If I guess right you have to own up. What do you say?"

"I suppose."

"O.K. First question. Do you have a boyfriend?" He narrowed his eyes at me. "That's easy, the answer is yes. And by your expression, I'd say it's somebody new. Am I right?"

"Well...." Despite my discomfort, I could feel how just the thought of Trent was pulling my lips into a smile.

"Come on, come on."

"I sort of met someone this summer," I said, the temptation to talk about Trent too strong to resist.

"On this trip? Who?" His tone – proprietary, eager – somehow pleased me.

"You know Lenny and Letitia in Boston?" I said. "They have a son...."

"Trent! I've heard about him! Good going!"

"How about you," I said, feeling awkward. "Do you have... someone?"

"I was faithful to your mother, if that's what you're asking," he said, his tone cold.

"I'm sorry," I said hastily, wishing I had bitten my tongue.

He went on as if I hadn't spoken. "Not just because I loved her. My situation makes me too vulnerable to risk any attachment. And believe me, fear is no aphrodisiac." He paused. "I don't know about your mother – whether she had men in her life. Given that we couldn't see each other often, I freed her from any obligation. But I don't want to know. Don't feel you have to enlighten me, Layla."

"She didn't," I protested. "Really. She had male friends – they would go to movies or meetings and things – but they weren't boyfriends. I'm sure, because I really wanted her to date, and she wouldn't."

He surprised me with a sudden laugh. "She told me how you called her a fishsicle." The reference was to one of my mother's favorite posters that read: "A Woman Without a Man Is Like a Fish Without a Bicycle."

We sat a moment, saying nothing. I was taken aback by how eager I'd been to spare his feelings. Everything suddenly seemed confusing and complicated.

A bare-chested teenage boy walked past, a white iPod cord dangling from his ear, singing off-key.

"Next question," my father said, "favorite type of music. Answer...." He made a show of wrinkling his brow, narrowing his eyes. "Not heavy metal or punk – but maybe my bias is too strong. Rap, jazz, classical – I doubt it. Opera? Not a chance. O.K., here goes: World music, some classic rock, pop. How did I do?"

"So-so," I said, not wanting to give in. "What I'm really into is female singers I guess you'd call folk rock."

"Like KT Tunsdale or more Dar Williams?"

"Tunsdale, yes; I'm mixed on Dar Williams," I said, a bit annoyed he'd heard of them. "O.K., my turn. You're classic rock all the way, and drippy Leonard Cohen folk – minor-key, angst music. Am I right?"

"She mocks me!" he threw up his hands, beaming.

"I figure your tastes are stuck in the '60s, just like the rest of you," I said, my tone a little snotty. I didn't want him to think he could win me over so easily.

O

Nina went off for a day's hike, leaving my father and me to each other. We played question and answer again as we scrubbed out the hot tubs and squeezed oranges for juice. We asked each other all the easy stuff – favorite movies, books, sports. Once in a while we were more probing – how did I feel about abortion, how did he feel about hunting – but mostly we kept it light. We called it Q & A, and we attributed points and kept score. We were psyching each other out, playing cat and mouse. It was almost fun.

Was it the game, the desert, the sun? Was it the sand, the mineral springs, the novelty? Something was happening, a melting down inside of me. I realized how tense I had been, how tight my muscles, how hunched my shoulders.

I actually liked being at the settlement. I liked the quirky mix of people, the shared chores and meals. It surprised me. It surprised me, too, that at times I liked being with this stranger who called himself my father.

It was bizarre, preposterous, of course, to believe he could have that irrevocable connection to me. Only when he turned his eyes—my eyes—on me, did I feel a jolt of belief. And there was a deeper sense—or sense is too strong a word—that he was as I'd imagined him. He told me that my mother had brought me to see him a few times when I was small, before I got too old for them to risk it, and I wondered if it was possible he was buried somewhere in my toddler memory. Still, I wondered who he really was, if he could have done what he had been accused of, if he was like me in any true or essential way.

So I watched him. I watched as he cut carrots and potatoes left to right in even chunks, lips pursed in a whistle of concentration. I watched as he unfolded his bandana to wipe a boy's sweaty face, watched the way he hitched his shorts and tucked in his T-shirt each time he stood up. He moved with a bounce, as if he were made of rubber bands, full of suppressed energy.

"I've really enjoyed being here," he said that second night. Once again we started off together after dinner without a word, as if the walk had been prearranged. He leaned back against a cottonwood tree, stretched his neck. "I've especially enjoyed being with you," he said.

"Me too," I managed. We both looked away. A few feet from us a small snake slithered in and out of some cactus plants, a little puff of desert dust pinpointing its location. The sky swirled violet and pink like thousands of tissue-thin ribbons playing against one another. It was true. I liked him. Or maybe I liked being the focus of so much energy and attention.

"This settlement is fun, isn't it? I've always enjoyed groups. Maybe it comes of being an only child. You're an only child – what do you think?"

"I've never been much for groups," I said.

"So much for that theory, then." He pulled at his beard. Unlike his hair, his beard was fully gray. I had not failed to notice that he tugged at it just the way I yanked at my hair.

"I like it here, though," I said. I wanted to give him that much.

"I'm glad," he said. "There's a sense of community, of being part of something. It's what drew me to politics. But I guess you know that, from my notebook. It opened me up."

"Look where that got you," I mumbled.

"What did you say?" he asked.

"Look where it got you," I repeated. "Your politics."

"If what you're saying is that now I'm more isolated than ever, maybe you're right. But think about it. For years now there's been a community of people who have helped me, cared about me, even risked their lives for me. Don't you think that's extraordinary? That people would risk so much for someone outside their circle of friends or family? How many people can say that? Could you say that?"

I looked away, wounded somehow. "No," I said. "I couldn't say that."

"Hey, I didn't mean it personally. They didn't do it for me, but because of what we all believe in."

"I knew that was what you meant," I said.

"I was thinking, Layla," he said after a moment, "that maybe – if it's O.K. – I'd hike out with you and Nina and then hitch a ride with you to San Francisco. It would give us a little more time."

We had been in one another's company for two days now. Alone together in a car, no longer surrounded by others – that would feel very different.

But I, too, wanted more time. I wanted, of course, to finally find out what had happened that had caused him to go underground. But it was more than that.

"Do you want me to call Philip, ask if you can stay, too?"

"Thanks, but that wouldn't be such a good idea. I try to jeopardize as few people as possible. I'll get a motel room somewhere."

I saw him in a dark room, slumped on a bed, changing TV channels. "Is it hard with" – what was I to call it? – "your circumstances – to have friends?" It was something I hadn't thought of before.

"Close to impossible," he said. "It's what I was saying, about attachments. I can't risk them. I make only superficial friendships because I move so often."

"Why couldn't you just stay in one place once you had the new identity?"

"I could have, that's what many others who went underground did. But I've always been afraid of getting too comfortable and letting down my guard. At least I usually stay long enough to contribute."

"Contribute to what, exactly?" I asked.

"Whatever I can find." He shrugged. "The last place I was living in, I joined a group that fought to keep a Wal-Mart from opening up and destroying the town."

"So you're still an activist?" I asked. "What you've lived through hasn't changed you?"

"Oh it's changed me, all right," he laughed. "But not in that sense. You always hear about the idealism of youth, as if to gain maturity means to give up your ideals. For me it hasn't been like that. I mean, the edges get worn with time, the metal gets tempered with experience – however you want to think of it. But I feel I've been true to my values, especially these days, with George Bush in office. I don't know if it matters to you that I can say that, but I'm glad I can."

I didn't answer. I felt his eyes on me even in the growing darkness.

"Well, Layla? Which would you rather it was? That I changed in those values or that I didn't?"

"I really can't say," I answered. My voice sounded cold and stiff. He was like my mother, then, another martyr to the cause.

"Oh, I'll bet you can," he said.

"No," I said emphatically, "I can't."

"You have no strong values or beliefs of your own, is that what you're trying to tell me?"

"Precisely," I said. "You've hit the nail on the head."

"But that's nonsense, you know."

"No, I don't know." The words came out in a rush. "I've never worked it out, not like you and my mother – your 'world views,' your 'perspectives.' I just have some basics – like I don't lie or cheat or steal. I don't believe in trampling over other human beings. I don't abandon people I love or have commitments to. I've got a nonaggression pact with the world – live and let live, something along those lines. Satisfied?"

He made a sound – an expelled breath of exasperation or frustration. He started to say something, but didn't. Seconds passed; I heard the scuff of his feet against the sand as he shifted positions. Finally he said, "Hardly. No, Layla, I'm hardly satisfied."

We walked back through the lines of tents in silence, and he bade me good night. The moon had come up, an enormous full white disk. But it wasn't a benevolent moon with a man smiling down at me. It was the kind of moon that desert coyotes would howl at during the long, lonely night.

O

If I were asked to describe who I was, and I owned up, angry would have been one of the words I would have had to use. Mine wasn't the righteous anger of my mother's at injustice. Mine was of the bitter, cynical variety, with a little temper tantrum mixed in. There were the pleasures of stomping around in a fit, being overdramatic, throwing my school books on the floor. Not least, of course, had been the fun of getting a rise out of my sane and competent mother.

But that night, after the exchange with my father, as I lay waiting for sleep, hoping to savor the familiar taste of that smoldering emotion, to fan it into a good hot flame, it didn't work.

"No, Layla, I'm hardly satisfied," my father had said, and that cut to the quick. I felt he was saying not only that he wasn't satisfied with the answer I had given him, but that he had found me wanting. His words hurt. But why? Why should I care what he thought of me? Who was he to me, after all?

I threw off the sleeping bag, then pulled it back up. By saying he wasn't satisfied, it was as if he were saying he expected a lot of me, and for some reason I couldn't fathom, some part of me wanted to meet his expectations. As if I was oddly dissatisfied with myself, too, in a way I hadn't been before. I couldn't let it go, I couldn't sleep, and I couldn't make any sense of it.

The next morning I awoke fuzzy-headed, out of sorts. I had slept fitfully, awakening from a recurring nightmare I hadn't had since grade school. I was at a racetrack, and my mother was urging me on. "You can do it, Layla! You're just as good as the others!"

The others were sleek horses, muscled and taut, straining to leap forward. I crouched low, ready for the starting gun. Off we went! I was dashing, legs outstretched, flying. What fun! But the others were pulling ahead. What was wrong? I looked down. Why, I wasn't a racehorse, I was something else, a dog it seemed, a terrier, frisky and eager, but with no chance of keeping up. They were galloping, tails like plumes, drawing farther away. I pushed harder, panting, running my heart out, but the others had become dots in the distance. I was getting smaller. I wasn't a dog at all, I was – a hamster? Yes, a hamster, racing madly on my little wheel, a crazy little rodent.

I crawled out of the tent to find everything quiet, Nina already gone. I headed to the open-air kitchen, hoping it wasn't too late for coffee. Along the path small yellow cacti were popping into bloom. There were so many kinds of plants in the desert. I liked their strangeness, their curious spikes, fuzzy hairs. It amazed me that they could survive in all this heat and dust, with so little water.

Outside the dining area I saw orange balls flying above the heads of a cluster of kids. As I got closer I saw with surprise that the juggler was my father. I slipped into the shadow of a willow tree to watch. My father's head was tilted up at the orange balls spinning from his hands in a fast furious whirl. Suddenly he spread his arms wide and let the balls fall to the ground to a gasp from the children. He bowed, gathered up the balls, and held them up, as the children applauded. "Who would like to try?" The children shrieked and shoved closer.

My father had seemed so quiet, so serious, with me. Now he was joking, tousling hair, playing the clown. Was this the father I would have known as a child, if he had not run away?

He was standing behind a small girl, his left hand beneath her left hand, his right beneath her right, a ball in each. He began to move her arms as if she were a puppet. For a second I felt the strange sensation in my own arms. One ball went up and the other, intended for her left hand, fell. The girl stomped her foot in frustration, just as I would have. My father laughed and gave her a hug. Without thought I found myself removing my camera from its bag, adjusting the telephoto. I snapped. My father turned to the next child. I snapped again.

Only a few people remained at the picnic tables. I went inside the dining area and snagged some granola and milk, and sat outside just as my father came loping down the path. His face was a little flushed, and he carried a mesh bag bulging with the juggling balls.

"Layla, hi, I was looking for you," my father slid next to me on the bench.

I started to tell him I had been watching him, then changed my mind. "I overslept," I said.

A Burl Ives lookalike loomed over us with a coffee pot. He held out his hand. It was big and meaty, with a strong grip. "Moe," he said. "Caf or De?"

"Layla," I said. "Caffeinated, please."

"The same," my father said, "Thanks."

Moe poured, then sat opposite us. "You look familiar," he said to my father. "Ride a Harley?"

"No, never," my father said. He took a teaspoon of sugar, stirred his coffee.

"Don't know what you're missing. So where are you from?" Moe's hair and beard were a faded red; the beard came midway down his chest.

"New York originally," my father said smoothly, accepting the granola I passed him. "Yourself?"

"Boulder," the man said. "Ever been there?"

"Afraid not."

"I'm sure I've met you," the man persisted. I saw my father's hand clench on his coffee mug.

"I have that kind of face," he said. His tone had gotten clipped.

"So you've never been to Boulder?" the man persisted.

"I've heard it's a nice city," I interrupted, but Moe ignored me.

"Maybe a conference once," my father said, finally.

"That's it," Moe brightened. "New Age healing and meditation?"

"Wow," my father said. "What an amazing coincidence." He sounded for real, but I wondered. Would a politico like him be caught dead in the New Age world?

"One of the best I've been to," the man said. "Did you go to the seminar on holistic medicine? I've put a lot of it into practice, I can tell you."

A thin, worried-looking woman looked up from the book she had been buried in. "Do you think holistic medicine really works?"

"Absolutely," Moe answered.

"What have you tried?" she asked. As Moe sidled over to her, I could feel my father's relief.

We cleared the tables, then carried one of the large rubber tubs full of dirty dishes to the wash area. The sun was already strong, the air saturated with something aromatic.

"That man made you nervous, didn't he?" I said.

"Anyone who says I look familiar, or who asks me too many personal questions, makes me want to shit my pants," my father said.

I laughed at his choice of words. "But by now...."

"Even now," he said.

"Was that the truth, about the Boulder conference?"

"Yes. I tell the truth as much as possible. Otherwise I get tripped up in the lies."

"New Age healing?"

My father laughed. "Your mother and I thought big hotels with conferences would be the safest places to meet, and we went to ones where it would be unlikely we'd run into anyone who knew us. Probably the funniest was the one for Mary Kay cosmetics.

But some were actually useful – car mechanics, for instance. All it took was to be on the run with a piece-of-crap car I couldn't fix to convince me I'd better be as self-sufficient as possible."

We wiped dry the dishes in silence, stacked them, and replaced the tubs. There wasn't a sound except for the splashing of sudsy water and clink of dishes as we worked. I noticed my father's hands were short and square, like mine. Suddenly I wanted to make amends. "I'm sorry about last night," I finally said. "I'm sorry if I seemed, I don't know."

"Feel like a walk?" my father said.

"Sure," I said. We headed past the hot tubs, circled the airfield, and headed for a cluster of rocks that gave, at this precise hour, a few feet of shade. We settled ourselves in a hollow and looked out over the desert, the flat expanse that led to mountains so large it was hard to believe they were miles away.

"People always talk about feeling dwarfed by immense spaces," my father said. "Immensity like this always makes me feel part of the vastness, somehow." He lifted his arm as if to make some sort of grand gesture, but merely reached for a stick and began poking at the sand with it. Christine had said how still he used to sit, how contemplative he was, but most of the time in my presence he was in motion. Was it me? Or was it that what had happened had changed him?

"If I believed in a religion, it would be Native American teachings," he said. "I did a wilderness course not long after I went underground. Like the car mechanics – I figured I needed all the skills I could get. I had a panic attack on the top of a mountain. Not even that high a mountain, either. I froze – I absolutely couldn't go backward and I couldn't go forward. I was sure I was going to die." His voice was light, self-mocking, inviting me to chuckle with him. "I think it was a metaphor – I had finally gotten it that I couldn't go back to the life I wanted. So I was going to have to find a way to go forward, to find a life for myself."

He was telling me the story to seem sympathetic, I decided, to show how he overcame his fear, how brave he was. "You really want to be a hero, don't you?" I said. He stopped poking at the ground and straightened, startled. "That's what's driven you from the beginning, isn't it?"

He let out a breath and shook his head. "That's not what I'm trying to say at all, Layla," he said. "Your mother was the fearless one. I just wanted to survive, survive and have a life worth living. Does that seem wrong? Selfish?"

"Not selfish, exactly," I said, confused.

"What then?"

"I don't know," I said.

My father's sigh seemed to drift off into the mountains. He licked his forefinger with his tongue and wiped the dust off his leather sandal, not looking at me. I didn't know what we were arguing about, and suddenly I didn't want to argue, anyhow.

"I saw you this morning, entertaining the kids. You were good. Where did you learn to juggle?"

"It's what I was saying before: Survival."

"Juggling?"

"When I first ran away, before I had new I.D., I was in Golden Gate Park when I saw a bunch of cops. I freaked. There was a troupe performing – you know, a juggler, clown, mime. I got behind the juggler and began to dance. The poor juggler had no idea why the kids were suddenly laughing. But the cops barely glanced at us. Juggling is a good diversionary tactic – I can start doing it on the spot if I think I'm in danger. Plus it calms me down."

"You get anxious a lot?"

"Let's just say I have to struggle with it." He paused. I thought of Moe and his questions, and felt a shiver, like a trickle of ice, down my back.

"The fact of being in hiding – well, in thinking about how to transform myself, I got into magic and magicians, sleight of hand, tricks. How what you think you see may not be what you see. How to manipulate reality."

My breath caught. I had been taking everything he had told me at face value. Trusting him. But what if manipulating was what he was doing with me, too?

I slid a little away. "Don't you find that unethical?"

"Unethical?" My father frowned in confusion.

"You're living a life of lies. Doesn't it all go against everything you say you believe in?" I had always felt uneasy with magic shows. I did not like the coins behind ears, coffins chopped in two, birds that appear only to disappear.

"I was only talking about in terms of staying hidden, Layla. Safe." He said it with alarm, an edge to his voice, as if he was only just getting it that I wouldn't necessarily understand and approve.

"How can you know it doesn't taint everything?"

"You mean in terms of other people, don't you? You mean in terms of how I relate, say, to you?" The creases around his eyes seemed to deepen.

I hesitated. As if my silence accused him, my father slouched over, ran his hands over his face and then dangled them between his legs. His legs were firm with long taut muscles, but his knees were knobby, like two bony hills with flat plateaus. Those silly knees tugged at my sympathy.

"I was deceived," I said. "I was deprived of even knowing I had a father."

"I know it was a horrible tradeoff in terms of you, Layla," he said, talking to the ground, fingering a medallion on a chain that had swung loose from his T-shirt. "But please believe me that I know the difference. I can trust myself to be authentic and honest where it counts. With your mother. With you." He looked up finally. "I don't feel that same loyalty to the United States government."

"But it has to exact a price," I said. "That kind of deviousness."

"Of course it does." He gave a deep breath, closed his eyes briefly. "My shrink calls it splitting. You become, in a sense, two selves, and the selves are not integrated. The me and the not-me. The authentic and the inauthentic."

"You go to a shrink?" I was shocked, as if I didn't really believe how desperate he must often feel.

"From time to time."

"Isn't it too risky?"

"I found someone who was an activist, who I could trust. He explained that, because I am trying not to get caught, I become obsessed with hiding. I obsess on good places to hide, how to blend in, how not to be noticed. So I become more observant. I watch people, I try and see who stands out and who doesn't, and why. What makes people get noticed. What excites curiosity about another person, what does not excite curiosity. I try to mold my behavior to those things that will make me one of those bland, boring, unnoticed people. I learn how to distract if attention is focused on me. I learn how to juggle in all sorts of ways, how to cry 'Fire!,' how to, if it becomes necessary, escape."

He was talking faster and faster, rushing to get the words out, his voice dropping to a whisper.

"Who is hurt by this?" he was saying. "Mostly me. I don't get to be my real self. I don't get to just open my mouth and say the first thing that comes out. So my real self becomes my truest enemy. Yet to lose that real self would be the cruelest loss of all, the real death. So how do I keep that self alive? I split it off. I allow it times and places where it can live. Times, for instance, when I would see your mother. In letters to a few friends. I allow parts out with people I feel I can trust – but only parts. Not the whole. Just enough of the real me so I experience some authenticity." His voice petered out, but it seemed to reverberate in my ears. Something in that voice tugged at me. Something I wanted to hold at bay.

He stared down at the sand, not looking at me. The rock we were sitting on bit into my flesh, but I didn't move, afraid to break the moment.

"I've always been shy, Layla. Politics brought me out of myself. But being in hiding, well, it's done the opposite, forced me back inside." He looked up and smiled then, but the smile was so pained it conveyed the opposite of what he intended. "That's another reason I like the juggling – I like being with children."

All but your own, I started to say. The others won't judge you. But this time I kept my unkind thoughts to myself.

○

It took us a day and a half to hike out of the desert, a day and a half of unmercifully hot weather that seemed to suck every drop of moisture from my body. My skin felt leathery, my lips cracked, my hair limp with sweat and dust. As we walked Nina usually led the way, my father took the rear, and I was in between. But once or twice I went first, to see if I could follow the trail, read the signs, keep the pace. I was proud of myself for holding up so well, proud of my bulging calf muscles, my new skills.

Because of the heat that first day we were forced to take a longer siesta and then walk later into the evening. We made a fire and sat talking, firelight highlighting the silver in my father's hair.

"I've been meaning to tell you, Nina," my father said. "Every year on the anniversary of the march we organized, I raise a glass and make you a toast."

"Wow, I'm touched," Nina said.

"It was a march against women being raped, a 'Take Back the Night,'" my father said to me, leaning back on his elbows. "God, that was great."

Nina chuckled. "Your dad and all the lezzies. He was cute, and your mother's boyfriend, so we tolerated him. But we thought he was a bit weird."

"Come on," my father frowned. "Didn't you think I was really cool? One of the rare, truly liberated, amazingly hip –"

Nina threw her head back, laughing. I thought of the gay women at Barnard, how they draped their arms around each other.

As I looked at my father's earnest face and tried to imagine him in their midst, a little spurt of laughter escaped.

"Oh no, you too?" he said. "Common, Nina, you're supposed to build me up in front of Layla. You're blowing it."

"Everyone liked him," she said lamely, and we all laughed again. For a moment, a warm feeling spread through me; the warmth of the fire, the laughter. Then I thought again of where all that activism had led, and the warmth was gone. My father promised to tell me his full story once we were alone. Strangely, the longer I spent with him the less eager I was to hear.

"I remember how windy it was that night, how the candles kept blowing out," he was saying.

"I remember being worried the paper bags would catch on fire." Nina turned to me. "You made cutouts in paper bags and carried the candles inside. It looked so pretty."

"It sounds like fun," I said.

"You look skeptical," my father said.

I thought of my mother's tired eyes, exasperated brow. Duty was what came to mind when I thought about politics. Responsibility.

"There was this coffee house in my neighborhood in Queens," my father said. "It was actually just a cruddy building squeezed between some abandoned stores that an old beatnik rented and fixed up, in imitation of the ones in the Village – it had the dayglow colors, the black ceiling, the whole bit. The regulars would come over every night and hang out. It was painted purple." He turned to Nina. "Remember that hippie purple? And black lights – the kind that made white extra bright? Talk about fun – getting stoned, talking politics, listening to music."

"The dancing parties!" Nina added.

They were like my grandfather, reminiscing with his World War II buddies at my mother's funeral. I yawned, exhaustion hitting me in waves. "I think I'm gonna turn in," I said.

"Save me some room in the tent," Nina said.

"Feel free to shove me over if you need to," I said.

I drifted to sleep to the murmur of their voices. Would I be sitting some day under a night sky with friends, talking about our college days? Which scenes would stay with me my whole life? Maybe even this night – the firelight on Nina's freckles, on my father's hair – would be one.

I woke up, sweating in the sleeping bag, to the sound of my father's voice. "If it hadn't been for friends like you, who we could count on –" his voice broke. "Just in case I haven't said it enough, thank you."

"Please, you know there's no need," Nina's voice was a whisper.

I began to fall back under the spell of the sound of the wind. It buffeted the nylon tent so that I felt I was rocking. But hearing my name stirred me awake.

"How do you think Layla is handling all this?"

"It's hard to tell," Nina said. "She's not one for talking about her feelings."

"So it's not just me?"

"It must be very difficult for her," Nina said. "But if you're asking me in my professional opinion is she O.K., I'd say yes. At some point she may want to see a therapist. But she strikes me as a very grounded, tough girl. Brave too, to be undertaking all this on her own. I've grown very fond of her."

"Me, too," my father said. "I cautioned myself not to expect too much. Instead I feel so much for her I almost can't contain it."

I felt my eyes water and pressed my face into the bundle of clothes that served as a makeshift pillow. My face was so hot that I flipped over the little bundle to get the coolness from the ground against my skin. But my tears dribbled out, and I had to flip my pillow over yet again.

O

We emerged from the desert the afternoon of the next day, like dinosaurs come back from extinction. Even though I had been in the wild only a week, the houses seemed strange, the light different, the air clouded.

"Layla looks stunned," Nina said to my father. "Having a little reentry problem, sweetie?"

"This must be a stage set!" I said, playing along. I pulled out my camera, took a last shot of the desert. "This must be Hollywood!"

"She's delirious," my father said. "Nothing a cold beer and a hot shower can't cure."

I groaned. I could feel the soapy lather, taste the burn of the beer.

Nina grinned at my father. "This is the most acute case I've seen." He smiled back, and in that moment, I snapped their picture.

My father's face dropped. "Oh Layla, I'm sorry, but you shouldn't have done that."

It took me a moment to realize what he meant. I thought of all the other pictures I'd taken unbeknownst to him over the last several days. I'd gotten shots of him juggling, sitting in the midst of a group of children, kneeling down to rub noses with a black Lab. I hesitated, but said nothing. I had been secretive not because I bought into his paranoia but because I wanted to capture him unselfconscious, private.

"Please – will you delete it?"

"Sorry," I said, "sure." I fiddled with the dials, pressed a button. "Gone."

I saw him wrestling with himself. Clearly he wanted to ask for the camera, to double check. If he did, he might see there were dozens in there already. I waited, ready to put up a fight, but he let it go.

"No more single-file," Nina said, grabbing our hands as we started up the block, swinging them back and forth. Messages were now coming in full-strength from my body to my brain, messages about thirst, a blister, my itchy scalp.

My father's hand jerked in mine. "What's going on?"

I followed his gaze. A huge crowd was outside near the safe house. Several men stumbled out of the house next door, carrying a sofa.

"Oh my God," Nina said. She started forward, then stopped. "It must be the neighbors – they were falling behind on the mortgage. I heard the bank was going to try and evict them. It's become a big issue around here; this is a working class Chicano neighborhood."

I wiped a trickle of sweat that was making its way from my forehead to my eyes, removed my cap and fanned my face.

"I can't be anywhere near the police," my father said.

"There's a back door," Nina said. "It leads into the kitchen. I think I left the backyard fence open." She passed him the key.

"OK," my father said. He sounded nervous.

We drew closer. A middle-aged woman and man, arms around several children, stood watching as possessions were removed from their house. Piled up on the scruffy lawn were several upholstered chairs and a dining table. The crowd was kept at a distance by a cop who stood with his arms crossed, facing them. People were yelling things at him in Spanish, but his face didn't change expression. Men brought out an avocado plant, a table lamp, a TV. When a toy chest was next, a skinny balding man gave a shout, raised a fist, and rushed forward, picked up a chair, and headed with it back into the house. A woman grabbed a lamp and followed. My father's hand tightened on mine.

The cop moved to block people from carrying more into the house. There was a crash. Suddenly the crowd surged, and we were squeezed forward by the vise of bodies. I heard shouts, the sounds of a scuffle, but couldn't see what was happening. Then there was the sound of brakes screeching and a truck pulled up, emblazoned with TV call numbers. A man jumped out, camera perched on his shoulder like an enormous black raven.

"I've got to get inside," my father hissed.

Nina began to wedge a path sideways through the crowd. My father ducked low, moving in a kind of half-crouch, as sirens began to wail.

It seemed only seconds before a police car pulled up and cops sprang out. They shouted through bullhorns, first in English, then in Spanish. "If you don't disband right now, you will be arrested. Please go home. You will be arrested."

We reached the back door of the safe house. I stood behind my father, as if I could block him from view. I looked back over my shoulder. None of the cops so much as glanced in our direction.

"I can't believe they can just throw people out like that," I said, once we were inside. "What will happen to them?"

"Probably end up in a homeless shelter," Nina said. "Hopefully some legal aid group will get everyone out of jail."

She and I watched the cops handcuff people and lead them off in police cars, the cameraman wandering among them like a clumsy, extraterrestrial bug. My father sat across the room, as far from the windows as possible.

○

In the morning we packed and tidied the safe house. I watched my father wipe every surface he had touched, and felt queasy. Nina was going home to San Diego; my father and I were headed to San Francisco.

"Thank you for everything," I hugged Nina.

"Come visit, O.K.? Here's my address. We'll do some more hiking." Then she drew from her bag an envelope I realized was from my mother and handed it to me. I had forgotten all about it.

"Come to New York," I said. "Don't underestimate the thrills of the urban desert."

My father and Nina hugged, too. "Until the next time," she said. "Whenever and wherever that may be. Stay safe."

I realized they didn't know if they'd ever see each other again. I realized in a matter of days the same would be true for my father and me.

It was a damp day, with a light gray rain falling, a rain that felt wonderful after all the sun and heat. I drove and my father navigated. He asked if it were O.K. for us to have our big talk once we were in San Francisco, so we could just relax and enjoy the drive. I was surprised at how eagerly I agreed. I didn't want to disturb the ease I was beginning to feel with him. So we played CDs. He liked Juliet Wyers, who I had heard at the PostCrypt, but wasn't crazy about; he was surprised I liked the Wreckers. "More country than I figured you for," he said.

"How do you know this music, anyhow?" I said.

"I worked with some at-risk youth a few years ago," he said. "I volunteered at a center." He hesitated, gave me a sidelong glance. "I wanted to have a sense of what you'd be like."

"You think I'm at risk?"

"Jeez, Layla, you are touchy," my father laughed. "Of course not. It was just a way to be around young people. I've done that since you were born."

"I don't understand."

"Well, when you were real little I helped out at a community day-care center. When you were older I tutored in an after-school program. This past year I helped kids at a community center set up a blog. I guess I was compensating for not having you. It gave me the feeling that I was connected. Silly, I know," he said, shrugging.

"No, no, it's not," was all I could manage. I thought again of his watching me from the schoolyard, the intensity of his gaze. I passed a jeep without signaling, and was blasted by a loud honk.

My father lifted my CD carrier onto his lap, opened the top, riffled through. "You have a lot of CDs for the iPod era. This is a surprise – I wouldn't have figured you for Tracy Chapman."

"That was my mom's – but I like her a lot. For a folkie."

"I love one of them – can't remember the title. Has something about 'free, free, free,' in the chorus."

"Oh, that's 'Freedom Now,' I said, "off her first album."

"Sing it for me," he said.

"I don't sing," I said.

"Of course you sing, everybody sings."

"Not me." I set my jaw.

"Layla, you're impossible, you know that?"

"Yeah," I said, "I've been told."

"Besides, I've heard you."

"You can't have, because I don't sing."

"You were singing in the desert that day. That's how I found you. You have a perfectly fine voice."

I shook my head no, stared straight ahead, focusing on the road.

"Why don't you sing?" he asked, after a moment.

"I just don't."

He paused. "It's O.K. You don't have to tell me why."

I hesitated. It seemed like such a minor thing, yet I'd never mentioned it to anyone. "I tried out for the school choir when I was a kid, and it was really awful. I guess I've just been embarrassed ever since, that's all."

"Let's sing," he said.

"I just told you –"

"Why you don't sing in public. Fine. I'm talking about in the car, just you and me. Come on."

"Look, I'm sorry, I just can't."

"O.K.," he said, and looked out the window. Perversely I suddenly wanted to give in. But I couldn't.

"What do you say we stop for lunch?" my father said.

A few exits later we found a small restaurant. We sat outdoors on metal chairs under a striped umbrella and ordered, the only customers in the place.

"I wanted to be in a rock band in the worst way when I was a kid," my father said, musing. "I forgot all about that."

"Is that what you would have wanted," I asked him, "you know, if all this hadn't happened?"

"Oh no, that was just a phase. I think I would have tried teaching, or some sort of organizing. But strangely enough, I've learned I really like working with my hands. I've worked repairing fences on ranches, and in auto-repair shops. I might not have discovered that."

"I like working with my hands, too," I said.

"That's right, photography," he nodded.

"Yeah, I like the physicality of handling the camera, the feel of it, the little dials. It's so – "

"Tactile?"

"Yes, so –"

"Concrete?"

We both laughed. "I find, when I'm immersed in a physical task, everything recedes," he said. "Thoughts, problems. It's like – "

"Meditation," I finished for him this time, and we laughed again. In my mind I was in the dark room, standing in front of the tanks of solution, snug in that tiny space. I liked turning paper and chemicals into images, of being, I suddenly realized, like my father, a kind of magician.

I thought of the photos I had surreptitiously taken of him. What truths would emerge when I uploaded them to my computer? My father met my gaze but said nothing, just let me study him – curly hair, green eyes, tiny worry lines, the mustache and beard that nearly obscured his mouth. Who would I see?

"I'm so pleased you're into photography. You know that little art box you had when you were little, and the Canon you got for your twelfth birthday? I sent you those. Your mother said you had artistic talent, and so I thought they would be good presents."

"You're kidding," I stammered. I didn't know what amazed me more: that the gifts came from him, that they were so thoughtful, or that my mother had thought I had talent. "I don't know what to say."

"You don't need to say anything," he said. "Your mother told me how much you loved them, and that's all that mattered to me."

"It means a lot." I said. "That it was you." I felt almost paralyzed with shyness. "I didn't know she thought I could be an artist. She never said anything." I had thought she gave me art materials simply to keep me out of her hair.

"She was afraid to encourage you."

"Why?"

"She said you could sometimes be a bit contrary. If she encouraged you, you were likely to do the very opposite."

I winced. "I guess that's true."

The seconds ticked by. My father ran his fingers up and down the chain he wore, as if he liked the feel of it against his skin.

"What is that medallion?" I asked.

He pulled the chain from his T-shirt, leaned forward, and held it out to me.

It had a medical symbol on one side. I turned it over. It said, "In case of emergency, call Dr. Audrey James," and our home phone number.

"It was a safeguard," he said. "She wanted to be notified in case anything ever happened. Seeing the word doctor, someone would assume she was my personal physician and call her." He looked down, as if embarrassed. "It's like my prayer beads." He gave a little laugh. "I used to pretend if I rubbed it she'd appear." It was too intimate, what he was saying; his vulnerability was too raw. I couldn't think of how to respond.

I watched him put sugar in his coffee cup, measure out a precise half-teaspoon. How constrained his life must be. How isolated he must feel, how interior his world. It seemed suddenly unendurable.

"What will you do now?" I found myself whispering. "Can you be – are you able to be – happy in this life of yours?"

His face seemed to drain of color. "You ask tough questions, Layla. The answer is, I don't know. Your mother was my lifeline, my center."

He said it so matter-of-factly, so without self-pity, that it seemed eons for his words to penetrate.

It was as if she really was his doctor, I thought. Crucial to his well-being. I wondered, suddenly, what the cost of all this had been to her.

We sat there, silent, across from each other, and I realized that we were united by the loss of my mother. Odd that it hadn't occurred to me before. I became aware of the precise distance between us, and looked down at his hands, caressing the mug that held his coffee. I drew my knees to my chin. He turned to look at me.

"Your mother used to sit just like that," he said. "Sometimes you remind me of her so much. Most times I'm glad that you don't."

I took a deep breath, looked away. My chest felt pinched, as if he had grabbed it and bunched it up in his fist.

"What do you think was the essence of the conflict between you?" he asked. "Your mother felt she failed you somehow, that she was never really able to figure out what you needed from her."

"She thought she failed me?" I said. I was shocked. "You're mixed up. I failed her. I was nothing but a disappointment to her."

"That's not true Layla, no. No you weren't. She just...."

"She just what? She wanted me to be like her, but I couldn't. She had such a complete world. There wasn't any room in there for me."

"She just wanted to share it with you. For you to be part of it."

"You don't get it," I said. "It wasn't about sharing. She wanted me to be like her, and I couldn't. She was a movement star, even to my friends. I just couldn't compete."

He shook his head. "Layla there was no need to compete. Your mother only wanted you to share with her who you are."

"Only if who I was happened to be who she wanted me to be!"

"I'm not sure you know who you are, Layla. I mean know yourself other than in opposition to your mother. She was a very strong personality. I can appreciate it would be hard to find your own way." He sighed, put down his coffee cup. "She's gone now. You don't want to live your life fighting against a person who no longer exists. You have to find some freedom, Layla."

He said it so gently, so caringly, I felt my eyes well up. A breeze blew my hair into my face and I busied myself twisting the short strands and fastening them with a clip. As if his words brought it into being, I felt as if I couldn't breathe, as if I was trapped in an invisible cage. How had he known this? How had he known what I hadn't? He seemed to read me in a way that was both terrifying and seductive.

Then a feeling of fear washed over me: How had I allowed this man I barely knew to become such a force in my life?

Chapter 9

We stopped that night near L.A. at a Best Western with two available rooms and a free, all-you-could-eat breakfast buffet.

I tossed my backpack and duffle on the bed and crossed to the window. My room overlooked the motel's parking lot and the back of a convenience store, where cartons were stacked in a high mound. I felt the energy leak out of me, as if the week in the desert – the stark lines and gentle slopes and clean light – had made me oversensitive, unable to bear such mundane ugliness.

My father and I were to meet for dinner in an hour, and I didn't know what to do with myself. I sat on the edge of the bed, leaning against my bags, and acknowledged to myself that I was depressed.

Depression is something I rarely own up to. I get grouchy, I get restless, I get bored, I get angry. But I don't get depressed. I had called Trent, bursting with the desire to hear his voice. Now I feared he was upset with me.

"Hey, girl, how are you?" he had said in his soft voice.

"Sore, sunburned," I said.

"Sore? Why? Where are you, anyway?"

"I was in the desert," I said. I started to explain, then stopped myself.

"The desert? Is that part of the quest?"

"No – I mean, it was just a hike." I faltered. "I'll tell you another time."

"Sure, fine," he said. His voice was flat. I knew he knew I was lying.

I made small talk, tried to get us back on track, but the conversation was forced, and finally we both said we had to go. I had a sick feeling in the pit of my stomach. I hated this; I hated being evasive in this way with someone I cared about.

I upended my duffle onto the bed, searching for clean clothes. Out tumbled the manila envelope with my mothers' letters. Had this been how she felt, lying to me? On the bed was her black leather jacket. I ran my hand over the soft, supple leather and thought of my father's question to me earlier, about the source of my conflict with her. It was so clear now that when I acted out it was a way of punishing her for rejecting me. But maybe she hadn't really been rejecting me. Maybe what seemed like emotional distance was really just what happened when you kept something hidden. Like what was going on now between me and Trent.

I picked up the envelope, started to open it, put it back down. I thought of what my father had said, that my mother felt inadequate. The mother who spoke to me through these letters – insecure, anguished – wasn't the mother I knew. Was my father right? Was it possible I had misunderstood? I had thought I had to measure up to her for her to really love me. Could it be that she loved me just because I was who I was? I tried to superimpose the woman of the letters onto the mother of my experience, to make them mesh in my mind, but the picture wouldn't come together.

I remembered a night early in the fall semester, when my mother was out of town, and I invited my new friends over for the first time. We were listening to music, hanging out, smoking dope, and I got the brilliant idea to make a cake, three layers.

The cake part was milk chocolate, the frosting, dark and sweet, and the filling a cocoa mousse like the inside of a 3 Musketeers bar. We traded bowls, flung whisks and beaters, stuck fingers into frosting. Then we had to wait, aroma filling the kitchen, everyone in paroxysms of desire. Finally the cake was done.

"The recipe says to let it cool before layering the filling," Jenny read.

"No, no, a thousand times no!" Robert, the group comedian, reached for the bowl of mousse.

Jenny and I snatched it first and slathered the mouse on the first half of cake, then sandwiched it with the other. Everyone took turns wetting the knife with cold water and smearing the frosting.

Clark, ever the leader, commanded us to sit. When we were all settled at the table he lifted the cake aloft with one hand, waiter-style. He approached the table, then suddenly stopped short. "Oh god, it's melting," he said; the cake was starting to slide.

"You're dropping it!" Rebecca shouted. Clark straightened, and the cake listed the other way. We could only watch, helpless, choking with laughter. Finally he managed to slip the plate onto the table. Something yellow and thick had pooled all around the cake, and the top layer was askew.

"It's disintegrating," Jenny said in a whisper, and we started laughing again.

That was when we heard the sound of the key in the door.

Everyone froze. I felt the laughter drain from me mid-laugh and I jumped up, as if I could erase the disaster we'd made of the kitchen. Steve grabbed the baggie of marijuana and darted from the room.

My mother walked in. "We were just −" I started to say.

"Hi sweetie," she cut me off. She was smiling. She walked over and kissed the top of my head. "Sorry to come back early − I called, but you didn't pick up. Hi Jenny, hi everyone. It's a pleasure to meet Layla's friends."

Not knowing what else to do, I introduced everyone. Then I watched, dumbfounded, as she pulled up a chair and dug into a piece of cake. She explained that because we hadn't let it cool, the heat caused the butter and other ingredients in the filling to separate. "Fabulous!" she said, licking her fingers.

But the most amazing thing was when my mother said, "I'd love to join you all in a joint, but I guess it isn't appropriate, so

I'll just toddle off to my room. Please don't leave – you'd make me feel awful."

I had never before seen this side of her, and I didn't know what to make of it. It occurred to me now that maybe this was what she had wanted from this trip – by sharing with me what had been secret for so long, I could know her in a way that hadn't been possible before.

I washed my dirty clothes in the sink and hung them around the room to dry, sorted everything else into piles. I opened a crumpled bag and removed the wad of pink tissue paper that held the little tin box I'd found in Burlington. It felt like months, rather than weeks, since I'd bought it. I ran my finger over the tiny holes and bumps of the surface, rough against my skin.

My father knocked. When he came in he saw the box in my hand, and his face drained of color.

"My mother collected boxes," I explained.

"I know, I used to send them to her – they were part of our code. That just gave me a turn – tin was our signal for danger."

I hurriedly wrapped the box back in its tissue paper. "That was how you communicated?"

"Oh, just one of the ways. We sent messages through newspaper personals, and friends forwarded mail to post office boxes. In the last couple of years we figured out a way to leave messages on blogs. Your mother even made up crosswords with clues in them for me." I saw my mother, head bent over her morning crossword, pen clicking in and out. Had nothing been as it seemed?

"I'm famished," my father said. "Let's go."

I grabbed the leather jacket from the pile on the bed.

"Wow. I gave that to your mother for her birthday a few years ago."

I stopped short. "I'll take it off."

"No, please. I love seeing you in it."

"Are you sure?"

"It looks wonderful on you. Besides, I don't really think she felt it was her."

An image of my mother at her closet door, head buried in the jacket as if she was inhaling its odor, shot into my mind. The gesture had disturbed me somehow, and I had hurried from the room so she wouldn't know I had seen.

"She loved it," I said.

My father and I drove through the small town, past nondescript houses, car dealerships, a full range of take-out places.

"I hate towns like these," my father said. "But they're good for disappearing in."

"You stay in places like this?" I asked.

"All too many. I've been all over. As I told you – I get anxious if I start to get comfortable."

"Is that why you went to a shrink?" I asked.

"Yes. In the beginning I got pretty depressed, and your mother would come and pull me out of it. But it wasn't fair to her. So I started to see someone."

"It helped?"

"A lot," he said.

"Good," I said

In the restaurant we ordered an inordinate amount of food and a small pitcher of Margaritas. My father regaled me with funny stories about life on the road. But for all his joking, he seemed a little down, too.

"This is on me," I said, picking up the check.

"No way," he tried to grab it.

"I insist," I said. I whipped out my credit card. He had been paying for everything – gas, lunch, the motel. I couldn't help but notice that he always paid in cash.

We drove back in silence. I was tired and stiff from sitting in the car all day, a little woozy from the alcohol. It suddenly occurred to me that I was due to leave for home soon. I thought of seeing Jenny and my other friends, but I couldn't summon up any anticipation. Maybe it was just fatigue.

"Layla?" my father said, as we pulled up in front of the motel.

"Yes?" I stifled a yawn.

"There's something I need to ask of you."

I toyed with the ignition key. Did he want me to take a message, carry something for him? I realized I knew nothing of his daily existence, all the little subterfuges and intricacies his life might require.

"O.K."

He leaned forward to turn off the radio, then turned to me. He took a deep breath, as if to steel himself. I stiffened. Now? Was he finally going to tell me everything?

"Could you tell me about her dying?"

I choked on my saliva. My throat constricted and I struggled to regain my breath. We were still strapped in our seat belts, and the interior of the car suddenly felt cramped. I watched the light of the motel's neon sign glance off the hood of the car and then retreat, glance and retreat.

"It was very fast," I said, when I could talk. "She didn't tell me that her cancer had come back until just before. She was always like that."

"My situation placed horrible constraints on her," my father said. "She wasn't always such a closed person." It was the first time he had acknowledged any lack of perfection in my mother, and it took me by surprise. "She didn't tell me she was back in the hospital soon enough for me to come," he said. "If I had known I would never see her again, I would have risked it."

I let that sink in, the idea that he thought visiting his dying wife would have risked his arrest. I remembered my mother whispering as she told me about the envelope in the drawer at her bedside. I was suddenly sweating, as if the car heater were on. "She said the room was bugged. I thought she was delusional – you know, from all the drugs."

"She would have assumed that the FBI had her room under surveillance, hoping I'd show up. She knew there was nothing would keep me away if I knew she was dying. She was protecting me to the end."

"She was very brave," I said. A feeling of exhaustion, like a great cloud of sleep, overwhelmed me, and I closed my eyes.

"I didn't get a chance to say good-bye," he said.

My chest squeezed tight with pain. In my mind I saw again the ochre stain on the wall across from her hospital bed, the stain I had stared at as I sat by her side as she slept, a stain I knew would never leave me. I saw the window, the spring breeze fluttering the blinds in a gesture of hope and escape, the lying flowers that had promised her a future. And I saw again the nightgown I had given her billowing out over her thin and wasted body.

"She just evaporated before my eyes," I said. "I had the chance to say good-bye, but I didn't."

My father's arm encircled my shoulders. I turned my face into his chest and began to cry. He said nothing, just held me tighter. His arm felt heavy and strange, but I wanted him to gather me to him and rock me like a baby.

I pulled away. "Sorry."

My father said nothing. His face was in darkness. Then the neon light flashed, revealing the wetness on his lashes, highlighting the streaks on his cheeks.

O

In the morning after my shower I stood naked in front of the bathroom mirror. My breasts were ordinary, but I liked them anyhow. They were round and solid but not so big they needed to be supported. I didn't want to lose them.

I lifted my right arm, put the middle fingers of my left hand into my right armpit. Slowly I circled my breast, kneading with my fingers, prodding and groping the soft mass of tissue, searching for what I didn't want to find. It was hard to slow myself down, not to rush to get it over with.

I felt nothing. I repeated the procedure with my left breast. I did this even though I was sure the disease would creep up on me anyhow, catch me off-guard.

"A family history means only that you're at higher risk than the general population," the gynecologist had told me. "It doesn't mean you're guaranteed to get it. New protocols and drugs are being developed all the time. Even if you do get it, it doesn't mean you will lose a breast."

Or a life? After her mastectomy my mother asked me if I wanted to see her chest. She said it didn't look so bad, that the scars weren't nearly as awful as I was probably imagining. But I couldn't overcome my horror, or my discomfort with the intimacy of seeing her naked.

"Well if you ever want to, just ask," she said. "If you get curious, or if you find it's troubling you, O.K.? Just let me know."

I pulled my T-shirt on and left the bathroom. I had been sure that the time would never come when I would want to see my mother's naked body – not whole, not mutilated. And then she was in the hospital, dying, and her body was like that of a 10-year-old's. Then she was covered by a white sheet, a sheet hiding a body I would never see again.

I took out all my mother's letters from the manila envelope and reread them in chronological order. When I was done I closed my eyes and listened to the sound of the air conditioner, letting myself absorb her words. My mother's letters now seemed the letters of someone trying to tell me something rather than those of someone trying to keep something from me.

After a while, when I was ready, I opened the new envelope, the one Nina had given me, marked "after the desert." Inside was another sealed envelope, marked, "For him," and a folded single sheet of paper.

Dear Layla,

I can't keep this thread going any longer. Much as I want to stay with you, I feel myself drifting. It is not unpleasant. They've given me more and more morphine and I'm grateful to hold the pain at bay. It takes the edge off everything, even leaving my life, leaving you.

He's a wonderful man, Layla, I hope you know this. I wish we could have been a family. How I looked forward to this trip, to us all being together, if only for a little while. I can't help but feel losing that chance is a kind of punishment I deserve for having kept so much from you for so long.

Do you understand what I mean now, Layla, by saying I wasn't perfect, that I made mistakes, that I was, perhaps, very selfish?

And courage. I thought, going together on this journey, we would have the space and time for me to tell you everything. When I got sick again, I waited, hoping I would beat the cancer. Then I knew it was too late, and I was back in the hospital, I couldn't talk freely. I was sure that they were waiting for him to show up, to snap the handcuffs on him. To protect him, I denied you yet again.

So I found this cowardly way to spare myself and to ease you into the truth. I planned it carefully. I wanted you to learn everything gradually, so it would be less of a shock, perhaps, easier to accept. That way at each juncture you would have the choice to go forward or not. My letters have been evasive and cryptic so that at no time could you jeopardize him inadvertently, before you fully understood.

You have reached that point, or else you would not be holding this letter. Now I can rest, knowing I put you into each other's hands.

I am with you always,

Love, Mom

I folded the letter and held it to my chest. This letter, then, was the last. I would have thought I'd have been glad to be free of all of it, but instead I felt bereft and lonely, like a small kite released too quickly into the sky. I wanted to cry again, but I felt empty, hollow-eyed and worn and old. Why had she had to die? Why had it had to be this way?

I went to my father's room. He answered the door with a towel around his neck. His hair was in damp waves from the shower, his lashes clumped together.

"How are you?" he asked.

Still fresh in my mind was the feel of his worn denim shirt the night before as I cried, my face pressed into the crook of his armpit. "O.K.," I said. I felt awkward. I watched him rub his torso dry, pull on a T-shirt. It struck me for the first time that he was an attractive man. I moved away.

I handed him the envelope.

"What's this?" he asked me.

"The envelope Nina gave me yesterday had this enclosed for you."

I had been eager to give it to him, but the raw longing on his face was somehow painful to see.

"Look," I said. "Why don't you come get me when you're ready."

"No, that's O.K.," he was saying, but I was already out the door.

He knocked on mine a few minutes later. He looked a little shaken.

"Are you O.K.?" I asked.

"It's a beautiful letter – I'll show it to you, if you like." I saw him glance at my pile of letters on the bed, and I began stuffing them hastily into my duffle.

"You can read all of hers to me, too, if you like." I said. "Do you want your notebook back? And your letters to her?"

"It's not a good idea to keep all this," he said. "Didn't she tell you to get rid of everything?"

"I just wanted to keep them a little longer. Believe me, they don't give anything away."

"I'm sure they are carefully written, but even so –"

"She never mentions your name, or what you did, or explains any of it," I said. I glanced at him.

"And I haven't either, I know," he said.

Over our all-you-can-eat breakfast I told him about my mother's death, her funeral. "My grandparents kept it private. They said that's how she wanted it."

"She was just playing it safe, I'm sure," he said.

"Why? Why would the authorities think there was still a connection between you?"

"They showed up after she gave birth to you, 12 years after I went underground, even though we obviously didn't list me on the birth certificate as your father. Believe me, they never give up."

My name, I realized. This was why I didn't carry my father's name.

"She said in her letter that she asked to be cremated. What did you do with her ashes?" my father asked.

"Actually I haven't done anything with them yet."

My father looked down at his fork, which he rotated between his thumb and forefinger. "You didn't happen to bring them, did you?"

I shook my head no.

"I was just thinking that maybe that was something we could do together." He put the fork down. "But it doesn't have to be her ashes. We could bury the letters maybe, have a sort of ceremony."

"Let me think about it, O.K.?" The idea made me queasy.

"Of course," he said. "I understand."

"I'm sorry."

We loaded the car and set off for San Francisco. It was an overcast cool day, a day for driving, a day for silences. We didn't talk much and we didn't put on any more CDs. As we got closer to San Francisco I could feel myself tensing up. I knew Philip would have dismissed my behavior toward him as nothing more than a reaction to my mother's death, but I couldn't let myself off that easily. And I was increasingly upset by the awareness that my father and I must soon come to some sort of parting. I was so jumpy I couldn't stay in one lane of traffic for a minute before I was signaling to change lanes again.

At the outskirts of San Francisco my father pulled out a map and a AAA motel guide. "Are you sure you don't want to come with me to Philip's?" I said, wishing he would.

"I'm sure." He unfolded the map.

"I know just the place for you," I said. I pulled over to the side of the road, took the map from him and figured out the directions to the Ho-Hum motel.

When we reached the motel, I parked on the other side of the hedges that blocked the pool from the road.

"This is where I learned that you were alive," I said. "This is where I learned that you were waiting for me, but it was too late."

"It's funny what gets attached to important moments," my father said. "That day as I waited, hoping you would show up, I was really thirsty. I had one raspberry popsicle after another. Now I'll always associate that flavor with disappointment."

"I'm sorry," I said.

"I'm just glad you came this time," he said.

"Me too."

"Well, better get a move on." We slid out of the car and went to see about availability. The only room was a suite, with a sliding door opening onto the pool.

"What about tomorrow?" I said.

"Let's meet at Buena Vista Park around eleven? That'll give me a chance to take care of a few things."

"Don't you want me to come pick you up?"

"No, public transportation is much easier."

"O.K.," I said.

"O.K.," he said. Then, awkwardly, we embraced, a quick, tentative, hug.

"See you tomorrow, then," I said.

"See ya," he said, and tousled my hair. Just like a father.

O

I drove slowly, trembly with tension. The afternoon was soft and misty and the edges of everything seemed blurred; I kept blinking to focus my eyes. The houses and stores and cars seemed flat, two-dimensional, a phony stage set. At some point, I realized I must have taken a wrong turn, for I was heading back south. I pulled into a gas station and got directions. I thought about phoning Philip but just got back in the car.

As I rang his bell I thought of the last time I had arrived on his doorstep, when he had taken one look at me and known I needed caretaking. What would he see in me now? The door flung open; Philip fairly jumped out at me. His expression was so agitated, almost hostile, that I took a step back.

"Philip?"

He made a motion as if to shoo me away.

"Should I come back later?" Did he have someone there, a woman, somebody half-dressed on the couch?

"Is that the young lady now?" a male voice called out.

Philip gritted his teeth and pounded a fist on his thigh, but his voice when he spoke was calm, almost pleasant. "Yes," he called over his shoulder, "she's here."

A sick feeling came over me then.

Philip threw me another anguished glance and went back into the house. I followed him into the living room where two men in dark suits and ties were standing. They were tall and slim and very polished looking, city men, the kind of men I hadn't seen in all the weeks I was on the road. And then somehow I knew.

"Ms. James," one of the men said, putting out his hand. "I'm Agent Keane and this is Agent Blair. We're from the FBI." He flashed a badge without giving me a chance to look at it. I turned to Philip.

"This is a joke, right?" I said.

"I'm afraid not, Ms. James," the one calling himself Keane said. "Or may we call you Layla?"

"No, you may not," I said, and crossed my arms over my chest.

"Please sit down, then, Ms. James," he said. I put my bags down and walked toward the couch. "What's all this about?" I looked at Philip again. "What have you been up to?" I said it jokingly, but I couldn't help but give him an angry glance, sure that he was somehow to blame. He caught the look and flinched.

"This isn't about Mr. Logan, and I think you know that," Agent Keane said. Agent Blair smirked and said nothing.

"I have no idea what you're talking about," I said.

"We're talking about your father," Agent Blair said.

"My father? What about him?" I said. "He's dead."

"Oh, I beg to differ."

"Huh?" I said.

"Look, you're a pretty cool cucumber, and it's very impressive, this little acting job. But you're not doing your father any favors. We all know he's alive and on the run. We're not here to hurt him. We're here to ask you to take him a message. He turns himself in and we'll work something out. Just tell him that."

"I think you're mixed up," I said. "My father's dead. I never knew my father. I only just learned from some old friends of my mother's how and why he died. It's none of your business, but I'll tell you how I feel anyhow. I despise all that they did and stood for. As far as I'm concerned, politics robbed me of a father. If he were alive, as you're suggesting, and he did what he was supposed to have done, I'd have no problem helping you out. I'd want him to rot in jail."

My voice was shaky; I took a deep breath and stared with all the defiance I could muster at Agent Keane. I thought I caught a look of confusion, or slight doubt, in his eyes.

"Your friend here," he indicated Philip, "professed not to be sure you were showing up. How long will you be staying?"

I turned to Philip. "Yeah, sorry Philip. I know I should have called. I thought I'd stay until Sunday – if that's O.K. with you?"

"Sure," Philip said.

"We'll see you before Sunday, then," Agent Keane said. "Here are my numbers." He handed me his card.

"Drop by any time," I said.

"Smart aleck," Agent Blair said to me under his breath as they walked out.

Philip and I just stared at each other.

"You can't think what I think you're thinking," he whispered. He seemed genuinely upset, but why would the FBI have come to his house if he hadn't given something away?

"I couldn't believe it when they showed up," he said, his voice loud. He placed his finger over his lips like a character in a spy movie. "I guess the FBI has nothing better to do than to concoct crazy stories to keep themselves busy."

"Well, I don't appreciate it, that's for sure," I played along, watching him peer under his coffee table, pull up the sofa cushions. Did he even know what to look for? "Let's just forget about it. I'm hungry. How about dinner? My treat."

"Sure, that would be lovely," Philip said, still with the phony voice.

"I'm gonna take a shower first, O.K.? I'm kind of grimy from the road."

The shakes hit for real as I stripped and stepped under the spray. It was preposterous, implausible, unbelievable that the

FBI was still looking for my father. I had to warn him – but how? Should I take a chance and use my cell phone? What should I do? I couldn't go to see him – what if they had me followed? I couldn't talk it over with Philip. I couldn't take a chance, though the notion that I shouldn't trust him made me physically sick.

What if I simply did not show up to meet my father the next day? Would he understand and leave, figuring something had gone wrong? Would he think that it was my way of saying good-bye? Or would he take a chance and contact Philip? If he did, the FBI would no doubt trace the call. I imagined them storming the motel. I imagined my father's face as he opened the door and saw them standing there.

No, no, no. Somehow I would have to make it to the motel. Yet if they did have us under surveillance, how could I possibly evade them? I couldn't risk Philip's knowing, but how could I pull it off without his help? It was impossible to do anything, impossible to do nothing. I needed time to think, to plan, but there was no time. My thoughts skittered about like a frenzied insect, alighting nowhere.

I toweled off, then rummaged through my bag for clean clothes. My hand touched the manila envelope with my mother's letters, and I froze. The whole time I'd sat talking with the FBI, this evidence had been just a few feet away. As I stood waiting for my heart to stop pounding, into my mind came an image: the little tin box. Tin, their signal for danger.

"I need to stop at one of those Federal Express places," I said to Philip, as we got into his car.

He narrowed his eyes in a question, but all he said was "O.K."

When we reached the FedEx office, another car pulled up behind us. "Keep an eye on that car, O.K.?" I said, "I'll only be a second."

"O.K.," he said again. He looked either shamefaced or aggrieved, I couldn't tell which. Right then I didn't care.

I thought it unlikely the car had anything to do with me, but I hurried anyway. The office was empty except for an overweight woman with bleached blond hair behind the counter.

"How fast to Oakland?" I asked.

She used a mechanical device of some kind to check. "Tomorrow morning, 8 A.M.," she said. I heard the swish of the door opening, the rush of hot meeting air-conditioned air. I made a show of unwrapping the tin box for the woman behind the counter. "I'd like to send this as fast as possible," I said, "a friend's birthday; I'm late." Then, pretending I'd only just realized someone was behind me, I turned to see a small man with a deep tan and a gold earring. He was the most unlikely agent one could imagine, but I wasn't taking any chances.

"You go ahead," I said to him. "I have to fill this out." Better not to risk having him see what address I wrote.

"That's O.K., I'm not in a hurry," he said.

I went to the side counter but he did likewise, busying himself with a form. He didn't seem to be paying any attention to me but just in case, I wrote in a large hand so he would have no trouble reading it: "Sorry not to be with you on your birthday. Can't *wait* to see you, Love Layla," and slipped it, and the box, in the envelope. The man still hadn't gone to the front. I ripped up the paper and started again, as if I didn't like what I wrote. Still he didn't budge. If he were an agent, and following me, there was no way to out-wait him. I wrote out my address in bold numbers.

"How fast can something get to New York?" I said loudly to the woman. As the woman checked, I leaned against the wall in a way that blocked the man's view and crossed out the address I'd written, replacing it with the motel's. If I hadn't gone there for a second time, I'd never have remembered the address.

"Tomorrow afternoon," the woman said.

"Really? That's great." I said. "I'm sending this there," I pointed. The woman, seeing Oakland when I kept talking about New York, began to say something, but I cut her off. "Yes, that's right," I pointed again. I turned to glance at the man, ready for a desperate maneuver to snatch the envelope back if he were close by and could see it, but he was on his way out the door. Either he wasn't an agent, or I had successfully convinced him that what I was mailing had nothing to do with my father.

"I have something else to go to New York another day," I explained to the woman once the man was outside. I didn't move until I saw my envelope safely tossed into a bin, then went back to the counter and smoothed out the crumpled form the man had left. It was covered with scribbles.

My heart began to pound. If he were a federal agent, could he march in here as soon as I was gone and demand to see what I'd mailed? I went to the door. He was at his car, cleaning the windshield. On the other hand, maybe it was more important to him to follow us, and so he wouldn't risk coming back inside. What should I do? I couldn't stay in here all night.

I went back to the counter. "I have a favor," I said, smiling at the woman. "That guy who was in here? I'm a little nervous about him. I think he might be following me. If he comes back in here and asks any questions about me, would you do me a favor and refuse to tell him anything?"

"Of course!" she said. "But sweetie, don't take any chances with men like that. You'd better call the police."

"Maybe I'd better," I said, biting my lip. "I'll go do that now – thanks so much for your help."

I walked slowly to the car. Thank god for female solidarity, I thought. The man barely glanced at me, but as soon as I was in the car he got in his and started it up.

"Drive really slowly for a block or so," I said to Philip, pulling a map out of the glove compartment. "I want to make it look as if we don't know where we're going. Watch to see if the car behind us follows us."

"You think – "

"Just being careful." I pretended to study the map and tried to spot the car in the side-view mirror.

"He's behind us, but so are a bunch of other cars," Philip said, a moment later.

"Shit," I said.

"Don't panic."

"Just don't tip him off that we suspect he's following us."

"That may very well be his intent," Philip said.

"What do you mean?"

"Maybe they want to shake us up. This could all be nothing more than a fishing expedition."

"You think so?" I felt a burst of hope. Maybe I just needed to stay calm, do nothing rash, and nothing bad would happen.

"Well I can't believe someone would suddenly have had a change of heart and betray him."

I thought of the letters I'd been carrying around, the letters my mother had instructed me to destroy.

"Did any of the people you've been visiting know where you would be going next?" Philip asked.

"Not that I know –" I started to say, then froze.

"Layla, what?"

My mouth began to form the name, but I couldn't. Trent. I'd given Philip's address to Trent. "Oh my God," I said.

"What Layla, what?"

"A guy. I gave him your address. But no, no way. He's political, like the rest of you. He wouldn't have notified the FBI. I refuse to believe he could have done it."

"How well do you know him?" Philip said.

It had all been so fast. Hadn't I known that it was improbable such a hunk didn't already have a girlfriend, if not dozens? Maybe he didn't really share his parents' values after all. I thought of our last conversation, how disappointed he sounded when I wouldn't say where I had been. No, I refused to believe this. It was too cold, too calculated. His voice had quickened with such excitement as he talked about the '60s. He couldn't fake that, could he? My instincts couldn't be so off, could they? I thought of everything else I'd been learning that I was wrong about, and groaned.

"Don't worry," Philip was saying. "Probably something about your mother's death triggered a new look at your father's file, and they decided to nose around."

"You think so?" I said, grabbing at the idea like a lifeline.

"It makes a lot more sense."

We pulled up in front of the restaurant. "I'm sorry if it seemed as if I doubted you," I said. "Earlier, with the FBI. I just got so freaked out."

"I would never do anything to jeopardize any of you," Philip said stiffly. "I can't believe you would question that."

I thought of him watching the sunset with me in Sausalito, throwing his head back, laughing, and felt a sharp pang of guilt and regret. "I don't, really I don't," I said. "I guess I just wanted to blame somebody."

"O.K."

I stuck out my hand. "Friends?"

We talked of other things over dinner, but it felt like treading water. It felt off between us, and I feared it might never be put right.

"Look," Philip finally said, leaning forward, twirling his swizzle stick in his drink. "In case you do know how to reach him...."

I stiffened, not wanting to admit to anything.

"What I'm trying to say is that if you need any help, let me know."

"Oh Philip." I squeezed his hand. "Thanks. But there's nothing. Really."

"Sure, fine." He looked away, and I winced. Who was betraying whom? He turned back to me. "You've changed quite a bit in the last few weeks, haven't you?"

"I guess," I shrugged.

"No, I mean it. You've done a lot of growing up."

"Thanks," I said, embarrassed, yet pleased.

"Just don't lose your edge, O.K.?" he said.

"I won't," I said. But I wasn't quite sure what he meant.

No car seemed to follow us back to the house, and Philip said those on his block were known to him. Still, I lay awake for hours. Around 3 AM I judged it safe and got up. I stood in his small backyard in my nightgown. Philip's street was one of a row of houses with narrow alleys in between, all with postage-stamp yards in back. Those on either side of his seemed to be separated only by high bushes. It should be easy to get at least a few houses down and exit from someone else's backyard, or from the crossroads at the end of the block.

The next 24 hours were excruciating. When it got close to 11 AM, the time my father and I had arranged to meet, I had to practically sit on my hands not to make a move, even though I assumed that he had received the tin box, understood its message, and, because I had underlined "wait," not left the motel. I went for a walk in the park and shopped in a toy store, all for show in case someone was watching. It was awful and eerie not to know, and it felt odd playing to an imaginary audience, what I imagined it must feel like to believe in an all-seeing, all-knowing God.

At the toy store I purchased three large dolls, all with long blond hair. It would have been simpler, of course, to have bought a wig, but too much of a tip off. I thought I shouldn't take anything for granted. After Phillip went to bed I removed the hair from the dolls and glued it to the inside of a baseball cap so that, with the hat on, the hair hung to my chin. I looked bizarre, but not certifiable, and I judged that in the dark, from even just a short distance, the disguise would pass muster. At 5 AM I put on my clothes, wearing extra to bulk myself up, and covered it all with an old jacket I found in Philip's closet. I grabbed some cheese and an apple, and left the house.

I had figured the best time to leave would be when it was still dark but early enough that if I were seen, it was plausible that I could be going someplace. Now I made my way out of the basement into the yard and stood a moment, afraid the FBI agents would pop out of the bushes.

It was dead quiet, the spooky, hollow quiet before dawn, with not a bird cheep or a car motor. Once my eyes adjusted to the dark I made my way through the shrubbery to the next backyard. There were no lights on; everything was silent. I waited a moment, then dashed across to the bushes edging the property.

A wire fence was embedded in the hedges. There was no help for it – I was going to have to climb over. The fence wasn't more than 5 feet high, but even so, I felt very exposed as I got close to the top. I was sure that if anyone was watching the front of Philip's house they wouldn't be able to see me, but even so my hands were so sweaty and my heart pounding so hard it took me awhile before I could work up the nerve to heave myself up and over.

I made it through one backyard to the next, until I reached the fourth one from Philip's. I had been outside probably only a matter of minutes, yet I was getting desperate to be on the street, and I had to force myself to keep to a slow, careful pace as I made my way around the picnic table and chairs to the bushes marking the boundary between the fourth and fifth backyards. I stopped, listened, and heard the unmistakable sound of trouble – a dog.

The barking pinned me to the hedges and I ducked down, shaking, sure that at any moment someone would be roused from the house. I raced toward the street, thinking I was far enough from Philip's to be safe. I slipped down the passageway between the houses, pressed up against the brick, and peeked out.

The four backyards had not put me as far away as I thought. The block was lit by streetlights, and I scanned all the houses and cars, especially those opposite Philip's. There was no movement that I could see.

Just as I was about to step out onto the street, the shadows of the house opposite Philip's seem to shift; in a flash I retreated.

I leaned back against the side of the house, heart hammering. I was going to have to deal with the dog – that was all there was to it.

I retraced my steps down the passageway and then, bracing myself for the barking, passed through the hedges and into the fifth yard. The barks sounded like gunshots as I raced pell-mell around a small aboveground pool and toward the sixth backyard. I prayed the barking wasn't arousing the suspicions of whoever might be watching Philip's house. I flung myself at the hedges and fell on the ground on the other side, panting. Belatedly I realized the barking dog had been inside the house.

The barking subsided. I stood, congratulating myself on my luck, and stumbled into something.

I let out a yelp and froze. An old black Lab struggled to its feet, tail wagging.

But this dog didn't bark. It just made a sound like an asthmatic's wheeze. "Hey there, pup," I said, cautiously, and held out my hand. I remembered the cheese and apple I had stuffed in my pocket. Did dogs eat cheese? I pulled out the baggie and unwrapped it. "Eat," I said. "Be still."

The dog gobbled greedily, slavered all over my hand, and whined for more. I petted its head. "Good dog," I whispered. I began to move on, and the dog did too. "Shoo," I whispered, "Shoo." I moved, and the dog kept pace. I couldn't seem to shake the dog. Then I had an inspiration.

I slipped through the tiny side yard between the row houses, my hand on the dog's collar. I was now only two houses from the end of the street, the crossroads only a hundred yards or so away.

I stepped out from the cover of the house. I pretended to bend down and adjust the dog's collar so I could give one last quick glance toward Philip's. Again I thought I saw something, a shadow, but if so, the shadow didn't move. Taking a deep breath, I walked purposefully, as if the dog was tugging me along.

I made it to the BART station without incident, without so much as a person or a car anywhere nearby. The dog whimpered when I had to leave her behind. I just hoped she could make it back home safely without my help. I loved that dog; I would have taken her all the way to the motel if I could have.

Chapter 10

Of everything about that awful, tense morning, the one unexpectedly easy thing was getting into my father's room. I simply went around the pool and slipped in through the sliding glass doors. It was 6:00, and my father was dead asleep. His breathing was completely quiet – no murmurs, no snores. It was unnerving.

I sat across from the bed in an overly soft chair and felt the tension leak out of me along with what seemed like every drop of water in my body. I took off my jacket and leaned back and closed my eyes for what I told myself would be only a moment. When I awoke my father was standing over me, saying my name. "I'm sorry to wake you, but I figured if you sent me the box and arrived in the middle of the night it's got to be serious."

"You shouldn't have left the sliding glass doors open."

"Escape route," he said. "FBI?"

I nodded.

He began to pace.

"They were waiting for me when I got to Philip's. Thank god you didn't come."

"What I don't understand is, why now?"

"Philip said maybe it's got to do with my mother's death, that maybe they got interested again."

"Maybe...." But my father looked troubled.

"You don't think Philip? Or Nina?"

"No way," he said.

We both nodded. I was shocked at how easy it was to be suspicious, to turn on someone you cared about.

"I gave Philip's address to Trent. I'm sorry. I shouldn't have."

"All of this – this trip – was much riskier than anything your mother and I ever attempted all these years," my father said. "Maybe there was some slip-up, something we failed to account for."

"If they caught you, what would it mean?" I asked. "What would happen to you?"

My father stopped pacing, looked at me. "I would stand trial," he said. "And then who knows? It'd be up to a jury."

"But wouldn't you get off? You've got to. A jury would see through the false charges by now, right?"

"What did the agent say, exactly?" my father asked.

I hesitated. I found myself reluctant to tell him, as if even repeating the message made me their allies, somehow.

"There were two of them – Keane and Blair. Keane did all the talking." I dug the agent's card from my pocket and handed it to my father. "He said they didn't want to hurt you, but that if you turned yourself in they'd make some sort of deal. Philip and I pretended we didn't know anything. I said you were dead. I don't know if they believed me." I felt my face flush, as if with shame.

My father nodded, waiting for me to go on.

"I said I didn't agree with your politics and that if you had really done what you were supposed to have done, that I'd want you to rot in jail. That shook them up a little," I tried to laugh. "You should have seen their faces."

My father did not smile at me in return. He regarded me thoughtfully.

"Layla, we need to talk."

I was suddenly anxious. "I thought we were talking,"

My father sat opposite me on the edge of the bed.

"I need to ask you this: Do you think I'm a murderer?" he said softly.

"What do you mean? What are you trying to say?"

"I've held off talking to you about what happened until you got to know me better. But we've run out of time. So I'm asking: Do you think what I did makes me a murderer?"

"Did you actually shoot that guard?" I burst out. I felt all my confusion flood back, and resentment that he was asking me this now, now when it was the last thing I wanted to be considering. I tried to bring myself under control.

"If I did, would that make me a murderer in your eyes?"

"I don't know. I don't know what to think! Why does it matter, anyhow? Either you are or you aren't. You tell me," I said.

My father let out a breath. "Fair enough," he said. "Someone died, and I was unwittingly part of that. But no, I don't consider myself a murderer."

"A part of that how?"

"I didn't mean to kill him."

"You did shoot him?" I sat bolt upright. "I thought you were framed!"

He winced, as if he couldn't bear the look on my face.

"I wasn't framed. But I didn't know the gun was loaded."

I stared at his hunched shoulders, squinched-up face, and could hear my breathing becoming labored. I hadn't realized to what extent I had come to believe he was innocent. He had really killed a man. I didn't know if I could stand knowing that.

"I've paid for it my whole life," he said.

"But you didn't stand trial. You didn't go to jail." These were things I'd always believed in – retribution, even, in some circumstances, the death penalty. I began to tremble, and hugged my arms to my chest.

"You know what my life's been. I did community service. I set up a fund for the guard's son. I gave up a normal life – work, friends, your mother. You."

"If you'd been in jail you could have had us both!"

"You want to know why I went underground. Why I did what I did. It's very hard to explain."

"Don't give me that," I said, enraged. "That's a cop out. You were scared, you didn't want to go to jail. Isn't that what it boils down to? You had time to think. You made a decision. You've made that same decision every day since."

"Do you know what they do to you in prison if you've killed someone in law enforcement? You're right, Layla, I was terrified. We're not talking about 10 years in jail reduced to seven for good behavior. You have no concept of what it was like back then. They wanted blood. It would have been life."

"You've been living a life sentence anyhow, isn't that what you've been telling me? At least in jail you would have been able to see my mother and me."

He was silent a moment. "I did see your mother, Layla. Not often enough, but it was as a free man."

The pain of what he was saying hit. It took me a moment to catch my breath.

"So it was only me, only not having a daughter. I guess my birth didn't make a difference."

"Of course it did. I didn't expect this to go on so long. But I just couldn't face being locked up forever. It just wasn't something I could do."

The silence went on and on between us. I felt oppressed by the room's hot, stale air, by my own stink. I became aware of the hideous shade of the room's green walls. I couldn't look at my father, and so I looked outside. Palm fronds slapped against the edge of the window. I felt faint from hurt and humiliation.

I wanted to say something, to wound him as he'd wounded me, but no words came.

"Layla, you have to accept that there's no going back, that no explanation can be good enough to explain it or to justify it or to give you what you never had."

I had a choice, I thought. All along, I had a choice. I could go or I could walk away forever. I stared at the door, willing myself to move toward it. The intensity of my ambivalence was like a fire. I couldn't remember ever before feeling I would burn up from sheer emotion.

"I need to explain a little more, and to tell you what happened, if you can bear to hear it."

I couldn't even lift my head to look at him.

"Layla, please?" He stood, pressed my shoulders down with his hands, as if to keep me there. "I know that what I'm admitting is that by staying underground I chose me over you. You've every right to feel hurt and angry. I would do anything to make it up to you. But please, can you let me get this over with?"

My face, my jaw, felt rigid; it was an effort even to nod.

"Thank you."

He removed his hands from my shoulders. "O.K.," he said. He began to pace, head down, as if he was addressing the carpet. "O.K. We were there to protest that a man – a friend of mine, Raul, who was in a group called NY – for Neighborhood Youth – was being unjustly accused and locked up. You'll probably say, why didn't you go through the system, file a complaint. But back then – the late '60s, early '70s – it was like a civil war. And it meant the rules of right and wrong were different, as if the rules of war applied, at least in the minds of many of us.

"I hadn't planned to do anything other than demonstrate. We thought of ourselves as part of a movement, that what we did was part of 'the struggle.' We learned Raul had been beaten – remember that he was being held without bail, and for doing nothing except exercising his constitutional rights – they called it plotting to overthrow the government.

"At the demonstration his brother Luis told me the NY members were going to try and free Raul and asked me to help. I didn't like it, but emotions were high; I let myself be swept along. And partly I guess I wanted to prove myself – my commitment.

"Raul was being transferred, and Luis had learned the route the van was to take, and when. It was early in the morning. We had two cars, and we made it look as if the cars had gotten into an accident. We blocked the road that way.

"I didn't have a gun, but it was rumored that the NY had guns, and I have to be honest and tell you that a part of me found it a little thrilling. It meant that we were serious. It meant we were willing to give our lives to the struggle. Do you hear what I'm saying? Not that I would take a life. I thought of it as being willing to die for what I believed in.

"It was stupid, ill-conceived, a horrible tragedy. I'm not proud of it, Layla. But I can't renounce what my beliefs were, and I can't denounce that overzealous younger self that made such an awful mistake. I've relived it thousands of times. Just as you say – I've relived it each and every day of my life.

"That morning, when the plan changed and the idea surfaced to help Raul escape, a few guns materialized. A man named Sam, high up in the leadership, asked me to hold one. He told me it was just for show, that it wasn't loaded. The point was just to hold it on the guards until Raul was freed. I had never handled a gun. I didn't even know how to check to see if there were bullets.

"We were out of the cars and in the road as the van drew up. Just as if there had been an accident, someone was on the ground and a few others were clustered around him. Luis, Sam, and I ran to the van, as if we were trying to get help. The van driver opened the door and we rushed him. Luis yelled to the guard to uncuff Raul. Raul's face was so bruised and swollen from having been beaten I almost didn't recognize him. I had been told to cover the driver, but I was so shaky I couldn't keep my hands steady, and I had to hold the gun in both hands. I'll never forget the look of terror in the driver's eyes.

"What happened next I've gone over and over in my mind, and I'm still unsure about it. There was a shout from one of the prisoners – a guard was aiming his gun at Luis. I swung around, and somehow the gun I was holding went off. That's how it felt – that the gun took over and went off. All I can think is that I must have squeezed the trigger inadvertently. I heard other shots, but I don't know if they were real or if my shot kept repeating in my mind. People were screaming. The guard was slumped over, groaning. Luis was on the floor, bleeding. I thought he was dead. Sam was grabbing my arm and saying, 'You've got to get out of here.' I couldn't move. He took the gun from me, shoved me off the bus, told me to find a phone, call an ambulance. Your mother thought that he took the gun because he planned to put the blame on me, but how can I ever know? Of course it never occurred to me to wipe the gun of my fingerprints.

"I can't describe to you what it was like, Layla. No nightmare, no matter how awful, has ever come close. How can a mind take in such a monstrous thing as killing another human being? How can you take in that lives are changed so profoundly in a second? You just can't grasp it.

"I got to a crossroad several blocks away and called the ambulance and then your mother. I took the subway back to Manhattan and we met at a greasy spoon on Broadway. We decided to wait and see how badly the guard was hurt. She arranged for me to stay with Lenny in Boston. You know the rest – the guard died. There were two bullets in him, only one from the gun I had shot, but they never found the other gun. It wasn't even established which bullet killed him, not that it matters. Luis was badly injured. He and Sam got 20 years; I would have gotten life. The gun with my prints was turned in. They could have wiped it, at least. But they needed to argue that I killed the guard or their own sentences would have been even harsher.

"I never intended to remain a fugitive. There were a lot of people who were underground back then, a network. Many people saw the jailbreak as an act of conscience. Everyone told me I would be crazy to turn myself in, that the system was corrupt, that no one would believe me that the guard's death had been an accident, that going to jail wasn't a way to make reparation."

My father sat back down on the bed, leaned forward and reached out to me as if to take my hands. When I didn't respond he put his hands on his knees instead.

"Layla, in my heart of hearts I don't know for sure why I ran, beyond sheer fear and panic. But as for the decision to go underground – that was to some extent a product of the times – of the political climate. Still, I'm not saying you should believe that. You can think me a complete moral coward, and I won't argue with you."

My father ran his hands over his head, as if to flatten his curls. I felt the shock, the repeated shocks, of his words go through my body. I unclenched my hands, my jaw. I understood now why he had procrastinated in telling me what he had done. In the silence I noticed dawn was beginning to creep into the room. I stared at my father's face. There was terrible pain in the way his head hung forward, terrible pain in the way his shoulders hunched toward each other. "I'm sorry," I said. My father nodded, looked away.

"So, Layla," he said, as if he was talking to the wall, "what's your verdict?" My stomach churned. Listening to my father's story, I had been pulled in to his tragedy; I had almost forgotten the man whose life had been lost. There must have been wife, children, people who loved him and suffered as a result of his death. Did the fact of his death outweigh the fact that my father didn't mean to kill him? Or did the fact that it was unintentional absolve my father? Even if the guard's death was an accident, it was an accident caused by actions my father had chosen to take because of his beliefs. If I felt my father's beliefs were wrong, did that mean I thought he should be condemned? If I believed my father's beliefs were right, did that mean I thought he should be absolved? Did I have to know my own beliefs to come to a decision? Or should I simply look into my father's eyes and allow myself to be swayed by his remorse, his humanity?

My father had killed a man. The newspaper photograph of the guard, grainy, black and white, had been so vivid as to be unforgettable. Life was sacred. But what did sacred mean, exactly? Freedom, justice; these were sacred, too.

I looked at my father, and as I looked I heard the echo of my words to my mother the night of our terrible fight: "I wish it was you who was dead, and my father who was alive." I remembered how the life drained from her face, the sound of her footsteps disappearing down the hall. I remembered how I had stood in the thundering quiet of the kitchen, waiting for her to return, finally daring to go to her room, holding the plate with the sandwich and the little paper flower I had made as an apology. I remembered how I had stood at her door and heard nothing in response to my timid knock and my fear that if I entered her room I would see only emptiness and the curtains blowing from an open window.

What if, when I had come in, the curtains had been blowing from the open window? What if she hadn't been asleep on the bed? What if I had rushed to the window and looked down to see her crumpled body? What if I'd had to live the rest of my life remembering that?

I could not begin to imagine. I could not bear to imagine.

"Layla?" my father was saying. "Am I a murderer? Would you convict me?"

The sun showed the weariness in his face, the early morning stubble on his cheeks before his beard began.

"No." I said. With the words I felt a great relief, as if something terrible in me had dissolved. "You didn't mean to do it."

My father wiped his eyes with the back of his hands. "Thank you," he said. The light made bright stripes on the carpet from the blinds; it was getting late. Decisions were going to have to be made, and soon. But I felt heavy, exhausted with the weight of my father's story, his sorrow and guilt. Any movement seemed false, trivial. "What are you going to do?" I started to say, but stopped myself.

"What do we do now?" I asked.

○

I now see that morning in the motel room as the moment in which my life changed, the moment to which all the moments of the summer, the small choices, had led. Because it was in that moment that I crossed over to my father's side. My words seemed to hang in the air, the world to have been struck dumb. It was as if we had been sitting frozen in a tableau, me in the upholstered chair, him on the edge of the bed, leaning toward me. Then the sound came back on: of doors opening and shutting, children's voices at the pool, cars on the road. The sound penetrated the bubble in which my father and I sat, and burst it.

I went to the window, peered out. I was shocked to see that the sun was fully up. "What do we do now?" I said again.

"That's going to be up to you," my father said.

"What do you mean?"

"Before, when I put you on the spot. I wasn't trying to be hard on you. There's something more – a reason you're really going to have to be clear about what you think."

More? I grabbed fistfuls of hair, tugged. It wasn't possible there could be more. My father gently pulled my hands from my hair and held them.

"I don't mean more about what happened – I mean about this trip, about why your mother and I wanted it in the first place."

"I thought it was for us to meet, for us all to be together."

My father pressed my hands more tightly between his. "Look, I need to backtrack a little. I haven't explained why your mother and I made the decision not to tell you about me. Why we didn't live together after you were born. There was my safety, of course – I mean, you were just a child – how could we expect you not to slip up? But it was also that having to keep a secret of such magnitude would have put tremendous pressure on you."

It took a moment for the point of his words to filter through. "You're saying the secrecy was for me?"

"Yes. We wanted as much as possible for you to have a normal life."

"Normal? A life of lies, a life without a father – normal?"

"What was the alternative, all of us living together underground? Can you imagine what kind of life that would have been for you? Or, if I'd been in jail, how it would have been visiting me in a maximum security prison?"

I started to protest, but what he was saying made a kind of sense. Still, I pulled my hands away from his. "Better than nothing."

"Layla, we really, truly, thought it was the right thing to do. We never expected this would go on so long. Look, we knew I was much more likely to get caught if we were together. Then when she got pregnant, and we wanted to have you, we talked it through all over again. But it was impossible. We knew it would be far too difficult and dangerous for us to be together. Think about it."

"Couldn't she at least have told me you were alive?"

"If we had told you that you had a father you could never know, could never see or talk about and the reason why – might that not have been more painful? Believe me, we agonized over this. We discussed it endlessly. What to say, what not to say. What age should you be when we told you – 10? 16? But if you feel we made the wrong decision – all I can do is ask your forgiveness." Forgiveness. I wanted to give it. I wanted to get past the obstruction in my throat, the tight grip on my chest.

"Well what do you think?" I said. "Was it the right decision?"

"Only you can answer that," he said.

"No. I mean in terms of you. Of what you lost."

He blanched, as if I had punched him. And I felt a ping, the kind of ping I felt when a frame fit one of my photographs so perfectly it was as if they were long lost lovers I was reuniting. A sense of rightness. What I felt now, the ping, was the words hitting the exact center of the pain inside me. A perfect match.

"I was your child," I said.

"God, Layla, don't you think I know that?" His eyes filled, and he sprang up, then sat abruptly back down. "Don't you know that I wish I could do it all over?"

"You mean that?"

"More than ever. You're real now, Layla." His voice dropped so low I could barely hear him. "Maybe you can't understand, but in some ways getting to know you…. It's been very painful."

I found there were tears on my own cheeks, and I wiped them away with both fists, like a child. "I'm sorry," I said again.

"No, don't be," he touched my arm lightly. "Don't be." He gave an embarrassed laugh. We both looked down. Our knees faced each other with just a few inches of space between, mine covered by the baggy pants of Philip's I'd borrowed, his poking through the holes in his threadbare jeans.

I felt his gaze, and looked up. "Layla, this brings us full circle. The real point of this summer. See, we had wanted to give you a say in the whole thing."

"I don't understand." His words were like a thicket I had to fight to get through. There had been too much information, too many revelations. "What whole thing?"

"Ever since I went underground, we planned to reevaluate the situation when you got older. So this summer, when we met, part of the reason was to discuss with you if I should turn myself in."

"Wait a minute! Are you saying that all along you've been considering –"

He just looked at me.

"I don't believe this!"

"We had planned to tell you sooner, but then 9/11 happened, and we thought we'd better wait. Now, with the upsurge in antiwar sentiment, the political climate has improved. You turned 22. We thought it was time. You were kept from having a father, kept from the truth long enough. We thought it was only fair that this be your decision. That's why I said you need to be clear about what you think."

"Are you telling me you want me to decide whether you're to be incarcerated or not?"

"If you want. It can be totally up to you."

I flung myself back in the chair. Every inch of my body ached from the two sleepless nights, the tension. I had imagined helping my father escape, a befuddled image of a father-daughter version of Thelma and Louise. I hadn't imagined us at a police station, my father in handcuffs. "I can't do this."

"Well we thought –"

"We this, we that," I snapped. "She's not a factor any more. It's just you and me now."

A flicker of a smile crossed my father's face, and he looked down as if embarrassed, began unraveling the hem of his T-shirt. "O.K.," he said. "Then, depending on what you want, I could walk away and we could never see each other again. Or I could reproduce with you the system your mother and I worked out. Or I could turn myself in and take my chances."

I felt the hairs rise on my arms.

"What would those chances be?"

"Well, I've been feeling things out this past year with a movement lawyer – there still are such people – and he thinks that sentiment may have changed enough that the risk might be worth it. The courts might be more lenient. Also, Sam and Luis are out of prison – there's a chance one of them will corroborate that they told me the gun wasn't loaded. Other fugitives from that time have turned themselves in – one was Katherine Anne Power – maybe you read about it? She got five years, but she didn't shoot anybody. I would get more." Five years? More? I wiped my palms on my pants, but the dampness just wouldn't go away.

I rocked back and forth in the upholstered chair, inhaling its musty smell and the smell of my own sweat. I had been sitting so long in the chair that little fibers of its wooly fabric were stuck to my skin. I lifted my clammy T-shirt slightly and fanned myself.

"Is it that you want me to know what it's like to be in your shoes? To have to live with a decision that has consequences for someone else?"

"Of course not!" my father said. "I just want to know what you want."

I had been furious to have been left out of their lives. Now I wasn't so eager.

"This is a lot to think about, Layla. I want to do whatever you're most comfortable with."

From outside came the sound of children's voices, a sound like the tinkle of chimes – innocent, beckoning. I went to the window, pulled aside the blinds, and stared at the zigzags and sparkles of light on the pool, the sudden bursts as water parted around small bodies and flashed white. I wanted to strip off my clothes, to feel the bumpy concrete of the pathway against the soles of my feet as I ran to the water, the icy cold silkiness as I dove in. I returned to my chair and sat down. My father was still sitting on the edge of the bed. He looked up at me expectantly, rolling his medal between his palms like a gambler rubbing the dice for good luck.

"I'd rather you were free, altogether free," I said. "But what if you get 10 or 20 years?" My voice quivered.

My father winced, looked away, but when he turned back his expression was calm again. "Layla, it doesn't make any sense to even think about that and to explore it further with the lawyer until you know how you feel, what you want. Are you sure you wouldn't rather I just stay underground? We could still see each other a little, stay in touch. Maybe that would be O.K. for you?"

I hesitated, a feeling of hollowness inside me at the thought of watching him disappear from sight.

"No," I said. "No, I don't want that. And I don't want to live outside society – I don't want to see you only once or twice a year in cheap motels, to not know where you are, how you are." How had I come to care this much? "But I don't want to be the one to lock you up!"

"It wouldn't be you locking me up, Layla," he said.

I felt my face get mushy. I took a deep breath, recovered myself. "Please," I said, "can't we decide this together?"

"Of course," my father said. "If that's what you want, of course."

"I need to know how you feel," I said.

My father looked down at the floor, rubbed the heel of his hand over the knee that poked from his jeans. "If you hadn't come to meet me, if we hadn't gotten along, I'd just have gone on as I have all these years. Without your mother, it wouldn't have made much sense to take the risk. But now there's you. What's important to me now is to have you in my life." He paused. "I think I would choose to turn myself in."

His words made a dull thud inside me, like the sickening impact of a bird against a window pane.

"O.K. then," I said, swallowing. "That's what I want, too."

"You're sure?" he asked. Was I? Was I sure this was what I wanted? We had been wrapped in a tight cocoon of days and time together. Back home, back in my own life, would I feel differently?

"I'm sure," I said. We fell silent, letting the reality sink in. My father seemed calm, but he was threading his fingers through his curls, making them stick up in little tufts, then twirling them in his fingers.

"What comes next?" I said. "Do you want me to call Keane and Blair?"

"No. If we decide to go ahead, I want to do it through my own lawyer. I'm not turning myself in to those agents. If I do it on my own terms, there's a good chance the sentence will be lighter."

I thought of something.

"My mother left me money – life insurance. We can use it for your defense."

"Layla, that's very generous. But it's unnecessary."

"She would have wanted that. I do, too. I mean it," I said.

"I know you do, and I appreciate it. But I won't need it. The lawyer is pro bono." He grinned. "I'm part of his political work."

"Promise you'll take it if – "

"I promise." He glanced up at the clock. Keane and Blair, I thought. They would be coming back to Philip's. He would have noticed long ago I was missing. I got up to use the bathroom. After I flushed I heard a retching sound coming from the other room. My father was leaning over the kitchenette sink. "Dad?" I said. "Dad, are you O.K.?"

"Just the jitters." He brought a handful of water to his mouth, rinsed, and spat it out, slouched against the sink. "Did you hear what you called me?"

I listened to the echo of my words. I let them settle between us. I put my hand on his shoulder. "We don't have to do this," I said.

"I know. But I think it's what I want, as long as it's what you want, too."

"I want you to live your life with no more fear!"

"I thought I was ready. It's just that it's only now really hitting me, you know?"

"Maybe we're being premature," I said. "Maybe this is just not the right time."

"We can never be sure it's the right time," he said, "that's just it. It's the devil you know versus the devil you don't."

My heart started thumping again. "What do we do now?"

"We wait. It may take a little time for a deal to be worked out."

"How much time?"

"I've no idea. I'll know better after I reach the lawyer, and he talks to the intermediaries. So you should go back to Philip's, act as normal as you can. Meet me tomorrow night. There's a big concert at Golden Gate Park. Near the bandshell there are bathrooms. I'll be in the ladies room. Just after the music starts. I should know a lot more by then and we can make our decision."

"Isn't that too risky? If the FBI is this close – ."

"I don't care. I've given you short shrift all my life, Layla. Not this time. We need to think this through together."

I stood up slowly, reluctant now to leave the claustrophobia of my father's motel room. I started for the door and then turned back. "Maybe I shouldn't leave at all. What if something goes wrong?"

"Try not to panic. If there's any problem, any trouble at all, I'll get word to you." He gave me a big hug. "Thank you."

"Thank me for what?"

"For coming here today."

"Of course I came," I said.

"There's no 'of course' about it," he said. "Think about it. You warned me that I am in danger. That says something."

"Well I could hardly turn you in!"

"I'm not so sure. After all, by not turning me in you lied to the Federal government. You aided and abetted a criminal."

I felt a shiver.

"You didn't even know yet the story of what happened, yet you acted to protect me. That means a lot to me. What you said to the FBI, about not believing in my politics, about how you think I belong in jail – that's probably what you really would have felt and thought a month ago. But maybe not now."

I felt a moment's dizziness, as if the floor had somehow tilted.

"You came here. Own that. Own your own instincts."

I felt a rush of fear: Had I been manipulated, reeled in like a stunned fish? Who was I becoming?

"I don't really know yet what I think."

"Maybe all you need to know right now is how you feel about me."

A lump formed in my throat, and I nodded.

"You'd better go." He gave me another hug. I took a deep breath and crossed the room. My hand on the door handle was slippery with new sweat. I felt weak and lightheaded, my stomach hollow. I turned back into the room.

"Go," he commanded.

I bit my lip, nodded. I slid the door open and stepped through. The sounds of the children and the pool merged into a roar of white noise and the air itself seemed to gather into a loud hum. I had a sudden fear that we were making a big mistake, a dreadful mistake from which we would never recover, a mistake whose outline we should be able to see, but somehow were blinded to.

Chapter 11

*O*utside it was so hot and bright I had to stay under the motel awning a moment for my eyes to adjust. It was late morning and the streets were quiet and picture-perfect, so peaceful it was almost frightening, as if it were orchestrated by the FBI to disarm and trip me up. I retraced my steps to the BART station, struggling to imagine what it would be like if my father turned himself in, but my mind stalled. I couldn't get beyond stock TV images: a courthouse fronted by tall columns, swarms of media people rushing up with cameras and microphones.

I tried to think clearly, but my thoughts skittered about in my brain. How could I have told my father I wanted him to turn himself in? How could I make such a momentous decision for someone else? My father was right: I needed to figure out my own mind. Not only because I might be asked by the judge or the FBI or the newspapers, but because I needed to know for myself what I truly believed about my father – what he had done, what he believed – everything. My parents had sealed their fates and mine when they were not much older than I was, but I had never before needed to think so deeply about anything.

I didn't have the habit of such thinking. I found myself looking at the other passengers on the train. That stout woman with the square chin – what did she believe in? What about that young blond couple with the baby. How had they arrived at their beliefs? Their parents? Their own experiences? I'd had plenty of opportunities to explore these kinds of ideas in school, of course, but I hadn't. I'd skimmed the surface like an ice skater, all flash and no depth.

Still, I seemed to believe in my father. In his goodness, his integrity. Could I just go with that? Maybe that's what many people did – people like me, who didn't really want to work at it. Maybe they found someone they admired and simply adopted their attitudes, sort of the way I had found myself agreeing with everything Trent said. Was that so awful? In my mind I placed the FBI men on one side, my father on the other. I detested them, I cared for him. Simple. But was that really good enough?

When I exited the BART I half expected to see the dog waiting for me. My race through the night, my terror, felt like a crazy, distorted dream.

About a block away from Philip's I passed a donut shop. I ordered a bakers' dozen and inhaled a cup of coffee and a chocolate-glazed while the clerk packed the other 12. The sugar and caffeine took only seconds to go right where I needed it.

I rang Philip's doorbell, still chewing.

"Layla, where have you been!" He looked furious. I realized I hadn't even left a note for him when I disappeared that morning.

"Here, peace offering," I said, thrusting the box at him. "I'm sorry, I know I should have called, but I didn't want to wake you."

"Wake me! It's 11:30!"

"Yeah, sorry," I said. "I couldn't sleep, so I decided to go to the beach and watch the sunrise." Too late I remembered it was sunsets you saw over the Pacific Ocean.

"Your friends are here."

I took a step back, my chest suddenly alive with thumping, a player piano gone berserk.

"Take a deep breath," he whispered. "Don't lose it now."

I did as I was told: deep breaths, one after another.

"Well, well, well, the prodigal daughter returns," Agent Keane said as I walked into the living room.

"Guys, I'm flattered," I said lightly, trying to keep my voice steady. "I didn't expect you, but there are enough donuts to go around."

"We were hoping you'd have something else to offer us," Agent Blair said.

"I got jelly for you, Philip. And what about you, Agent Blair? Coconut custard?"

"Skip the bullshit, O.K., Ms. James?" Agent Keane said.

"I don't think we've had a satisfactory answer about where you took off to," Agent Blair said.

"I don't recall owing you an explanation as to my whereabouts," I said.

"Since you went to such lengths to slip away unseen, it suggests your father is near," he went on, as if he hadn't heard me. "Do you have a message for us?"

"I told you before, I don't know what you're talking about." I said.

"Look Ms. James," Agent Keane said. "It's a little late to be covering up. You should have been more discrete all along."

"What are you talking about?" I could hear a twinge of fear in my voice.

"Agent Blair, could you oblige Ms. James with an excerpt?"

I looked at Philip and then back at Keane. I tightened my hands into fists and stuffed them in my pockets.

"Let's see," Agent Blair was smirking, unfolding some papers from an envelope. I let out my breath only when I saw they were not my mother's letters.

"Conversation, July 10th, between Layla James and Jennifer Tisch. Ms. Tisch: 'Are you sure you're O.K.?' Ms. James: 'Yeah, it's just …I've been learning some heavy stuff about my parents. Shocking, actually.' Tisch: 'Shocking? Your mother?' James: 'Well, more my father. You're going to flip out. It turns out he was involved in a violent crime.' Tisch: 'You're kidding! What happened?' James: 'It was a sort of civil rights thing. You can't say anything about this to anyone, O.K.?' Tisch: 'O.K., I promise, but Layla, you're making me nervous.' James: 'It's just a long story, kind of complicated. I'd rather tell you in person, that's all. I just don't like talking on the phone.'" Agent Blair grinned, refolded the paper.

My face was burning. The silence seemed to go on forever. "So what," I finally managed.

"Ms. James?" Agent Keane said. "Why don't you sit down."

I sat.

"Pretty suggestive, don't you think?"

"You tapped my phone conversations," I said. I still didn't get it. I had talked to Jenny from my cell phone.

"We've had your mother's phone tapped ever since your father went underground. Routine." He said it carelessly. I looked at him and in that moment I knew what hate, real hate, was. Some clerk with the FBI had listened to every conversation of my mother's and mine all my life, and he tossed it off as if it were nothing. "It was just a lucky break for us that your friend is staying in your apartment this summer and that you two are so chatty," he was saying. "It was fairly easy to figure out what was going on."

"Nothing is going on." It took an effort to speak.

"Just a rendezvous with a known fugitive," he said, his voice hard, all the phony politeness gone.

"I told you – I've been staying with my mother's friends to learn more about her and my father since her death," I said. My anger had given my voice a little of its strength back. "I learned about my father's past this summer – that's what I was talking to my friend about. That's all I was talking about. There's nothing in that conversation that says otherwise, and you know it." I crossed my arms in front of my chest and glared at them. It was a toss-up whether I would maintain my stance or burst into tears.

Blair and Keane looked at me. What they had wasn't proof, and they knew it. Suggestive, yes, but that was all. No proof. I tried to focus on that and not the awareness that I had put my father's liberty at risk. Even if he did decide to turn himself in,

I wanted it to be on his terms, not because of a blunder on my part. My mother's notes had repeatedly cautioned me to keep my mouth shut. I felt the hairs at the back of my neck rise: It was sheer luck the FBI hadn't followed me into the desert and captured my father, before we'd even gotten to know each other.

"Ms. James, we'll be watching. It's just a matter of time." They turned, headed for the door.

"Mr. Keane," I called out, just as his hand was on the knob.

He turned back, expectant.

I waited a moment. I wanted to make him sweat, if only a little.

"Please, won't you take a donut?"

The slam of the door was his only response.

I collapsed onto the sofa and glanced at Philip. Under his expressionless stare I grabbed a cushion and pressed it to my face. Still he said nothing. I became aware of the ticking of a clock mounted above me on the wall, a cruel, unnerving sound. I removed the cushion.

"What can I say?" I blurted out. "I – ."

Philip gestured toward the door. I had forgotten that we were acting under the assumption that the house was bugged. "You should have let me know where you were going," Philip said loudly to the invisible audience. "I was worried."

"Please don't make things worse than they already are," I said, once we were in the backyard.

"The last thing I want is to make things worse," Philip said.

"Philip, I really am sorry. I doubted you, and all along it was me."

"Hey, don't be so hard on yourself." He shoved me into the wooden double rocker that was his sole piece of lawn furniture and nudged me with his hip to make room for him. "You only hurt my feelings a little bit."

I sank deeper into the swing. "If something terrible had happened –"

"Well, it didn't. You were lucky. He was lucky. And aren't you pleased that nobody betrayed anybody?" I thought of Trent, how I had doubted him, too. "You didn't understand why it was so important to be careful. Enough self-recrimination. Time to move on."

He was right. Over the next 24 hours I would have plenty of time to dwell on my failures, to be stabbed by sudden moments of terror like those free falls that shoot you upright in bed, gasping, just before you fall asleep.

○

Philip drove me to the public library where I scrolled through databases, Googled key-word combinations: FBI and arrests, FBI and fugitives. I wandered through the stacks. The history of the FBI was next to the True Crime section, plenty of murder and mayhem, all of which I avoided. There was a book about how the FBI tracked a killer through 10 states, one about a gang of fugitives caught after 18 years; they were sentenced to 10 years in jail reduced to 7 for good behavior. I went back to the computer and typed in student activists, 1960s' protestors. I found books on communes, on the FBI's covert activities against antiwar activists, on Abbie Hoffman, an autobiography by Jane Alpert, one of the Weathermen. I located an article in *The New Yorker* on Katherine Anne Power, the fugitive my father mentioned who had turned herself in and gotten a five-year sentence.

I had not imagined there were so many antiwar activists who had gone underground. A few had fled after an isolated deed like my father's, but most, like the Weather Underground, had done so as part of their political strategy. They believed the Vietnam War was integral to a corrupt system that only revolutionary action could dismantle, and engaged in acts of sabotage, usually blowing up draft centers or robbing banks for money to purchase guns. Most had been caught or had turned themselves in after only a few years in hiding. There seemed no particular pattern to what sentences they got, although I was relieved that those who turned themselves in usually received lighter ones that those who got caught.

I had only wanted to know what happened afterward, but I got more than I bargained for. The activists talked about the loneliness of life underground, the constant fear, the loss of identity. "Anxiety, isolation, vigilance," one psychologist was quoted as saying, "are the symptoms of depression. And yet these are exactly the qualities fugitives must cultivate in order to survive."

Abbie Hoffman committed suicide after he turned himself in; Katherine Power had been on suicide watch in jail at her own request. She had married while underground and had a son. It was because of her son, because of the strain of keeping her identity secret from him, that she had finally surrendered. But the judge, in order to punish her, refused to allow her to be transferred to a prison near her family. Her son stopped visiting her in jail; it upset him too much to see her.

I couldn't read any more. I clicked off the computer and went to the bank of chairs where Philip and I had arranged to meet and slouched in a chair. The afternoon was warm, the library barely air-conditioned.

If my father went to prison would he, too, become suicidal? I had watched him the morning we hiked out of the desert, staring off at the mountains. He loved open space, wilderness. He had said he was terrified of being locked up. He was prone to depression. How would he bear it?

Near me a mother enfolded her daughter in her lap, balancing a storybook.

I closed my eyes, tried to breathe deeply to steady myself, concentrated on the sound of her voice as she read.

"Layla?" Philip was shaking me. "Sorry to wake you. The library is closing. Ready to go?"

I nodded, groggy. I had been dreaming, and I wanted to hold onto the dream. Something to do with my mother and my father and me, and a kind of wholeness and contentment I couldn't remember ever feeling.

○

Posters were everywhere for the concert at Golden Gate Park. It would be a protest concert to end all protest concerts – against the war, against oil drilling in the Arctic, against rain forest destruction, against child labor overseas. I was glad when Philip said he and some friends were going; tagging along would be cover.

Until then I stayed indoors, skimming the books I had taken out of the library on Philip's card. I wanted to learn everything I could about the '60s, as if the more I knew, the clearer I'd be about what decision we should make.

Philip had been outside working in the yard, and his threadbare yellow tank top was spotted with soil. He hesitated by the doorway of the guest room and then came in, picking up one of the books. "History?" he said.

Stories of my mother's past were now termed history.

"I was reading about Kent State. My mother said your college campus was in turmoil over it, but I didn't realize."

He flopped onto the bed. "Realize what?"

"400 college campuses were shut down or had riots – that's huge!"

"Well yeah, I thought you got that," Philip said.

How could I explain? I thought it had all been exaggerated. But I was beginning to see that what my parents had lived through – the scale of it, the heightened sense of urgency – was a different order of magnitude from what I had imagined. I was more cautious and conservative than my parents, but I realized if I'd been alive during the Vietnam War, I probably would have gotten involved, too. It would have been easy to have gotten swept up and carried into too-deep waters.

"What is it you're looking for?" Philip said.

"I'm just trying to make sense of it," I said. I couldn't come right out and say, I'm tying to figure out if my father should turn himself in. "So much time has passed. It's hard to believe it could still have so many ramifications."

Philip hesitated. "Layla, don't underestimate the other side."

The other side. The old Us against Them. Had I bought into that too? I thought of the FBI agents. I supposed I had.

"Are you saying...." How much had he guessed? Was he telling me it would be a mistake for my father to turn himself in?

"I'm just saying you have to remember that, like it or not, what operates is power. Back then we had gotten too much – they were afraid we could actually stop the war. They fought back, in every way they could – above and below board."

"And now?"

"Jeez, how can I say?" Philip pushed himself upright. "Look, I'm assuming you met him. If so, maybe you should break off contact. For both your sakes."

I could only stare at him, chilled. I thought of the plan to meet my father later. I was beginning to understand the kind of risk he was taking to see me again. If I were followed, and led the FBI to him, he would lose all his bargaining power. Maybe the caring thing, the brave thing, would be not to show.

○

I bought a gigantic map of Golden Gate Park and memorized the pathways, identifying the bathroom where my father said he would be. That evening I followed behind Philip and his friends – three couples, two straight, one gay – nipping at their heels in my anxiety to hurry even though it was way too early. The night was balmy, misty and cool, and streams of people were straggling along with chairs and coolers, hoards and hoards of people. How would I ever meet up with my father? I searched the crowds hoping to spot him in the mass of color and noise and movement, knowing it was impossible. The crowd was a hodgepodge, from ravers to old hippie freaks to dumpy middle-aged rockers, wearing fringed leather vests and tie-dyed T-shirts and head wraps and billowing flowered skirts. The light was dimming in the west, and all around us candles were being lit. I checked my watch every few minutes, until I noticed one of Philip's friends giving me a funny look. I jumped up, saying I needed the bathroom, and went to scope out the location. What I saw made me quake: Long lines snaked around the building. Why in the world had my father chosen a ladies room? How could he hide in there? How would we talk? I went back to the blanket where Philip and his friends were, hoping once the music was underway the line at the bathroom would dissipate.

Philip's friends had brought chilled ceviche with scallops and mango, wild rice salad, tortellini with pesto, and chocolate brownies, but I couldn't eat and I couldn't concentrate on the conversation. My stomach felt as if I'd swallowed a hundred Mexican jumping beans. It seemed as if I waited an eternity for darkness while people came and went on the stage, moving equipment, saying: testing one, two, three, one, two, three, one, two, three.

Finally I couldn't take it any longer. I stood up. "I have to go to the ladies' room," I said to Philip.

"Didn't you already go? You'll miss the music!"

"The lines were too long before."

"Here, take my flashlight, then," he said. "It's getting dark." The crowd behind us had grown vast. I picked my way past blankets, an infinity of blankets, an infinity of chairs, trying to orient myself so I could find my way back in the dark. A loud cheer went up. I looked back. No one seemed to be following. On the stage, five skinny men in torn leather were stomping around.

I reached the bathrooms. They were now deserted, as if the crowd and the noise had created a kind of vacuum and sucked everyone away. I found myself shivering violently. I rubbed my hands up and down my arms, over goose bumps, trying to steady myself. I pushed the door. It swung open on rusty hinges, seeming to echo in the damp emptiness, and the pungent odor of urine was overpowering. The bathroom was empty. I checked back outside. No one.

I peered under the stalls and spotted at the far end a pair of black leather boots. "Hello?" I said. "It's me, Layla."

"Were you followed?" came a whisper.

"I don't think so."

"Good. I got here hours ago, to be on the safe side."

The door swung out and a tall woman with long black hair, tight black leggings, a micro-mini, and an oversized Grateful Dead T-shirt under a jean jacket stepped out. I gave a little yelp. If I hadn't known from the voice that it was my father, I would never have recognized him. His face was made up and his eyes were hidden behind gigantic pink-framed glasses. I burst out laughing.

"Come on, I look fabulous," he said.

"You look like a transvestite!" I sputtered through my laughter.

"Are you ashamed to be seen with me, honey?" he said in falsetto and struck a pose.

"Great legs," I giggled. There was a burst of applause from outside.

"You like the get-up?"

"Very effective," I said. "I guess you really learned your stuff – what you were telling me, about transformation."

"It's like the purloined letter," he said. "Sometimes you don't see what's in front of your face." There was a crash of chords, and then a loud screech of guitar.

"I know it stinks like holy hell, but I think we should talk in here. I'll stay in this booth, and if anyone comes in you say, 'sorry,' and close the door, O.K.?"

"Got it," I said. My father sat on the toilet. He looked so silly that I giggled again. My jitters were threatening to spill over into hysterical laughter. I tried to calm myself.

"Did you reach the lawyer?"

"Yes. The D.A. in New York is willing to make a deal. There's an offer."

"Offer? I thought this was going to take a while."

"I know. I had barely tested the waters before this. But –"

There was a squeak of hinges; my father shoved the door to his stall shut in my face. I backed up and stood stupidly immobile as a chubby teenage girl in denim overalls walked in. She glanced at me curiously and went into the adjacent stall. I busied myself at the sink even though there was no soap and only the merest trickle of water. The girl gave me another look as she left. "Hurry up in there, Susie," I called out. "I want to get back to the music."

I waited a moment after the girl was gone and then knocked lightly on my father's door. "It's O.K.," I said. "Just a teenager."

My father sat back down on the toilet. I came into the stall, closed the door behind me, and dropped to a squat opposite him. "Tell me," I said.

"As soon as the lawyer told his contact person that I definitely wanted to come in, everything accelerated."

"What would the deal be?" I asked.

"The charge against me is murder. I could plead not guilty and take my chances with a jury. Or I could avoid a trial by pleading guilty to manslaughter. That carries a recommended prison term of 10 to 12 years. I'd be eligible for parole in something between five and eight, depending on the sentencing judge."

I sat back on my heels. "Eight years!" I felt myself lose my balance and tipped forward. My father reached out to steady me. I ended up with my face pressed against his knees. He stroked my hair. "Layla, Layla, it will be O.K."

"This is too fast. We need time to think."

"I'm sorry, Layla, there just isn't time. The FBI is too close. Once word gets out through law-enforcement circles that I've been in negotiations to surrender, they'll be in a frenzy to capture me first."

I inhaled, my nose stinging from the stench of urine.

"It's a one-time offer, the lawyer says. Now or never."

"Can you trust them?" I said.

"The lawyer? Absolutely."

"No, the judge, attorney general, whoever. Will they keep to the agreement?"

"There are no guarantees. But I think I have to assume they will hold to whatever gets worked out."

"What does the lawyer think you should do?"

"He thinks that if I do want to give myself up I should plead not guilty."

"Why, because he thinks you can get off entirely?" I jumped at the possibility. "Because it was an accident?"

"No. Because he thinks my actions should be looked at in the context of the times. In effect, he wants to put the Vietnam War on trial, especially now, with public sentiment turning against the war in Iraq. He also thinks it could be good for me emotionally – to talk about it on the stand, before witnesses." My father grimaced. "Like a confessional."

"But what if they find you guilty!"

"Probably life," my father said.

"That's too big a risk!" I scrambled to my feet. "You can't take that chance!" My father tilted his head back to look at me, fingered a strand of the long black hair. The contrast between what we were talking about and his absurd get-up made me want to weep.

"A trial seems the more honorable way to deal with this whole thing – in a way I feel I should be forced to go through it. It makes me feel slimy to be cutting deals." He hesitated. "But I don't think it's a luxury I can afford."

"Thank you," I exhaled.

"It'll be O.K., Layla, really it will."

Maybe not, I thought. He would be put through plenty, trial or no trial. The press hounded Katherine Anne Power after she turned herself in. People stalked her, she got hate mail, her life was threatened.

"It's not too late, is it? We can still change our minds, forget the whole thing, can't we?"

My father stood up, cupped my face with his hands. "Since you left yesterday, since we talked and since I spoke with the lawyer, I've started to feel a sense of relief. I think I'll feel it even more as time goes by. It's really hitting me how hard this has been all these years – the lies, the fear, the disguises.... I'm older now. I'm not as afraid as I once was. To plead guilty of manslaughter is fair. I did kill someone, even if I didn't intend to. It'll be a kind of closure."

I looked at him. Was it just the make-up? Or had the muscles relaxed, the fine lines softened around his mouth?

He dropped his hands from my face. "By the way. My lawyer told me that because of the informal feelers he put out this past year, the FBI guessed the fugitive in question might be me. That's why they renewed the search. They hate the embarrassment of having failed to catch a fugitive."

I realized that I hadn't told my father about the FBI's visit the day before. I hesitated, hating to let him know how careless I had been. But I wanted no secrets between us.

He just shrugged it off. "Please don't beat yourself up. It really doesn't matter at this point. In fact, it helps confirm that I've got to act, and act quickly."

"How quickly?"

"I'll set it in motion tomorrow."

"Tomorrow?" Was this to be it, then, the last time I would see him as a free man, this meeting in a stinking bathroom? "It's unfair," I said, though I didn't know what I meant.

"It's what is, Layla. It's what we have to work with."

I opened my mouth to protest further, then closed it. He was right. There was nothing more to say, to do. For the next five years I would be meeting him on the other side of a glass divide with a phone to my ear. If we were lucky.

"Can you take a peek outside?" my father said.

I opened the door. No one was nearby. I stepped out, strolled the perimeter of the bathroom and came back in. "All clear, as far as I can tell," I said. There was a burst of loud cheering, then silence. Tracy Chapman's voice came over the loudspeakers; she began to sing "Freedom Now." My father and I looked at each other and smiled. He opened the door of the bathroom. Tracy's earthy voice was so clear she could have been under the tree opposite, singing just for us. Free, free, free. The irony was too much. My father reached for my hand. And then I found it wasn't hard at all. It was easy, in fact. We stood in the doorway of the bathroom, and along with a thousand others, we sang.

The song came to an end, and my father leaned down and tapped his forehead to mine. "Thank you," he said. "That was lovely."

"It felt good," I said.

"I'd better go."

"Not yet," I wanted to say, but didn't.

"Keep an eye on me to see if anyone's following. If anyone is, cause a commotion. I'll know to run like the wind. Think you can manage?"

"When will I see you again?"

"My lawyer will contact your lawyer," he grinned. "No, seriously. I'll find a way to get a message to you. Since the crime was committed in New York, that's where I have to turn myself over to the authorities. I'll go with the lawyer – with you, too, if you want – before the judge."

"So this is it?" I whispered.

He nodded. His eyes seemed to get larger behind the eyeglasses. I threw myself against him.

"Be careful of the make-up, sweetie," he said, and I choked on my laughter, but still held him tight, inhaling his dreadful perfume.

"You're not a moral coward," I said into his denim jacket. "Never think that."

"Huh?"

"In the motel room – you said that you wouldn't blame me if I thought you were a moral coward for running away. I just want you to know I don't think that. I would never think that."

"What are you saying?"

"In case you can't go through with it. In case you get cold feet. I'll understand."

"I won't get cold feet," he said. "Now, watch my back, O.K.?"

He disappeared out the door. I fixed my eyes on him as he melted into the crowd. He got plenty of looks, but no one set off after him. I trailed him until I felt satisfied he wasn't being followed, unwilling to lose sight of him. Finally I turned and headed back.

I had to pick my way through the crowd, from small patch of grass to small patch of grass. Tracy was singing another old favorite, "Subcity," and people were dancing on the blankets and on the grass in between. "Sorry, sorry," I kept saying, as I blocked someone's view or stepped on someone's foot. The ground seemed to throb underneath from the music, and the air was thick with the smell of marijuana.

In the darkness, with the lights from candles and lanterns flickering, with arms and bodies swaying like seaweed in water, I felt part of an unearthly religious ceremony. I thought of my father being pulled like a threaded needle through the crowd in the opposite direction from me. I held in my mind my last image of him – his tipsy swagger in the stack-heeled boots, flinging the long hair over his shoulder. Was I right? Had there been something joyous in his walk?

I found I was smiling even before I spotted Philip, dancing with a friend, wearing a plastic halo that glowed in the dark. He pulled me into their circle, and I danced and danced and danced, twirling around until I was dizzy. And along with everyone else, I sang at the top of my voice. There was no stopping me now.

Chapter 12

New York in summer is a sultry, sulky city, August the slowest of slow summer months. Heat shimmers off buildings, flecks of mica shine shards in your eyes. Your head swells and throbs, your blood simmers. In doorways, sullen teenagers gather as slow and thick as drunken flies just begging to be swatted. Children, skin moist with sweat, adhere to their mothers' bare legs.

From my bedroom window seat on the 15th floor I can look down on the trees that stand like guards outside our building. The trees have large leaves that droop from the branches with a kind of graceful ease, like the dangling legs of cats resting on their stomachs. I watch the wind flutter the leaves, and the rain pelt them. I watch the plastic bags that get stuck in the branches swell with air and then deflate. When I left at the beginning of the summer the leaves were the bright green of Granny Smith apples, young and naive. When I returned they were the dark, mature green of late summer.

High up in my perch above Broadway, I sat listening to the air conditioner's low grumble and watched the city below. I watched and I waited, waited to hear from my father's lawyer.

I had turned in the rental car in San Francisco and taken my flight home as scheduled. Philip saw me off. I had been brave when I said good-bye to my father. I was not brave with Philip; he didn't know what to do with me except squeeze me tighter and tighter, until I finally had to stop crying.

Jenny met me at the airport, and on the way back to the city from JFK I told her what I could – about what my father had done that sent him underground, and that I had met him. Jenny was thunderstruck. "There's more," I said, cutting off her questions.

"I really want to explain, but I can't. Everything should be clear by the time you and Steve get back." She and Steve were going to Europe for a few weeks. I told her to read the New York papers while she was there, and she'd understand.

Alone in the apartment, I paced like an animal getting used to new surroundings, unable to settle in. I went out as little as possible. I did not see friends. I postponed calling Trent. I worried the FBI could monitor my cell as well as the landline.

I busied myself unpacking the cartons I had filled at the beginning of the summer and sorting through all my photos from senior year. It was so much clearer, with a few months' distance, which ones weren't so bad and which were worthless. I was on the floor, sliding the photos around, when the phone rang. I stumbled to my feet, and reached the phone just in time before the machine picked up.

"Is this Layla James?" an unfamiliar voice asked.

"Yes," I said, trying to catch my breath.

"The book you ordered will be in on Wednesday."

"I'm sorry, what did you say?"

He repeated it. I hadn't ordered any books.

"You can pick it up at the 83rd Street Barnes and Noble. We open at 10:00." I heard the click of the receiver being replaced.

It took a full five minutes for my heart to stop pounding.

○

10 AM. The Barnes and Nobel superstore. The last time I had seen my father he had been dressed as a woman. Who would he be now? I roamed the store from floor to floor but didn't see him. Then, in the café, I spotted a man in a ponytail and three-piece suit talking to another man whose back was to me. I knew that back, the shape of that head. I started to rush and then forced myself to slow down so as not to attract attention. My father turned; he looked thinner, his eyes dark against a forest-green

oxford shirt. His beard was gone and his hair was cropped short, stealing all his unkempt curls.

He jumped up and held me for a moment, not speaking. Then he brushed my cheek with his lips and introduced me to the pony-tailed lawyer.

"We'll be going to the precinct, where your father will turn himself in," the lawyer said in a low voice. He went on; I sat at the edge of my chair, straining to concentrate, but his words seemed to come and go, as if I kept falling asleep and waking up over and over again. My father squeezed my hand, to steady me or to give both of us strength, I don't know. "He will be taken into custody."

"O.K.," I said. I took a deep breath. I felt very shaky, even though this was exactly what I knew to expect. I stood up. "I'm ready."

"Layla, I'm not sure it's a good idea for you to come along," the lawyer said.

"I don't understand," I said, sitting back down. Why wouldn't I come along? Neither of them said anything. I looked from the lawyer to my father and back again. My skin felt hot and flushed, and a painful throbbing was beginning above my eyes.

"He'll be processed – fingerprinted, handcuffed, and put in jail to await his arraignment."

"I want to be there." I waited, but still my father didn't say anything. The ache beat like a pulse just above my eyebrows. I reached for my coffee.

"I think I'd rather you didn't see all that," he said finally. I started to protest, then bit my lip, hard. He was trying to tell me that he would feel humiliated to be placed under arrest in front of me. I nodded, but didn't meet his eyes. He leaned over and kissed my forehead, as if he knew how much it hurt.

"The arraignment will be within 48 hours," the lawyer said. "You can be present then, if you like."

I trailed them down the stairs and through the store. Outside the lawyer hailed a cab. My father gave me a brief hug, and then he was inside the cab, being whisked away. I stood watching until he was out of sight, a knot in the pit of my stomach. I had been waiting, so tense, for so long, that the anticlimax was disorienting. I leaned again the wall, spent, as crumpled and damp as a sweater rung hard to dry.

O

My father was arraigned the next afternoon. He was in and out of the courtroom in a matter of minutes, as if it were a mere bureaucratic detail. He didn't request bail – he refused to let me put up any money from my mother's insurance policy. It would have been set too high, millions, anyhow. I watched as he was taken away.

Outside the cool, fragrant air was a shock after the stuffy courtroom. I stood on the steps, at a loss.

"Are you all right, Layla?" the lawyer asked.

"I guess," I said.

"I know this is very hard on you," he said as we walked to the subway. "I'll call you as soon as the hearing with the sentencing judge is set up. Try not to worry."

"Would I be right not to worry?"

"I think it will go about as planned," he said, then added, "but that doesn't mean it will be easy."

"How do you mean?"

"The publicity." He paused. "No one knows who you are in relation to him. Maybe it would be better if you stayed out of the picture altogether."

"I want to be there for my father," I said.

"Of course you do. But you can remain in the background. Otherwise you could be setting yourself up for a lot of grief."

I didn't say anything.

"You have time to think about it. It will be weeks before he goes before the judge."

"Weeks? Why weeks?"

"They have to review all the records, notify the victim's family. In a case like this, they have to be scrupulous about all the details. But that's not necessarily a bad thing. It'll give us time to prepare."

"What do you mean, prepare?" my voice squeaked. "I thought everything was already agreed to."

"Relax, Layla. I'm talking about how things play in the court of public opinion. That will influence how things go for your father from now on. But look, you let me worry about all that, O.K.? I'll be in touch. Call if I can help you with anything. Anything at all." He gave me his card; I tucked it into my pocket.

I got out of the subway a few stops early so I could walk a little and clear my head. I didn't know how I was going to stand the tension between now and when my father's situation was resolved. How would he find a way to stand it?

I stopped at the photo lab where I used to work to pick up copies of my pictures from the trip. Back at the apartment, I spread them out on the kitchen table, separating out the ones I had surreptitiously taken of my father from the rest. There he was with his arms flailing, eyes squinting, orange balls in the air. There he was sitting next to Nina, toasting her with his wine glass. There he was lifting a little boy high enough for him to see the flavors of ice cream, Ike's plane in the background. There he was sitting on a boulder, elbows on bony knees, staring into the sunset.

It was surprising to see how clear it was what I was saying with the photos. Even from the beginning I was telling myself that I liked him, that, despite everything, I thought he was fundamentally a good man. I didn't know where that sense of trust came from, but it was there. Still, I was unclear exactly what I thought about what he had done. The lawyer had given me an out: I could choose not to reveal my connection to him. We did not share a last name. No one need know. I imagined myself standing before the judge, the judge asking me what I wanted to say. In my mind I stammered and hedged.

Suddenly I realized there were two calls I had to make. Now that my father was arraigned, it would be all over the news. I went outside and walked up Broadway looking for a functioning pay phone.

My first call was to my father's parents in Florida. My father had told me that he had written to them over the years, but that he had not seen them since going underground.

"Grandpa, it's me, Layla," I twirled the black cord around my wrist, around and around.

"My, my, child, how are you?" my grandfather said. His voice had the creaky sound of old age, the wavering tremulousness of a voice echoing from underwater.

"Grandpa I have something shocking to tell you, so you need to be calm."

"I'm calm, baby doll. At my age calm is pretty much it."

"My father turned himself in." I waited, but there was just silence. "To the authorities. I don't know how many years he will get or where he'll be sent."

There was nothing on the other end of the line except a wheezy breathing.

"Are you O.K. grandpa? I'm so sorry to tell you this way, but I didn't want you to see it first on television."

"How? –" he started to say, and then stopped.

I heard my grandmother's sharp voice in the background, saying, "Roger, what is it?"

"I met him this summer. I hadn't even known he was alive. He's fine." There was silence. "Maybe now you and grandma can see him."

The silence went on so long I began to get worried. "I don't know if that will be possible," he finally said.

I heard the sharp intake of my own breath and felt pain just below my breastbone.

"Well, I guess I'd better go," I said.

"Come visit," he said.

"I will," I said. But I think we both knew that I wouldn't.

Next I called my mother's parents.

"Grandma, I need to prepare you for something," I said.

"Stacy just called me, she heard it on NPR. Did you know about it?"

"NPR, already?" I took a moment to digest this. "My mother arranged for me to meet him this summer," I said.

"Your grandfather has never forgiven him for how he ruined your mother's life. We didn't want yours tainted by the terrible thing your father did. I can't believe you would get mixed up in this."

"He's my father," I said.

"I can't talk about this now," she said. Her anger and disapproval stung; it had never been directed at me before. Before I could say anything, she hung up.

I sat a moment cradling the phone, and then did what I'd been longing to do for days. But there was no answer at Trent's apartment and he didn't pick up his cell. I was too shy to leave a message.

Loneliness hit, then, sharp and hot. I went back home and plopped down at the kitchen table, fingering the salt and pepper shakers, the napkin holder, the oil and vinegar cruets. I heard my mother's voice: "Could you please stop fidgeting!"

I leaned back, closed my eyes. I concentrated on conjuring her image – the dark hair, parted in the middle, the thick stern black eyebrows, the twitch of her lips as something I said both amused and exasperated her.

How could she have left me alone with all of this?

The shrill blast of the doorbell jolted me. I didn't want to answer it. I couldn't bear to deal with anyone. But the ringing didn't let up.

I opened the door. In front of me, even more beautiful than my memory of him, was Trent. I just stood there, mouth dropped open like a trapdoor.

"Oh my God!" My hands flew to my hair; why hadn't I washed it? I was growing it out again, and it was driving me crazy.

"Are you O.K.? I heard on the radio –."

"I just called you. I can't believe you're here. I look like a slob. My hair – ."

He started laughing. I started laughing too. I grabbed his hand and pulled him into the apartment.

"You look gorgeous. Really. I like it longer, and that tan suits you."

I held my arm next to his arm, and we compared pigmentation.

"I hope it's O.K.," he said, "but once I heard, I had to come. I figured if I called first you'd be brave and sensible and tell me to wait."

"I'm sorry I didn't call you when I got home, but I couldn't. I was sure the FBI was tapping my phone."

"I understand, Layla, of course you couldn't."

"I am so happy you're here." As I said it I felt the full weight of everything and flung myself at him.

Once we extricated ourselves I sat him down in the living room and got us each a beer. I stared at him over my glass – at the sharp angles of his cheekbones, the lovely sweep of his eyebrows. How strange that here was this creature I hardly knew, yet I felt such comfort in his presence. It came over me that he was the only person – besides my father – I could bear to be with just now. So our shared background did matter. Some day, after I talked everything over with my friends, after time had passed and I had gotten used to what life would be with a father in prison, I was sure I would feel like myself with them again. But for right now it was as if I had crossed to the other side of some chasm, and only he was there.

"Talk to me," he said, reaching for my hands.

It was such a relief for me to tell Trent everything that once I got going I couldn't stop. Finally I wound up. "His own parents are furious with him. I'm so afraid the media is going to massacre him."

"We won't let that happen," he said. I could only look at him. We? That cinched it, I thought. I loved him.

Trent followed me into the kitchen for another beer. The photos were spread out on the table.

"Wow, are these who I think they are?"

"My father." As I said the word my voice sounded hushed, even to my own ears, proud like a new parent, thrilled to have a father to show off.

"These are wonderful," Trent said. He picked up one after another, examining them closely. Finally he put them down. He looked at me. "Layla, I think you're going to have to testify."

"What do you mean? Why? Why would anything I say matter?"

"Everything you've been telling me about him – it makes him more real, more likeable. That's important in how people see him. How he'll be treated."

"But I'm just telling you stories, showing you pictures."

Trent paused a minute, looking at me. "Exactly," he said.

○

So that's how it came to be that I wrote an article for a magazine about meeting my father, complete with photographs – Trent's idea. The lawyer not only gave his O.K., he thought it was inspired. Somewhere along the line, I seemed to have decided: I was on his side. I would like to think that it was a well-thought-out decision. But it may have been this simple: I wanted a father. I wanted to be loved as a daughter.

I tried to make the story sincere and true, but the editors gave it the Disney treatment. Still, the point was to get sympathy for my father. I was learning from my father, it seemed, learning to be a practitioner of artifice, of indirection. With the article I drew attention to myself – and away from his deed.

When the day of my father's sentencing finally arrived, I was terrified. Something about the finality. Something about standing to speak in front of a judge, about being in the public spotlight. In the months since that day I've tried to block the memory of it from my mind. But some nights I wake up from nightmares, those horrible anxiety nightmares that leave you shaking, and I know that it will be a long while before the effects fade.

The moments in the courtroom before my father arrived were the worst. My hand was slippery in Trent's, my stomach cramped.

Across the aisle from us sat a middle-aged woman and a man of about 30. When my father was brought in and I saw him glance at them and flinch, I was sure who they must be, and my heart seized. I had arranged ahead of time to give a statement and I guessed they had done likewise.

The court clerk asked us all to rise, and the judge entered. She was tall and slim and severe looking. The folds of her skin did not soften her face. My father's lawyer had told me that she was considered fair, but, looking at her, I wondered if he had lied to reassure me.

My father's lawyer, in a voice and manner too smooth and confident to my ear, summed up my father's crime, his life. He mentioned the scholarship fund my father had set up for the son of the guard. He handed over the affidavit he had managed to secure from Sam, one of the other men who had been involved in the shooting who was out of prison now. Sam wrote that he had lied to my father that the gun he gave him wasn't loaded. It was our best hope at bolstering my father's chances.

When my father rose to make his statement, his voice was so soft the judge barked at him to speak up. My father coughed, and resumed. He said how sorry he was that he had killed the guard. He said he would do anything to bring back his life, to make amends. He turned to the woman and her son, and asked for their forgiveness. He said to the judge, "I am grateful for whatever leniency the court is willing to bestow on me."

My father sat down. There was a sound in the courtroom as if everyone let out their breath at once, and I sensed he had swayed the crowd. But then the wife of the slain guard stood. She was dignified, wearing black, as if still in mourning.

"Your honor, I lost my husband that day," she said, her voice cracking. "I don't care what this man was protesting for. I lost my husband. I would be lying if I said I wasn't happy to take the money he sent. But that doesn't give me back my husband. It doesn't give my son back his father."

A heavy silence seemed to fill the room. I felt my eyes smart and my skin burn with painful emotion. The judge motioned me forward. I felt a film of sweat on my upper lip, along my hairline.

I stood. I wiped my palms along the seams of my dress.

"Your honor." I paused, swallowed. "Your honor, my name is Layla James. The defendant is my father. I grew up believing he was dead. I only learned about him and met him this summer, after my mother died.

"Because of what happened, I grew up without a father, too. In some ways I think my father stayed underground because of that. I think he felt it was fairer. He took a father from a son and wife, and so he took from himself a wife and daughter. I think he was trying to punish himself."

I glanced at my father. He was open-mouthed.

I turned back to the judge. "A man is dead. There is no bringing him back. But I think the rest of us have suffered enough." I turned to the family. "I understand how much pain you have endured, and I'm so terribly sorry. I know it's only fair that he goes to prison. But I just lost my mother. Please, please let me have my father soon."

I sat down. There was complete silence in the courtroom. I didn't know what that silence meant, what impact, if any, I had had. I stared fixedly at the back of father's bowed head while we waited, squeezed Trent's hand so hard he had to gently loosen my grip. The judge leaned forward and began to speak. She talked about the '60s, about how they were a time of extreme politics and emotion. She talked about the sanctity of human life. With every remark I swiveled between hope and despair. Then she looked directly at me. "I find myself swayed by the testimony of your daughter. I hereby sentence you to nine years, eligible for parole in five and three-quarter years." It was the lowest possible sentence under the terms of my father's surrender.

There was a loud roar engulfing me, and for a moment I sat, stunned. Then I leaped up, ran to my father, and held on until I was peeled off of him. A guard on either side of him, he was led away, metal clanging on metal. "Dad!" I called out, but he was already out the door. The paper the next day showed a picture of me, wild-eyed, open-mouthed. The caption read simply, Layla James, fugitive's daughter.

○

The route upstate to visit my father in prison is the one I took to visit Karen and Ben at the beginning of the summer. I own a car, now, a little navy-blue Honda just like the rental one I got so attached to on my trip, and already I have my habits well-established. There is the Hess gas station on Route 17 in New Jersey on the way to the Thruway where I stop to tank up because I like the station's green and white colors and the fact that they have an accessible bathroom. There is the funky general store in Raybrook, the little town near the prison, where I like to stop for magazines and candy or whatever suits my fancy to bring to my father on a given day, just as I used to do for my mother when I visited her in the hospital. I always bring real food, too, from Manhattan – bagels and cream cheese, Valhrona chocolate, salsa and chips – something strong to kill the taste of prison food.

As I drive into the parking lot the tremors begin, the same every time. In my hands, then in my legs. As I walk to the entrance my legs feel as weak as limp stalks of celery. First comes the nausea, then the shivering. Every time.

Today I sit waiting, as I do most Saturdays, in this dreary prison room, feeling my anxiety build. I rub my hands over my goose-pimpled flesh. The door opens, and a man in uniform beckons. I stand so quickly that I bang my knee, but it clears my head. As he leads me to my father I feel the impulse to cry. Each time it takes me a few moments to adjust to how he looks – too pale, too thin – and then to feel reassured that, so far at least, he seems O.K.

I sit down opposite him. It's different between us now, different in a way I can't yet put a name to. It's as if we're meeting for the first time all over again, starting again at our beginnings. We sit and talk softly. I tell my father stories about growing up, and the stories now are of the happy moments, the special times with my mother. I feel more strongly how much I miss her. There's so much I wish I could say now. I wish I could tell her that she was right – how much the '60s and the Vietnam War, which changed the course of their lives, changed mine as well. But maybe she knows.

My father tells me about berry-picking at Alley Pond Park as a kid, about fishing Long Island rivers. We've decided that the park is where we'll bury my mother's ashes. We'll do it together, the day he is released.

More often these days we speak of the present – of my graphic arts job for a small magazine, of his friendships with some of the men in jail. But I don't tell him about the hate mail, or how the visits curtail my fledgling relationship with Trent, and I know he keeps from me the more unsavory aspects of his experience.

Over time I've gotten to know a few of the other regulars, mostly girlfriends and wives. From them I've heard the kinds of stories my father doesn't tell me. And so I joined a prisoners' support group. The group has petitioned the governor to continue to allow prisoners to take college courses, and we are planning a mid-winter demonstration. When I tell him this, or talk about my involvement in a peace group, he says nothing at all, just smiles.

Today I show him the rough draft of the poster I'm doing for the prisoners' rights demonstration. I'm doing the PR, too. I have a few press contacts, after all. I'm still a little bit of a celebrity. It strikes me as very ironic that it's because of him that my first photographs were published.

Too soon, it seems, our time is up. We say our good-byes, and I choke up when he tells me he loves me. Then I remove my camera from my backpack. I am making a record of my father's time in prison. Each time I limit myself to two shots, an exercise in restraint, in making choices. Today I take one of him with another prisoner high-fiving each other. The other shot is a close-up of the lines, thin as a spider's filament, around my father's eyes, the exact color of mine.

My father gave me my eyes; it's up to me to develop a point of view.